GLIMMER TRAIN
STORIES

EDITORS
Susan Burmeister-Brown   Linda B. Swanson-Davies

CONSULTING EDITOR
Roz Wais

COPY EDITOR
Scott Stuart Allie

TYPESETTING & LAYOUT
Paul Morris

ADMINISTRATIVE ASSISTANT
Kaylin Elaine Dodge

COVER ART
The Three Brothers, Riga, Latvia, *by Jane Zwinger*

PUBLISHED QUARTERLY
in spring, summer, fall, and winter by Glimmer Train Press, Inc.
1211 NW Glisan Street, Suite 207, Portland, Oregon 97209-3054
Telephone: 503/221-0836   Facsimile: 503/221-0837
www.glimmertrain.com
PRINTED IN U.S.A.
Indexed in *The American Humanities Index*.

©2005 by Glimmer Train Press, Inc. All rights reserved. No part of this periodical may be reproduced without the consent of Glimmer Train Press, Inc. The magazine's name and logo and the various titles and headings herein are trademarks of Glimmer Train Press, Inc. The short stories in this publication are works of fiction. Names, characters, places, and incidents are either the products of the authors' imaginations or are used fictitiously. Any resemblance to actual events, locales, or persons, living or dead, is entirely coincidental. The views expressed in the nonfiction writing herein are solely those of the authors.

Glimmer Train (ISSN #1055-7520), registered in U.S. Patent and Trademark Office, is published quarterly, $34 per year in the U.S., by Glimmer Train Press, Inc., Suite 207, 1211 NW Glisan, Portland, OR 97209. Periodicals postage paid at Portland, OR, and additional mailing offices. POSTMASTER: Send address changes to Glimmer Train Press, P.O. Box 3000, Denville, NJ 07834-9929.

ISSN # 1055-7520, **ISBN # 1-59553-005-3**, CPDA BIPAD # 79021

DISTRIBUTION: Bookstores can purchase *Glimmer Train Stories* through these distributors:
DEMCO, Inc., 4810 Forest Run Road, Madison, WI 53707 ph: 800/356-1200
Ingram Periodicals, 1226 Heil Quaker Blvd., LaVergne, TN 37086
Peribo PTY Ltd., 58 Beaumont Rd., Mt. Kuring-Gai, NSW 2080, AUSTRALIA
Source Interlink, 27500 Riverview Center Blvd., Suite 400, Bonita Sprints, FL 36134
Ubiquity, 607 Degraw St., Brooklyn, NY 11217
SUBSCRIPTION SVCS: EBSCO, Divine, Blackwell's UK

Subscription rates: Order online (www.glimmertrain.com)
or by mail—one year, $36 within the U.S. (Visa/MC/check).
Airmail to Canada, $46; outside North America, $59.
Payable by Visa/MC or check for U.S. dollars drawn on a U.S. bank.

Attention established and emerging short-story writers: *As of October 1, 2005, we pay $700 for first publication and onetime anthology rights. We welcome your work via our **online submission procedure: www.glimmertrainpress.com***

Glimmer Train Press also offers **Writers Ask**—*nuts, bolts, and informed perspectives—a quarterly newsletter for the committed writer. One year, four issues, $20 within the U.S. ($26 beyond the U.S.), Visa, MC, or check to Glimmer Train Press, Inc., or order online at www.glimmertrain.com.*

We dedicate this issue to past contributing authors and artists whose words have appeared in *Glimmer Train*'s pages, and who've since moved on to other realms.

Joan H Bohorfoush 1951–1997

Harold Brodkey 1930–1996

Jack Cady 1933–2004

Michael Dorris 1945–1997

Andre Dubus 1936–1999

Andrea King Kelly 1953–2005

We continue to value their contributions
as we miss their physical presence.

Linda & Susan

PAST CONTRIBUTING AUTHORS AND ARTISTS

Many of issues 1 through 55 are available for thirteen dollars each.

Robert A. Abel • David Abrams • Linsey Abrams • Steve Adams • Diane King Akers • Daniel Alarcón • Susan Alenick • Rosemary Altea • Julia Alvarez • Brian Ames • A. Manette Ansay • Margaret Atwood • Kevin Bacon • Michael Bahler • Doreen Baingana • Aida Baker • Russell Banks • Brad Barkley • Andrea Barrett • Kyle Ann Bates • Richard Bausch • Robert Bausch • Charles Baxter • Ann Beattie • Barbara Bechtold • Cathie Beck • Jeff Becker • Janet Belding • Sallie Bingham • Kristen Birchett • Melanie Bishop • James Carlos Blake • Corinne Demas Bliss • Valerie Block • **Joan Bohorfoush** • Robin Bradford • **Harold Brodkey** • Danit Brown • Kurt McGinnis Brown • Paul Brownfield • Ayşe Papatya Bucak • Judy Budnitz • Susanna Bullock • Christopher Bundy • Jenny A. Burkholder • Evan Burton • Robert Olen Butler • Michael Byers • Christine Byl • Gerard Byrne • **Jack Cady** • Annie Callan • Kevin Canty • Peter Carey • Ioanna Carlsen • Ron Carlson • H.G. Carroll • David Cates • Brian Champeau • Vikram Chandra • Diane Chang • Mike Chasar • Xiaofei Chen • Yunny Chen • Robert Chibka • Chieh Chieng • Carolyn Chute • George Makana Clark • Dennis Clemmens • Aaron Cohen • Robert Cohen • Evan S. Connell • Joan Connor • Ellen Cooney • Rand Richards Cooper • Lydia E. Copeland • Michelle Coppedge • Rita D. Costello • Wendy Counsil • Doug Crandell • Ronald F. Currie Jr. • William J. Cyr • Quinn Dalton • Bilal Dardai • Tristan Davies • C.V. Davis • Laurence de Looze • Toi Derricotte • Janet Desaulniers • Tiziana di Marina • Junot Díaz • Stephen Dixon • Matthew Doherty • **Michael Dorris** • Siobhan Dowd • Greg Downs • Eugenie Doyle • Tiffany Drever • Alan Arthur Drew • **Andre Dubus** • Andre Dubus III • Stuart Dybek • Wayne Dyer • Melodie S. Edwards • Ron Egatz • Barbara Eiswerth • Mary Relindes Ellis • Susan Engberg • Lin Enger • James English • Tony Eprile • Louise Erdrich • Zoë Evamy • Nomi Eve • George Fahey • Edward Falco • Anthony Farrington • Merrill Feitell • J.M. Ferguson Jr. • Lisa Fetchko • Joseph Flanagan • Charlotte Forbes • Susan Fox • Michael Frank • Pete Fromm • Daniel Gabriel • Avital Gad-Cykman • Ernest Gaines • Tess Gallagher • Louis Gallo • Elizabeth Gallu • Kent Gardien • Ellen Gilchrist • Mary Gordon • Peter Gordon • Elizabeth Graver • Lisa Graley • Jo-Ann Graziano • Andrew Sean Greer • Gail Greiner • John Griesemer • Zoë Griffith-Jones • Paul Griner • Aaron Gwyn • L.B. Haas • Patricia Hampl • Christian Hansen • Ann Harleman • Elizabeth Logan Harris • Marina Harris • Erin Hart • Kent Haruf • Daniel Hayes • David Haynes • Daniel Hecht • Ursula Hegi • Amy Hempel • Joshua Henkin • David Hicks • Andee Hochman • Alice Hoffman • Jack Holland • Noy Holland • Travis Holland • Lucy Honig • Ann Hood • Linda Hornbuckle • David Huddle • Sandra Hunter • Siri Hustvedt • Quang Huynh • Frances Hwang • Leo Hwang • Stewart David Ikeda • Lawson Fusao Inada • Elizabeth Inness-Brown • Debra Innocenti • Bruce Jacobson • Andrea Jeyaveeran • Ha Jin • Charles Johnson • Leslie Johnson • Sarah Anne Johnson • Wayne Johnson • Allen Morris Jones • Nalini Jones • Thom Jones • Cyril Jones-Kellet • Elizabeth Judd • Tom Miller Juvik • Jiri Kajanë • Anita Shah Kapadia • Hester Kaplan • Amy Karr • Wayne Karlin • Andrew Kass • Kate Kasten • Tom Kealey • **Andrea King Kelly** • Jenny Kennedy • Thomas E. Kennedy • Tim Keppel • Jamaica Kincaid • Lily King • Maina wa Kinyatti • Carolyn Kizer • Carrie Knowles • Clark E. Knowles • N.S. Köenings • Jonathan Kooker • David Koon • Karen Kovacik • Jake Kreilkamp • Erika Krouse • Marilyn Krysl • Frances Kuffel • Mandy Dawn Kuntz • Anatoly Kurchatkin • Victoria Lancelotta • Rattawut Lapcharoensap • Jenni Lapidus • Doug Lawson • Don Lee • Frances Lefkowitz • Peter Lefcourt • Jon Leon • Doris Lessing • Jennifer Levasseur • Debra Levy • Janice Levy • Yiyun Li • Christine Liotta • Rosina Lippi-Green • David Long • Nathan Long • Salvatore Diego Lopez • Melissa Lowver • William Luvaas • Barry Lyga • David H. Lynn • Richard Lyons • Bruce Machart • Jeff MacNelly • R. Kevin Maler • Kelly Malone • Paul Mandelbaum • George Manner • Jana Martin • Lee Martin • Valerie Martin • Daniel Mason • Alice Mattison • Jane McCafferty • Judith McClain • Cammie McGovern • Cate McGowan • Eileen McGuire • Susan McInnis • Gregory McNamee • Jenny Drake McPhee • Amalia Melis • Askold Melnyczuk • Frank Michel • Paul Michel • Nancy Middleton • Alyce Miller • Katherine Min • Mary McGarry Morris • Ted Morrissey • Mary Morrissy • Bernard Mulligan • Abdelrahman Munif • Manuel Muñoz • Karen Munro • Kent Nelson • Lucia Nevai • Thisbe Nissen • Miriam Novogrodsky • Sigrid Nunez • N. Nye • Ron Nyren • Joyce Carol Oates • Tim O'Brien • Vana O'Brien • Mary O'Dell • Chris Offutt • Jennifer Oh • Laura Oliver • Felicia Olivera • Jimmy Olsen • Thomas O'Malley • Stewart O'Nan • Elizabeth Oness • Karen Outen • Mary Overton • Patricia Page • Ann Pancake • Peter Parsons • Roy Parvin • Karenmary Penn • Susan Perabo • Dawn Karima Pettigrew • Constance Pierce • William Pierce • Angela Pneuman • Steven Polansky • John Prendergast • Jessica Printz • Melissa Pritchard • E. Annie Proulx • Eric Puchner • Kevin Rabalais • Jonathan Raban • George Rabasa • Margo Rabb • Mark Rader • Paul Rawlins • Yelizaveta P. Renfro • Nancy Reisman • Linda Reynolds • Kurt Rheinheimer • Anne Rice • Michelle Richmond • Alberto Ríos • Roxana Robinson • Anya Robyak • Andrew Roe • Paulette Roeske • Stan Rogal • Carol Roh-Spaulding • Frank Ronan • Julie Rose • Elizabeth Rosen • Janice Rosenberg • Jane Rosenzweig • Karen Sagstetter • Kiran Kaur Saini • Mark Salzman • Carl Schaffer • Robert Schirmer • Libby Schmais • Natalie Schoen • Adam Schuitema • Jim Schumock • Lynn Sharon Schwartz • Barbara Scot • Peter Selgin • Amy Selwyn • Catherine Seto • Bob Shacochis • Evelyn Sharenov • Sally Shivnan • Daryl Siegel • Ami Silber • Al Sim • George Singleton • Floyd Skloot • Brian Slattery • Roland Sodowsky • Scott Southwick • R. Clifton Spargo • Gregory Spatz • Brent Spencer • L.M. Spencer • Lara Stapleton • Lori Ann Stephens • Barbara Stevens • John Stinson • George Stolz • William Styron • Virgil Suárez • Karen Swenson • Liz Szabla • Mika Tanner • Lois Taylor • Paul Theroux • Abigail Thomas • Randolph Thomas • Joyce Thompson • Patrick Tierney • Aaron Tillman • Tamara B. Titus • Andrew Toos • Pauls Toutonghi • Vu Tran • Patricia Traxler • Jessica Treadway • Doug Trevor • William Trevor • Rob Trucks • Kathryn Trueblood • Jennifer Tseng • Carol Turner • Christine Turner • Kathleen Tyau • Michael Upchurch • Lee Upton • Gerard Varni • Katherine Vaz • A.J. Verdelle • Daniel Villasenor • Sergio Gabriel Waisman • Daniel Wallace • Ren Wanding • Mary Yukari Waters • Jonathan Wei • Jamie Weisman • Lance Weller • Ed Weyhing • J. Patrice Whetsell • Joan Wickersham • Lex Williford • Gary Wilson • Robin Winick • Terry Wolverton • Monica Wood • Christopher Woods • Leslie A. Wootten • wormser • Celia Wren • Callie Wright • Calvin Wright • Brennen Wysong • June Unjoo Yang • Nancy Zafris • Jane Zwinger

CONTENTS

*I'm the one holding the Coke. It's 1976 and a historic moment
for our family. We're at a stadium in Portland, Oregon awaiting
the entrance of the Timbers, a pro soccer team. My mom assures
me now that I was not wearing a leash around my neck.*

Gina Ochsner's short-story collection, *The Necessary Grace to Fall*, was selected for the
Flannery O'Connor Award and published by University of Georgia Press. A second
collection, *People I Wanted to Be*, was published this year by Houghton Mifflin. A lifelong
resident of Oregon, Ochsner lives in Keizer and teaches at George Fox University.

A CLOUD FOR A CARPET

Gina Ochsner

One day, just before quitting time, while looking for a fresh roll of toilet paper in an ordinary broom closet of the Riga Two Star Hotel, Valdis accidentally fell through the closet wall. First Valdis's hand punched through the plaster, and before he could right himself, his shoulder, his head, and then his torso had gone through. Wedged in the hole, it was with tremendous effort that Valdis managed to pull himself out of the wall. When he did, the sheeting crumbled and long white scales of plaster flaked to the floor. All this happened in complete view of Valdis's boss, Kajer Sevudis, who sat drinking a cup of tea.

Valdis shook his head, brushed his shirt, and watched wisps of insulation and bits of chinking fall to the floor. A strange smell clung to his skin and under his fingernails—mud. Valdis brought his fingers to his nose. The mud smelled of dark earth and something else Valdis couldn't name. Kajer sneezed, and downed the last of his tea with a swallow. Then Kajer rolled his eyes to the sagging particle-board ceiling and pulled on the beaded chain attached to the light bulb, extinguishing the light.

When Valdis got home to his mother's apartment, the next-door neighbors, Alla and Rein, were sitting at the table with his mother, Viivi, and eating *pirogi* baked with a fresh skin of soot.

"Latvian Jews are the loneliest people on the planet. Not only are we outnumbered by every other group, but now we are making the papers for our zero population growth," Viivi complained.

"At least we're doing better than the Estonians," Alla said.

"I don't know. That girl downstairs is eating a lot of turnips." Rein tapped his fingers over the table top.

"Okay. So the Estonians are beating us." Alla sighed. Alla had gray hair that had been dyed brick red, which looked good enough on the girls downtown, but seemed ridiculous somehow for Alla, a middle-aged woman with doughy ankles that spilled over the tops of her shoes. If that weren't bad enough, she had poor eyesight and wore three sets of eyeglasses on three different chains. Rein, her husband, who never spoke lest he spite her, sat in quiet contemplation of the vodka bottle before him.

"What surprises me," Viivi turned to Rein, "is that you don't smell that fish stink. It's like stale urine." Now they were discussing the Koreans who lived upstairs, had recently emigrated from Tashkent, and whom Valdis knew his mother held in utter contempt. "But then I can smell the slightest scent of any contaminant." Viivi sniffed, as if a foul odor were underfoot. Everyone else in the room sniffed, too, and then Alla chimed loyally: "Yes!"

But Viivi shook her head slowly. "No. It's something else, something even worse than usual." Viivi corkscrewed in her chair. With a weary and threadbare gaze she studied Valdis.

Valdis brought his hands to his face, smelled the mud. Then he tiptoed around Rein and crossed the kitchen for his desk, a refrigerator box that had been pushed into the corner, and sat in a metal chair.

"Those Koreans are so stupid," Viivi continued, with a quick adjustment of her wool wig. "They probably think life is good."

"They speak four languages," Rein offered quietly.

"That's right—they're speaking Russian in the home now. It's not right," said Alla. "And why they think a rat is a dog, I'll never know. That woman even knitted it a sweater and walked it on a leash."

Valdis recalled the animal, a magical dog on account of its black droppings, shiny as gems and completely devoid of odor, just like the droppings left by the rodents in the subbasement of the Two Star. Valdis pressed his fingers to his left side—always the left—and fed a blank sheet of paper into his typewriter. It was a Soundless, the same kind Lenin had used. Excepting the fact that the machine had no ribbon, it was as fine a typewriter as one could wish for, especially if one were typing an imaginary book, as Valdis was. It was a Latvian lexicon of how to disappear while acting as if you were happy about it, disappearing being the best way to avoid the attentions of those who would happily exterminate you. In it Valdis intended to catalogue every useful piece of advice he'd received: namely the lessons his late father, Martin Berzins, a refrigerator salesman, had tried to teach him one day, several years ago.

Valdis tapped at the keys, squinted at the blank piece of paper. The paper was open like a field leveled by wind and water, like the field behind the stretch of communal apartments where they lived—that same field they went to one day, because his father had important things to say to Valdis, and the field was where people went to talk. It was spring, and, that day, Valdis's feet sank into the mud, and he remembered that, even then, at ten years of age, he had pains in his left side.

"Don't worry. That's just your ma's cooking," his father explained with a wince. "But listen. Three things a boy like you ought to know." Valdis kept his fingers dancing over the keys, remembering how the kite slapped at his father's head. The first lesson: don't eat tinned meat. The second lesson: never bow to the Russians. Valdis stopped typing and rolled his hands over, examined the meat of his palms. This is what his father had done, just before he closed them into tight fists, which he then shook high in the air.

"Why are you doing that?" Valdis had asked.

"To scare them!" Martin grabbed Valdis's hands and folded them into fists. Overhead the clouds were assuming strange shapes of swollen rags, of hammers, of internal organs and thunder.

"And what if they don't scare?" Valdis asked.

Martin beat his fist against his open palm. "Then crush them!" But they were speaking Latvian in a field where no one could hear them, and, if they could, likely would not understand. And Valdis, a boy then, only wanted to trace maps with wax paper and ride a squeaky bike through town without getting beat up. He liked to look at the sky, consider the clouds. This is why his father made the kite, such a trifle—paper and string—that flagging kite being, of course, the third thing his father was teaching him.

So how could he have missed it—that lone rogue of a cloud hovering at the scrim of the horizon? Viivi had asked him after they'd buried Martin in the back of the cemetery. But boys don't think what clouds can do, not boys like Valdis. And then from the sky a spindly leg of light had come stringing down, a skinny thing, moving quietly with such a seeming lack of ambition that Martin and Valdis couldn't really take it seriously.

"It's so hard, so hard," his father had been saying, touching his chest in a most Latvian way, "to believe in much anymore. And I am frightened of death." At that very moment the tip of the lightening bolt touched his father's head, and he fell to the ground.

Valdis lifted his fingers from the keys. From the kitchen came a scraping of chairs. Alla turned her eyes, wide and rudderless behind her three sets of glasses, toward Valdis. "You must be so proud," Alla whispered to Viivi. "Valdis is so smart."

"It's just the typewriter," Viivi said with a sniff. "Besides, he has a bad kidney."

The arguments of a kidney are loud and insistent. A kidney lacks patience. A kidney blares, announcing its faults with a pain that pulses out of tune. In this way the kidney makes its unhappiness understood. It pines for and suggests the impossible, aspiring to grand proportions and the relevancy of, say, a symbol. But for all its bad points, the faulty kidney has a few good ones, too, Valdis decided as he waited for Kajer at the service entrance of the Two Star. The kidney kept him out of the Russian army. The kidney kept him home with his mother. The kidney got him in good at the hotel where Inspector Netsulis didn't give a damn about the quality of a man's kidney so long as he kept the bathrooms at all times stocked with fat new rolls of toilet paper as the

Japanese and American tourists, it seemed, couldn't have a satisfying crap without them.

"What do I do with the half-used rolls?" Valdis had asked Kajer once.

"Give them to your ma—a gift from me to her," Kajer had said, his voice expansive.

Valdis stamped his feet, wished he had a better coat, then lit a cigarette. Ever since Kajer's wife had bitten him on the neck, then fled through the Kurseme forest, Kajer had developed some interesting ideas about giving and getting gifts. For instance, as a gift, Kajer arranged the job for Valdis at the hotel where Valdis was master cleaner of the toilets, and, of course, in charge of keeping them well stocked. It was also Valdis's job to turn down bed linens with fresh sheets, hang towels and fluff pillows, empty trash bins, and drag a listless vacuum cleaner over the tired rugs. All this he did on account of his bad kidney, which rolled and pitched like a cork in water. All this he did because Kajer had two good kidneys. Because Kajer was so healthy he could lift a horse, if he wanted. Because Kajer had a thing for Viivi, who had clucked and cooed when Kajer told her the story of his erstwhile wife who thought she was a dog. Because Kajer had found in Viivi a somewhat sympathetic ear, and, so desperate for the touch of a woman, might be willing to part with one of his perfect kidneys. It may take some persuading on Valdis's part, Kajer informed Valdis, but he was a reasonable man, Kajer, who said things and ordered Valdis around lest Valdis take the offer of a kidney for granted—this same kidney which, Kajer said, would become lonely if not kept near its mate. "It will work out," Kajer said to Valdis. "You'll see." But how, Valdis had to wonder. By no stretch of the imagination could anyone consider Viivi's heart spacious. To think of the energy Kajer would expend to wear Viivi down wearied Valdis. And honestly, some days Valdis just wished he were dead already.

"Dog Shit. Tie my shoes." Kajer jogged Valdis's elbow.

Valdis stubbed his cigarette, bent, and knotted Kajer's laces.

"You know what's wrong with the world?" Kajer punched Valdis in the shoulder, hard. "There are people in it." Kajer unlocked the back door to the hotel and bowed slightly at the waist. With a munificent sweep of his arm, he ushered Valdis through the corridor and to the

broom closet where Kajer nodded at the mess on the closet floor
and handed Valdis a broom. "Sweep," Kajer said, then turned for the
corridor and for the service lift that would take him upstairs to the
vending machines.

Valdis picked up the broom and pushed the plaster flakes and chinking into a chalky mound in the far corner. It was important to work
hard. If you didn't work hard, it was important to make a show as if
you were. This because of the tinned meat, that first thing his father
had taught him. In certain places no one could point to on a map,
but places every Latvian knows exist all the same, men's hands are cut
off in punishment for not working hard enough, and are ground up
and potted in small tins. All this his father explained just before that
bolt touched his head.

Valdis turned to the heap in the middle of the floor, bent, and
scooped handfuls of the plaster and dry wall. From inside that hole
in the wall, Valdis could smell that mud, metallic and elemental, rich
with the smell of all the things that make mud in the outdoors smell
good while making mud indoors, say in basements and closets, smell
bad. Valdis peered at the hole. It reminded him of his kidney: brooding and broken. Valdis lifted a leg and stepped over the jagged lip of
plaster. The hole seemed to have grown: he had only to fold his body
over like a question mark to fit in it now. Valdis reached into his hip
pocket and lit a match, held it to the darkness. He was not in a small
hole at all, Valdis could see now, but in a long tunnel. Rivulets of water
trickled down a mud wall and emptied into a small trench. All this in
the subbasement of the Riga Two Star Hotel!

"Dog Shit!" Kajer's voice came from outside the hole.

"In here!" Valdis cried. Kajer kicked at the mouth of the hole with
his boot and climbed into the tunnel. "Look there," Valdis pointed.
At the end of the tunnel Valdis could see a faint shaft of light. Kajer
hooked a finger through a belt loop on Valdis's trousers and, doubled
over, they walked toward the pale light. As they stepped out of the
tunnel, the light turned heavy and like liquid, pressed against Valdis's
skin. Valdis straightened and craned his head. Gone were the cracked
and dripping ceilings. And where they should have seen brick or

plaster, joists or mortar, angles and edges—all the things that suggest dimension and proportion—there was nothing, only cloud and, here and there, hints of bluing, of sky.

Kajer shouldered his way around Valdis.

"Fog." Kajer held his palm outstretched as if feeling for rain. "This looks serious."

Valdis gulped, choked on a mouthful of cloud. "Maybe we should tell Inspector Netsulis."

"That pudding ass? No." Kajer stamped his feet again and pulled on the brim of his cap.

The cloud bank lowered and Valdis could sense more than see movement, a shifting darkness at their shins and ankles. White and gray and glossy black dogs skirled at their feet, threaded in between Valdis's legs, pressing against him as they panted and whipped his shins with their tails. Valdis bent and stretched his hand to a hairy shepherd of some kind and felt for himself the whiskers against his cupped palm, saw the bits of cloud caught in the guard hairs.

"Don't stick your hand out for a dog. Not these anyway," Kajer said, lifting his right boot and examining a fresh pile of manure gummed in the treads of the sole. Kajer set his foot down and, immediately, a short-haired gray crapped on the laces of his left boot.

"Okay," Kajer muttered. "This is really getting serious. Maybe I will tell the pudding ass about it." Kajer turned for the tunnel.

In the distance the fog thinned to tails and patches. The dogs swirled around Valdis, propelling him gently. Valdis grimaced, clutched his side. Dentures for false gums, his kidney was really biting now. He could hear Kajer snapping his fingers and calling for him, and then the angry thuds of his boots through the tunnel. But it was easier, Valdis decided, to let the dogs move him where they would. Valdis steadied himself, a palm flattened on the broad back of the shepherd dog, and kept walking. Just ahead he could see large flat stones pushed up from the ground. Clearly it was a cemetery: near the tops of the stones, photos of the dead were preserved and mounted in plastic. Valdis read the names aloud: Ilyin, Brkic, Kalmins, Kaipaks, Mintz. The cemetery was arranged in the same ugly way their city was arranged: Russians here,

Latvians over there, Jews stacked ten deep near the back next to the Gypsies and other undesirables. He could hear them, heavy sleepers, breathing deep and even. Odd, Valdis thought, because every cemetery he had seen (and in Latvia there were more than he had thought possible) there was mud, yes, but at least some bunch or crab grass, such sociable varieties both. But here there was only this mud, which, Valdis suspected, was comprised mostly of dog manure.

The dogs twined around his legs then, shaping and reshaping the air until Valdis couldn't tell where sky, where mud, and he found himself in front of a heaping pile of used appliances: toasters and vacuum cleaners, and, near the top, an unbelievable find—a typewriter. The machine was one of the newer models of the Soundless, and a thin banner of ribbon unspooled in an unseen breeze, catching every invisible movement of the fog. The TVs, though good, had bent antennas and fraying cords. Here and there were sets of crutches, grip pads worn, and work boots, tongues peeled back and cracked. A few yards beyond the pile Valdis could see a tall metal fence. As if reading his mind, the dogs wheeled him toward it. The fencing was orange with rust, and a lock big as a man's hand latched the gate closed. A sign hung next to the lock:

Freedom is within our reach.

Valdis pressed his face against the fence and thrust his hand through the gaps, but he couldn't quite squeeze his body through. Beyond the fence he could hear laughter and see the most amazing sights: rows of Danish gabardine overcoats suspended from fishing wire, healthy kidneys—beautiful and dark marbled pink—fields and fields of kidneys beating wetly in the mud. Overhead in the cobalt and periwinkle skies he heard the sound of wings beating in the air. Birds! He cried aloud—oh, the birds!—species he'd only seen in books, and other birds that used to live in Latvia—and wearing all natural colors, too.

Valdis rattled the gate. Beside him the dogs sat on their haunches, their shiny eyes watching him.

"Pssst! Over here!"

The dogs scampered away and Valdis leaned into the fog, feeling his way toward the nearest stone. From the mist a shadowy figure slowly materialized. There before him, sitting on his own grave stone, was his father, Martin. From the top of his head a thin wisp of smoke curled up into the air. At his feet lay the tattered Moscow Aerostar kite.

"Father!" Valdis cried.

"Does your ma miss me?" Martin's smile was tight and uncertain. Smoke trailed from a nostril.

"No."

"Don't try to sweeten it any. Just tell me how it is. She's still broken up about me, isn't she?"

"No." Valdis shifted his weight and pinched at his side.

Martin spat, kicked his heels soundlessly against the marker. "Well, she's toxic. But God help me, I miss her cooking." Martin rubbed his head. The dogs returned then, pressing tight against Valdis's calves, and propelled him toward the tunnel. Martin picked up a handful of mud and flung it at one of the dogs. "Wait!" he called, his voice trembling to liquid.

It took two bottles of Stakliškes and a visit from Kajer to convince Viivi, Alla, and Rein of the strange weather system that filled the secret subbasement of the Two Star. And nobody, not even Kajer, would believe Valdis when he described the cemetery populated by the likes of Martin, who had, after all, been a bad refrigerator salesman, selling his product in remote villages that did not yet have electricity.

"What did he say?" Viivi pressed her lips together in a bloodless look.

"He misses your cooking."

"You're sure he was dead?" Kajer frowned.

"Pretty sure." Valdis pinched his left side.

"Swear on a piece of iron!" Viivi raised a frying pan above Valdis's head.

"I swear, Mother."

Alla switched glasses and peered at Valdis. "Who else was in the cemetery?"

Valdis shrugged, trying to recall some of the names. "Lots of people, but they were all asleep." Alla's daughter had died for lack of penicillin tablets a few years ago and now, he knew, it was all she thought of, and the reason why Rein quietly drank so much.

"What else?" Kajer punched Valdis's shoulder.

"Some used appliances, a few pairs of boots, and—" here Valdis looked around the table cautiously "—I think I saw heaven's gates."

Viivi folded her arms across her chest. "And?"

"That's all I could see. The gate was locked."

"Why is it locked? Aren't Jews allowed?" Kajer asked.

"Of course we're allowed, stupid." Viivi adjusted her wig and turned to Kajer. "He couldn't get in because he's not fully dead yet."

"Yes," Rein thumped his chest with a fist. "I myself feel only half-dead."

"Gates. Pah! We will trampoline our way in. It's so simple even a child can do it." Kajer glanced at Valdis. "Well, it's relatively simple, anyway. Most children could do it."

"Appliances!" Viivi cried, and in her excitement she launched the frying pan, clipping Valdis in the jaw.

The next morning before the shift change of the service staff at the Two Star, Valdis and Kajer led Viivi, Alla, and Rein into the basement broom closet. Kajer widened the hole so that Rein could push through with the wheelbarrow loaded with a collapsible trampoline while Valdis led the way, punching at the darkness with the hotel's highest-power flashlight. Once they'd cleared the tunnel, they wandered amongst the stones. Rein found a tall obelisk belonging to a Russian major. A big red star burst from the crown of the monument, and tacked on the other side were rows of war medals, some which might bring them at least fifty *litai* if they stood outside the train station.

Viivi found her Aunt Ilka and Auntie Triforyev's headstones and switched them. The mutual confusion would, Valdis supposed, bring the two fractious women together at last.

Meanwhile, Alla clutched the photo of her daughter tight to her chest and combed the rows. She had spotted the children's markers and moved from stone to stone, the picture of her daughter held aloft as a beacon. "Ausra!" Alla called, her voice swallowed by the fog.

16

Viivi looked about for a while, then pointed her nose in the unfamiliar air. "Where are the appliances?"

Valdis shrugged. "Closer to the gates, I think." No sooner had he said the words than the dogs reappeared, yipping and panting, swarming Valdis, who let them lead him through the fog. At the sight of the glistening heap Viivi gave a shout and Rein rushed with the wheelbarrow. A kid's tricycle hung to drip-dry from an invisible wire. From the handlebars dangled a sign:

The meek shall inherit the earth.

"Isn't that a famous quote?" Alla turned to Rein. "Who said that?"

"Jesus, I think." Rein held up a pair of work boots and examined the cracked soles.

"Well, I don't think he really said that. And if he did, I don't think he really meant it. And if he did, it doesn't apply to us—we're Jews!" Kajer said, working his feet into a pair of boots.

"Wasn't Jesus a Jew?" Valdis pinched his side.

"Not the same thing. He wasn't as Jewish as he could have been. Look where it got him." Kajer snorted and Viivi, entranced by a vast assortment of wigs—some quite natural looking—paid no attention to Valdis, who found himself escorted by the dogs back to the rusty gates.

"Pssst!" Martin hissed. Valdis parted the fog with his hands, as a swimmer at the breaststroke. There was his father, face pressed against the gate, hands gripping the metal. Valdis leaned and peered through the fog. If he squinted he could make out the forms of angels, their wings unfurled, skating in those old skates with the metal shanks that you strapped to your feet and tightened with a key. They were playing hockey with, impossibly—yes—their golden crowns. At the places where the points of the crowns knuckled through the glass, pinholes of light leaked up into the air. Star light, Valdis realized.

Valdis craned his neck. He could see the Rilkis family who had died of food poisoning three summers ago—all twelve of them—juggling lemons and oranges over grass so green it offended the senses. They stopped every now and then to fill china plates with pickled herrings. If Valdis's kidney didn't scream so, he might have felt actual hunger.

Instead Valdis couldn't stop blinking. Heaven, it seemed, was a big picnic. Who knew!

"Do you see that?" Valdis turned to his father.

"What?"

"The Rilkis family. The pickled herrings." Valdis stood on tiptoe. "And now they're playing badminton with a ruby the size of a plum."

"Well, if *you* say so, I believe you. After all, they were idiots, eating those potted meats as if they'd go out of style. But to be honest, I can't see that far through the fog." With each word another tendril of smoke curled out of his nostril. It was hard for Valdis to ignore it, hard for him to get used to the figure his father cut, a man who had known so much in life and now seemed so wholly unaware of his situation in death. "But then," Martin dropped his voice to a stage whisper, "I don't believe in all this anyway." Martin motioned with his thumb as they turned from the gates and paused by his stone. "I'm an atheist, you know."

Viivi's voice pierced the fog. "Oh, shut up." Then she materialized, a bright red wig on her head. "You're a Jew and the sooner you start admitting it, the better off you'll be." Viivi yanked Martin by the elbow and pushed him into the mud. "Settle down now and be quiet." The mud folded around Martin even as he thrashed and chuffed. "I still love you!" he sputtered.

Viivi turned to Valdis. "God, what a pest!"

Alla, out of breath, emerged from the fog, two of her glasses perched in tandem on her nose. Her eyes, magnified by the lenses, swam in confusion. "Did you say you saw lemons and oranges?"

"Yes. It's like a big supermarket over there," Valdis said. Rein jumped for the wheelbarrow and began wheeling the trampoline in the direction Valdis had just come.

"How much did they cost?" Alla asked.

"That's just it—everything's free," Valdis replied.

"Impossible," Kajer said, waving Rein back.

"Valdis always was one for visions." Viivi tucked a used lipstick into her bra. "So don't pay any attention to him. Besides, it's getting late and my feet hurt," she announced. With a synchronous grunt, Kajer and

18

Rein each lifted a handle of the wheelbarrow and followed Viivi.

Alla grabbed Valdis's elbow in a fierce pinch. "You're the smart one, tell me: why do some people, like Martin, get to move about the cemetery and others do not?"

Valdis studied Alla's eyes, which were shiny and wet. He knew she had not found Ausra, and likely never would. "I don't know," Valdis mumbled, and an ugly taste filled his mouth.

The next morning Viivi sat at Valdis's cardboard desk and fingered the shiny curls of her new red wig. "I'm not so sure about this color with my complexion. Chestnut would be better, don't you think?"

Valdis, under the kitchen table, curled his knees into his chest and moaned. Never in his life had he hurt like this. "I don't know, Mother," he groaned.

"Yes, chestnut would be better. We should go back to the pile."

"So go," Valdis clutched his side.

"Oh, no. We all go together," Viivi said, picking up the phone and ringing Alla. "Besides, you're the only one who can see where you're going."

Valdis moaned. What his mother said was absolutely true: while the others could see the cemetery, the household heap, and even Martin, only Valdis could navigate the fog, and this only because of the dogs. And none of them, except Valdis, could perceive anything beyond the rusty heavenly fencing.

"My side," Valdis gasped.

"Oh, don't be such a baby," Viivi said, reaching for her frying pan.

It only took a moment for Kajer to write up Valdis's absence as a sickness and leave a note asking the new girl from the overnight shift to stay on and cover Valdis's rounds. That done, they trudged through the mud tunnel, Rein with his Soviet army-issue duffel strapped to his back, Alla her three sets of glasses and that photo of Ausra, and Kajer with a slightly larger wheelbarrow. Viivi brought the plastic shopping bag she used for a purse, only instead of tissue and her umbrella, she'd stowed her super-strength spirit gum, the strongest adhesive she could find for the backs of the wigs. At the far lip of the tunnel they stepped into a thick band of cloud, which was heavy and, like wet wool, clung to their skin and clothes.

As soon as they spied the heap, Alla veered off for an unexplored portion of the cemetery, her arms extended like a sleepwalker feeling for foreign objects. Rein, Viivi, Kajer, and Valdis stood in front of the heap with postures of consternation. The pile, it seemed, was growing. At their feet an accordion sighed and Valdis noted how the open snaps of women's compacts, which weren't there the day before, glittered like jewels, duplicating their bewilderment.

"What can this mean?" Rein cautiously walked the circumference of the heap.

"Who is leaving all this behind?" Viivi looked to Valdis for an answer. But Valdis could only cough into his sleeve, and wince.

"Oh, who the hell cares. It's ours and no one else has to know about it!" Kajer said, and began loading up the wheelbarrow. Rein reemerged from the fog; in his hands leaky bagpipes wheezed and complained with his every movement. Viivi draped an assortment of wigs, scalp sides turned out, over the handlebars of a child's bike, and began applying the spirit gum. She had been a beautiful woman once, and in a glance Valdis understood then how hard it was for her to give up that former notion of herself. Rein had finished with the bagpipes and uncapped a bottle, suspended it over his open mouth. Watching, Valdis began to see how when Rein drank it was like tonguing the moon in the bottle, and that burn of vodka, that was like swallowing the wet acid forests.

Valdis stood on tiptoe. Above the fog line he could see the green, fescue and sedge, aspen and willow. The birds trilled and whistled, and in the lower left corner, all those pink and friendly kidneys turned in their furrows, waiting patiently for him. Valdis pinched his side and sat down on a toaster. At his elbow was the Soundless, and beside him those gadgets and trinkets, the clumsy artifacts that he knew meant everything to a man like Kajer, who was, even now, piling as many of them as his wheelbarrow would allow. It wasn't as if Valdis, too, didn't feel the pull of all these things. Valdis bit his lip imagining the great profundities he might type on such a machine as this Soundless; imagined, too, that the typewriter might long for the touch of his fingers, and that the ribbon, beautiful and thick with new black ink, breathed the currents of air. But he was tired, weary in his blood of this life, and him not even an old man. And he was tired of being alone, something you could not say in the company of other people.

The kidney pinched and Valdis doubled over and retched violently. The dogs sat on their haunches, watching. When Valdis wiped his mouth on his sleeve, they followed him to where the others stood.

The fog had lowered, gloving them all in dew.

"We should go back. People will wonder," Kajer grunted behind the wheelbarrow.

"It is a miserable land, a miserable life," Alla said, the photo of Ausra crushed against her chest.

"Yes, but it is still our land and our life." Rein capped the bottle and tucked it into his waistband.

Viivi sniffed suspiciously. "You're right. We can't stay here," she announced. In the set of her jaw Valdis realized she would never leave it behind, that old life, would never see what he could, an immutable landscape painted in the impossible colors of pure joy. Nor would she hear as he could the music of the aspens shaking their paper coins, or the soft sounds of Latvian carried in the understory of the birch and willow. There would be no way to coax her or anyone else closer to these gates they could not see. But it wasn't their fault, Valdis decided. They weren't dead yet. Then Valdis realized with a jolt that he was. Valdis plugged a finger into the soft flesh below his left rib cage. He squeezed his eyes closed waiting for the buzz of neon lights cartwheeling him to pain. Nothing. Valdis opened his eyes and turned for the gates.

"Are you coming, or what?" Viivi straightened her wig. Amber, the color of weeping bark, a color not so bad for her.

"No."

"If you don't come back, you don't get my kidney!" Kajer's voice was thin and spectral. Valdis shifted his weight from one foot to the other.

"Oh, forget him. Let's go." Viivi held a finger to her nose, rolled her eyes at Kajer. "Heaven has a bad smell."

• • •

Valdis found his father leaning against the fencing and rubbing the spot where the sky had dented his head. "It's so hard, really, to find any good conversation. Especially here." Martin indicated the cemetery with a jerk from his thumb. "And I'm really quite tired. Atheism is so exhausting, and now all I really want to do is sleep." Martin slumped. He was fading, as an image on a TV screen sheeted in static and snow. Martin drew his knees to his chest and Valdis bent, put his hand on his father's shoulder. Then Martin was gone, the tired kite all that was left to suggest he'd ever been there in the first place.

Valdis knelt at the gate, sank to his knees in the mud. Though a clever man in possession of good and true advice, his father—God rest him—had not learned much in his years here outside the gates. But it didn't have to be that way, Valdis decided, as he buried his hands in the mud. A life could be lived in revision. In this way it was possible to receive a distillation from the heavens, a dispensation to leave off with old gestures, leave behind all trappings of a former life. An end to weariness, an end to pain; this was how quiet healing came, in spite of what one knew or thought they knew.

Valdis clawed at the mud, pulling handfuls up at a time. Beside him the dogs dug with their forelegs, rooster tails of wet dirt flying out behind them. After a few minutes of digging, Valdis sat and wiped at his forehead. The dogs raced along the fence, stopped here and there to raise a leg. Valdis squinted, watching a terrier piss at the base of the latched gate. Something about the gate was different. Valdis straightened. How could he have missed it? The lock had sprung and the gate fallen open. All he had to do was give a little push and it would swing wide on its hinges.

Valdis wiped at the mud on his knees. He did not know exactly what would happen to him next, only that he would walk through that open gate and never once look back.

Valdis took a step and was immediately caught in a whirlwind of dogs. The air was so fibrous now, it wobbled to full saturation, and Valdis, buoyed up on the backs of the dogs, allowed himself to be carried in.

FICTION OPEN AWARD WINNERS

1ST PLACE

Gina Ochsner receives $2000 for
"A Cloud for a Carpet."

Ochsner's bio is on page 6 preceding her story.

2ND PLACE

Sean Beaudoin receives $500 for "Winter Kills."

It was still raining in the morning, just as hard, fractured sheets of water draped from the roof across the window, leaving Germanic shadows on our arms and legs.

Sean Beaudoin lives and works in San Francisco. He holds a completely useless degree, he says, in photography from Antioch College. Other writing will appear in the upcoming issues of *Floating Holiday* and the *New Orleans Review*.

3RD PLACE

Susan Engberg receives $300 for "Margaret."

"And you, Maggie dear, how are you?" Lolly asks finally, sounding spookily like her mother Rosemary, poised either to pity me, or save me from what her family calls the godlessness of ours.

Susan Engberg's stories and novellas have appeared in many journals and anthologies and have been collected in three volumes: *Pastorale* (University of Illinois Press), *A Stay by the River* (Viking Penguin), and *Sarah's Laughter* (Alfred A. Knopf). A recipient of a Creative Writing Fellowship from the National Endowment for the Arts and other prizes, she lives with her husband in Milwaukee, Wisconsin.

We invite you to visit www.glimmertrain.com to see a list of the top twenty-five winners and finalists. We thank all entrants for sending in their work.

My literary mentor, brother Tom, at nine. We were riding the ferry across the Mississippi River from Iowa to Illinois. It was 1953.

Lucia Nevai's short fiction has been published in the *New Yorker*, *Zoetrope*, the *Iowa Review*, *New England Review*, and other periodicals. Her novel, *Seriously*, was published in 2004 by Little, Brown. She has published two collections of stories, *Star Game*, which won the Iowa Short Fiction Award, and *Normal*. Born in Iowa, she now lives in upstate New York.

EMILE

Lucia Nevai [signature]

Lucia Nevai

At two o'clock on the day before Thanksgiving, the stranger came to the Department of Environmental Conservation, looking for information. He had a letter from a child he had fathered in his youth, then immediately lost track of, who was now seventeen and resided in a state-run home for the deaf outside Albany. This being the biggest travel day of the year, almost no one anywhere in the state offices was at their desk.

Gretchen was the department head. She had worked her way up from grade-five assistant by applying a rigid Scotch-Irish work ethic, softened with an informal Christian generosity. She would not tolerate lateness, sloppiness, or mistakes, but she forgave absences of any length necessitated by love—a sick child, a spouse in OR, a parent in ICU.

To her credit, Gretchen looked more like a person, less like a boss. She was clear eyed and rosy cheeked, sturdily built with no surface sensuality, an energetic being in whom socialization had occurred early, quickly, and without a price. Her choice of apparel was subordinate-friendly—quality suits and slack sets that reflected self-respect without ostentation. These she personalized with costume jewelry that invited comment without inspiring envy. Everyone knew she collected spoons and grew brown-eyed susans; her husband bred and trained border collies. Accordingly, these were the themes of her adornment.

Gretchen had turned off her computer and wanted to go home, but the stranger was deferentially approaching her desk, letter in hand. His name, he said, was Liske, Foster Liske. He was supposed to visit his son, Emile, this evening, but Emile, in error, had been bussed to a handicapped jamboree. No one at the home felt qualified to release information regarding Emile's destination.

"You want the office of Health, Education, and Welfare," Gretchen said.

"Ahh, yes," the stranger said. "The seventh floor of building C." He'd been there. Everyone was gone.

"I don't have access to those records," Gretchen said. "This is Environmental Conservation."

The stranger lowered his head, smiling a strange, ironic smile, the smile of a man who keeps losing at life. He was a withdrawn man. He was blond, with a bit of premature balding at the temples, irises that were gray-green and looked as if they had been recently removed, rinsed in sorrow, and replaced. His trench coat was of the belted, double-breasted, expensive, European variety. On his right hand he wore an interesting ring—not quite fraternity, not quite Masonic. Gretchen read the letter.

Emile was born deaf in New York City, August 17, 1985. Six weeks later his mother died of pneumonia. She was estranged from his father, whose whereabouts were unknown. Tuesday morning, Emile had found his father on the internet.

Gretchen called her husband and told him to meet the 4:45 p.m. flight from Kansas City. Her son's in-laws were coming for Thanksgiving. She offered the stranger a bottle of distilled water, which he declined. He sat down, still in his trench coat, and read a French newspaper. She put on her bifocals, booted up her computer, and hacked her way into the welfare records.

Gretchen had two adult children, a son and a daughter. Both lived nearby and were married, with good jobs. Her daughter had three daughters, all pretty, healthy, and athletic. Her son's wife had given birth over the summer, to a brown-haired baby boy who was—she shivered to admit it—perfect. The boy slept through the night, was strong, breast fed effortlessly, with never a moment's colic or indigestion. His complexion was creamy and clear. When he smiled, he beamed a celestial happiness, punctuated with what Gretchen liked to consider a masculine pair of dimples. He was named Will, a name equally delighted in by everyone on both sides of the family.

The arrival of a grandson had pleased Gretchen's husband, also a Will, more than the arrival of any of his granddaughters. It spawned an appreciation for their daughter-in-law; he became both demonstrative and useful. "He never swept my kitchen floor when I fed you," Gretchen would say to her son every time Will snatched up the broom at the close of a family meal as her exhausted daughter-in-law lingered at the high chair with unbrushed hair and blue bags under her eyes, spoon in hand, feeding Little Will.

Gretchen was not introspective as a rule, but she could not help noting that the addition of Little Will to the family had driven the tiniest of mental wedges between herself and her daughter-in-law, creating the mildest, the faintest scorecard with God: her daughter-in-law now had it better in the family than her daughter. Gretchen made sure not to allow any by-product of this small, contained grudge to infect her feelings for Little Will. She was doing well along these lines when things went wrong in the world and of the six National Guard units called up for tours of duty in Iraq, one included her son. Now she had a very big scorecard with God.

Her brain began to time-release memory after rich memory of her twenty-seven-year-old son as a child, each one looming before her in queasy, vivid colors, drenched with high-fat poignancy and choked down in the heart-rending new perspective of unforgivable danger. During these days, her productivity declined. She forgot appointments, paid for prescriptions then left them on the drugstore counter, dropped glass jars of food on the supermarket floor, had a fender bender, deleted an irretrievable file. Gretchen didn't go to church, but she lived her life by Christian ideals. She had not really paid that much attention to God before. Now she was asking him for a biggie. She wanted God to guarantee for her son total intactness of body, mind, and spirit. There could be no maiming. She would not accept any Post-Traumatic Stress

Syndrome. A very small depression might be tolerated upon her son's return home to domestic bliss—part and parcel of a decompression period psychologically appropriate after eighteen months of riding through sandstorms in helicopters, waiting to be picked off. December 4, he would be deployed.

Gretchen hastily arranged a christening for the Sunday after Thanksgiving. Her son's in-laws decided to fly out from Kansas City to attend. They were to stay with Gretchen at her son's request—his home was too small. Thanksgiving dinner would be held there, too, for the same reason. It was a lot.

There were two handicapped jamborees being staged in New York State: one in Pottstown, four hours north, and one in Jamestown, seven hours west, as far west as you could go and still be in New York. Gretchen picked up the phone and did her department-head thing. Emile was expected in Jamestown. She wrote the address and telephone number of the facility on a scrap of paper for the stranger.

It was six o'clock when she drove out of the state-employee parking lot. She turned on the radio to get the news. *A ceasefire has been ordered in Iraq today*—those were the words she irrationally dreamed of hearing every time she punched the on button. Today, she had missed the war news, or there was none: just an electrical fire that killed some children in a cabin, a drug-related stabbing death, and, bad news for travelers, a snowstorm was on the way.

The traffic light before the on-ramp was red. She came to a stop. Standing right there where no pedestrian ever stood was the stranger, hands in his pockets, looking lost. She rolled down the passenger window and called out to him, addressing him only as *you* because she couldn't remember which of his two names was first and which was last. "Can I take you to your vehicle?"

"I don't have one," he said.

"Can I drive you to your motel?" she said.

"I don't have one," he said.

"Where are you going?"

"I don't know," he said.

The light turned green. "How did you get here?" she said.

"I took a taxi from the airport," he said. "I came from Paris—just now."

"Get in," she said.

He bent at the waist, looking into the car, carefully reading her eyes to see if he had correctly understood her invitation. "I don't want to be a burden," he said.

She opened the passenger door for him, saying, "Please."

Gretchen drove the stranger to her house. The message her husband left on the answering machine warned her that the in-laws' flight was delayed indefinitely. Gretchen sat the stranger down at the dinette table in her kitchen with the telephone and the Yellow Pages. She told him to go down the Lodging list until he was able to book a room.

She went into overdrive, preparing foods for the feast. She chopped sweet potatoes, minced onions, peeled carrots, pared turnips, parboiled potatoes, sliced apples, shelled pecans. She rolled out pie dough for six pies and mixed three fillings: apple, pumpkin, and chocolate pecan.

The stranger's voice was passive, nearly inaudible. His telephone manner was overly formal. A simple, immediate, *Do you have any rooms?* would do, but he had to explain that he'd been caught unexpectedly without hope of shelter and was telephoning from the home of an extremely kind stranger to investigate the availability of accommodation. Yes, for tonight. The answer was always the same. Nothing was available until Friday.

The stranger was asleep on the sofa in her husband's pajamas by the time the plane landed and her husband had found the in-laws' lost luggage. The in-laws were rattled and drunk. Gretchen had met them only once, at the wedding. They were both teachers. She made them comfortable. When their door was shut, she and her husband fell into a spontaneous embrace both had needed all day. "I don't know if I can do this," she said. Neither of them had ever heard this tone in her voice—there was gravity, desperation, assault, suffocation. After she said it, he permitted himself a single inaudible sob.

Early Thanksgiving morning, the stranger was standing outside on the deck in his trench coat with his back to the sliding glass doors, looking at the blue hills to the west when Emile called. The stranger's voice came alive with emotion. It was only the second time the two men had spoken to each other. Apparently, the resident manager could not release Emile unless the stranger appeared in person with the letter. Gretchen got on the phone. She confirmed that the driver of the bus could not return to Albany until Friday when the roads were cleared. "Send Emile back with him," she said. "I'll take responsibility." She asked the stranger to have Thanksgiving dinner with them.

Gretchen got out the good china and set the table for thirteen, a number she superstitiously regretted. The phone began to ring: first her daughter to say the girls were sick—they all had fevers and diarrhea; then her daughter-in-law, who wished to speak to her parents. Daughter and daughter-in-law called every half hour. For the first time in her life, Gretchen understood how an introverted person might dread even a friendly voice on the phone for the way it ruptured the stabilizing, self-preserving counsel one kept with oneself.

In the end, five places were removed from the table. There was food enough on the sideboard for thirty when Gretchen, her son, Big Will, Little Will, the stranger, and the in-laws sat down to say grace. Because the missing people were the noise-providing ones—all three grand-daughters chattered, interrupted, told jokes, gossiped, teased, complained, competed, and cried—the meal was eaten in silence.

Gretchen kept looking over at her son and seeing a brown-haired man of twenty-seven with his father's speckled eyes, his mother's rosy cheeks, and his own quiet manner. He was hard working, orderly, and fastidious. He wore a pink oxford-cloth shirt with a button-down collar which flattered him—pink was his color—but which Gretchen regretted today because she remembered him as a twelve year old, choosing pink in the men's department for the first time.

Except for an infrequent coo from Little Will, the only sound during the feast was the clink of silver against china as her guests filled their plates, then passed dish after dish after dish around the table. Gretchen could have used a bit more bubbliness from the in-laws. She could have used a compliment or two. She could have used a hand. They were exhausted, they were hungover, yes. But they had slept until noon, showered and dressed, then both sat down to read the paper without asking if there was anything they could do. They were concerned with their own comfort and pathos first and foremost; they were unaware that their hosts were people who both had full-time jobs and whose son was going to war.

Gretchen took a hard look at both of them across the table in the light of the bland November noon. Her daughter-in-law's mother was small, dark, moody, and self-satisfied. She taught high-school chemistry. The father taught elementary social studies. He was lighter of complexion and he had the potential to bring brightness into the conversation. At least he had praised her husband for their beautiful view of the Catskill Mountains.

Gretchen resented the way the woman ate with her elbows on the table, staring straight ahead into space and chewing methodically as if she were alone. Her husband on her right and her daughter on her left were both anxious to make sure the woman had everything she needed. "Butter, Mom?" Gretchen's daughter-in-law said in a tone so "positive" it was eerie. The woman nodded. Her daughter put two pats on the plate for her mother, as if she, not Little Will, was the helpless one.

Gretchen looked at her husband to see if he had noticed this. If he had, they could laugh about it later. If not, she was on her own. There was no explaining nuances of behavior to him after the fact. Her husband looked distracted. His plate was half full, but he had stopped eating. His stomach was bothering him again. He laid his silverware neatly across the plate, knife parallel to fork, leaned back in his chair, and said to the stranger, "Tell us about your son."

The stranger spoke in French-inflected English with an occasional Swedishism. "When I was seventeen," he said, "I took a freighter from Gottenborg to New York. I stayed with an aunt. I had no green card. I fell into a lucrative but very dangerous situation. I hand-delivered illegal skins."

"Skins?" Gretchen's husband said, taking a fold of his own along the forearm. The stranger had pronounced it *skeens*.

"Yes," he said. "Endangered species. Animals that were poached in Africa and Thailand. They were killed and skinned and smuggled to a very small storefront on a little street near the Bowery. Celebrities came to this store to buy skins from an old man. The old man was Russian. He had to be eighty. He was religious. His clothes were long and black, but they had this smell—the smell of sweat, leather, glands, blood, grease. Truly, it was the smell of murder. His breath smelled too, of strong things like whitefish or herring.

"Jewish," the father-in-law whispered to his wife. The stranger eyed him for a moment.

"Yes," he said. He went on. "When I came into the picture, the old man's big customer was a tax attorney with a fancy office next to the Hilton Hotel. The attorney's wife cut the skins into beautiful coats, and had them sewn together however these celebrities wanted them sewn. Tiger was the big thing when I was in the picture. Zebra was *outre*. The attorney was . . . a new kind of man. Immoral. Lean. No smell—maybe just the faintest English aftershave. He didn't eat. He didn't go to the Synagogue. He went to the Hamptons. His clothes cost a fortune. I took these skins in a steel briefcase in a taxi. From the old man to the new man, it was twenty minutes. The attorney would see me the minute I arrived. He took me into his office. There were floor-to-ceiling windows, looking all the way up the Avenue of the Americas to Central Park and all the way down to the Village. He flipped open the sprockets and inspected the skins. Then he paid me—a lot. I don't even want to say to this day how much. This went on every two to three weeks.

"Many times when I walked past the Hilton Hotel, there was a beautiful, dark-haired girl standing next to the service entrance by the laundry vents. She wore a starched pink uniform, very proper, very innocent, but she leaned against the granite of the hotel, smoking, with one leg bent at the knee and the sole of that foot pressed up against the granite. She leaned there in the midst of these great, white, clean clouds of steam, smoking a Gaulois and holding the blue pack.

"I got up my courage one day and said, *Bonjour, ma belle jolie.* There was a slight delay. She could read lips. She was deciding whether or not to respond and how much to reveal. She decided to reveal everything. She signed something like, *Where does a Swede just off the boat learn such pretty French?* We began to have conversations, me speaking French, she reading my lips and signing something back. We understood each other so perfectly—we both forgot she was deaf.

"I began to bring her very expensive gifts. We fell in love. We would meet in the fancy Hilton suites on the high floors after the guests were gone. She knew when and how to steal the key. We were careless. Emile was conceived. We were both seventeen. We didn't have green cards. What could we do?

"I offered to pay for an abortion, but she had a better plan. She would get her green card and we would marry. I would be legal and our baby would be an American citizen. I went along with it, though I never dreamed it would work. She tried to convince her boss to sponsor her, but he wouldn't, not unless she slept with him. She refused. Then as the baby began to show, she panicked. It was too late to get rid of it. She decided to go ahead with it, with the boss thing. She was in America, and in America, this is the way things were done.

"I agreed to it, but after it was over, I was destroyed. It ruined everything—her, the baby, America. At least the boss was true to his word. She got the green card. We were free to marry. I couldn't even look at her. I took a freighter back to Gottenborg."

"Before Emile was born?" Gretchen asked.

"Yes," the stranger said. "She listed me as the father and put my whereabouts as unknown. Emile was born deaf. And, six weeks later, she died! She died of pneumonia she caught in the hospital, this beautiful, dark-haired angel who never hurt anyone."

In the morning, Gretchen drove the stranger to a long, brown strip motel off the Northway. His room was poorly heated, dark, noisy, and stale. Heavy draperies hung from a bent curtain rod across an expanse of glass overlooking the Northway, while the wall that faced the woodlands behind was windowless. The toilet tank continually filled with water, trickling like a maddening, "mood-adjusting" desktop waterfall. Gretchen removed the tank lid, reached into the cold water, and adjusted the lever on the suction cup at the bottom of the tank. The noise stopped. They said goodbye.

Saturday she fell apart.

Her sister's church was charming enough. The stained-glass windows at the front and rear were old and exceptionally beautiful, with rich reds, saturated yellows, emerald greens, and cobalt blues. Gretchen was grateful that the design featured doves, lilies, irises, roses, and ivy. She preferred stained-glass windows without people in them, including Jesus. He never looked right. The pews were new. The hymnals were, too—they smelled of glue.

Gretchen's son wore a white shirt with a navy-blue tie. His cheeks were rosy. His manner was calm. Her daughter-in-law had dressed herself in black and Little Will in red. Gretchen was floored. What kind of a woman would wear black to a christening and dress her baby boy in red?

As Gretchen looked over her shoulder to see which of her son's best friends were showing up, the stranger entered, his hands in the front pockets of his trench coat. He hesitated at the rear. His eyes caught hers. She waved him over. She wanted him to sit with the family.

The Reverend was a balding man with heavy eyebrows and a some-what handsome smile. The Simon Says aspect of the church service had always bored and baffled Gretchen. Please rise; please be seated. Turn to hymn number this; turn to hymn number that. Even as a child, she wondered why anyone with a choice in the matter would voluntarily spend an hour doing this on their day off. The choir sang, straining equally over high notes and low. In his mother's arms, Little Will began to fuss. The red cotton suit made him resemble a miniature old man in red flannel longjohns. Gretchen's son took the boy. She was pleased at the way, chest to chest with his father, the boy became instantly calm. Little Will looked out over his father's shoulder directly at the great round stained-glass window. It pleased him. He cooed, waving his clean pink fist in small circles at the sight, as if mixing the colored light into the plain.

Little Will's father was watching this. The boy felt his gaze and turned to him. They were nose to nose. They both smiled. People whipped out their disposable cameras. There was a soft, percussive flurry of clicks, accompanied by a phosphorescent flashing of bulbs high over the pews. Little Will's mother decided to feed him.

When the choir sat down, the Reverend called the young family to the altar. "We are here today," the Reverend said, "to witness the coming to Christ of Bill."

His name is Will, Gretchen thought. *Someone correct him*. But no one did. The Reverend took the baby from his mother, grasping the boy firmly along his ribs. Little Will looked alarmed. Air bubbles in his stomach attempted to rise to his throat. He grimaced. The Reverend called him Bill again. The baby turned a light green. His father snatched him away in time. A small, white jet of formula arced onto the red carpet. A forgiving noise arose from the pews, a soft, domestic *uh-oh*. The choir director bent at her waist as if staying out of a snapshot, hurried forth to dab at the spit-up with a coarse, brown, institutional paper towel. The Reverend made quick work of the rest, dipping his hand in the holy water, placing it on "Bill's" head, pronouncing him baptized in the name of the Father, the Son and the Holy Ghost.

The reception was at Gretchen's house. Finally, her home sounded like it should. Her granddaughters were there to chatter, cry, interrupt, compete. Two of her son's three best friends had driven up from North Carolina, adding a gentle, jocular bass tone to the gathering, the intimate sound of adult men in unguarded camaraderie. At last—lovely familiar family noise.

The sideboard was groaning anew with easy snacks and comfort food—lasagna, chili, turkey pot pie. The football game began. The men moved, each with an open bottle of beer, toward the large-screen TV in the den. Gretchen felt comforted by the sound of the game, the stadium crowd, the two announcers, the men in the den, urging, warning, cursing, yelling, always reacting as one. It had a harmless, nostalgic ring, like a big-band swing tune on a scratchy 78.

At one point, Gretchen needed air. She swept through the kitchen to the garage that functioned as her pantry. She intended to just take a moment for herself, but someone was already there—her son. Still in his white shirt and navy tie, he was arranging the soft drinks by brand. Suddenly, she was afraid for him. "What are you doing?" she said, unable to keep a casual tone.

He continued lining up the twelve-packs for a moment before answering. "Oh...nothing," he said.

Two nights later, at her daughter-in-law's insistence, they staged an early Christmas. Her daughter-in-law put up the tree. Gretchen baked Danish butter cookies and gingerbread men. She roasted the traditional Christmas pork tenderloin. A fluke in the weather made Tuesday the hottest winter night in a century. Everyone was sweating in their Christmas outfits as they went through the motions of opening gifts, acting surprised, acting happy. Then that, too, was over. Her son was deployed.

The first communications from Iraq were encouraging—his voice was as clear as if he were right down the street. They spoke twice. Then in January in Fallujah, his Black Hawk was shot down and all nine soldiers aboard were killed.

Throughout the jobs of death—getting the body back; writing an obituary for the paper; making the arrangements with the Reverend who'd done the christening; throughout the hollow service and the hollow reception afterwards at the home of her sister, while Gretchen moved forward step by step, carrying that great, gray weight which was the rest of her life—something spiritually interesting nagged at her. Until it revealed itself, she bore a grudge. Yes, she was a lukewarm Christian, but God wasn't a Christian at all.

Then one afternoon in the office, when she was pausing over a cup of tea, she realized that all along she knew. She knew he would die. The in-laws knew, too—that's why they kept to themselves. His friends knew—that's why they drove ten hours up and ten hours back for two hours of lasagna and football. The stranger knew. That's why he showed up at the christening, though it took two eighty-dollar cab rides. Even the weather knew, producing a night as hot as Iraq for their false, rushed Christmas. The only one who didn't know was Little Will, and he wouldn't remember.

It was painful, like a shard of glass in an open wound, the way she and the stranger had helped each other through the Lost Son Relay. When they met, she was running her lap. He was jogging in place, waiting for the hand-off. But the pain of that came to seem too coy. Gretchen began to relax into a great, unholy, metaphysical indifference. According to the stranger's emails, he and Emile were getting on famously.

This is my sister and me dressed for church. Recently my sister let me stay at her house for a few weeks when I was broke and had no place to live. I still love to dress up in nice clothes and my sister is still beautiful and kind to her little brother.

Matt Bondurant currently lives in Alexandria, Virginia. He has previously published stories in *Prairie Schooner, Gulf Coast,* and the *Hawaii Review,* among others, and the first chapter of his first novel was published in the *New England Review* spring 2003 issue. A Bread Loaf waiter and staff member in 2000 and 2001, he received his PhD at Florida State University where he was a Kingsbury Fellow. His first novel, *The Third Translation,* was published by Hyperion Books in the spring of 2005.

TELEMETRY

Matt Bondurant

I had two thousand milligrams of blue-green algae surging through my intestines when Scotty Marin's mother called me at work for the fifth time. Her brother, the sheriff's deputy, was going to kill me.

I was on the kitchen extension, back by the dish station. It was the middle of the dinner shift and the place was steaming with clattering hordes of diners tucking into cheap pasta. I was holding a tray of drinks when Genny the hostess said I had a phone call. This was in the winter of 1994. I was stuck in Staunton, Virginia. My short-wave radio set, the most important thing in the world to me then, was in hock at Billy's Gun and Pawn. I was in love with a hippie college girl who sold algae to pay for pot and booze.

You don't touch my boy, Scotty Marin's mother was saying. My brother is a sheriff's deputy. He's gonna find you and *git* you.

The cooks, a line of heavily tattooed and pierced teenagers, were looking at me sideways, as they prepped lasagna plates and slid trays of frozen stuffed peppers under the giant cast-iron broilers.

Find me? I said. You called me here. You know where I am *now*.

You shouldn't *never* laid hands on my boy.

I'm right here, I said. C'mon over any time.

Now all the cook's ladles paused in mid-scoop. The ice in my drinks was melting fast and I needed to check my tables.

Matt Bondurant

Look, I said, you know where I am, and when I'll be here. You keep calling me but nothing happens. If you like, I'll give you my home number and you can threaten me there.

Scotty Marin was this twenty-year-old punk, another waiter working with me at the Olive Tree in Staunton. It was because of him that I ended up working as a collector for Mahoney and his Pink Mafia.

So maybe I was a little edgy about being back in Virginia again, with my set at the pawn shop, but this kid Scotty Marin really pushed it. I was just asking for help with the side work that he was assigned to do anyway. The place was jammed and we had no salad plates. The motto at the Olive Tree was *Eat it and beat it*; you had to turn the tables to make any money.

Scotty Marin kept saying, Yeah, whatever. Several times he did this.

Then in the kitchen I said to him, look, you gotta help me out. Stack those plates from the washer and prep the salad station. Which is supposed to be his job anyhow.

So he looked right at me and jabbed his finger in my nose.

Fuck! You! Kaiser! he said.

Scotty Marin was not a big guy, a bit short and skinny, and he wasn't scaring anyone. I'm six-three in my boots and maybe two hundred pounds. Not an imposing fellow necessarily, but at the time I was doing a hundred push-ups and a hundred sit-ups a day. I was thirty-four years old then, more than ten years his senior.

I dropped my tray and grabbed him with both hands, right there in the kitchen, one hand bending that finger down and away and the other hand tearing his fake tuxedo shirt down the front, the buttons popping off in all directions. I brought his hand with the finger behind him in a chicken wing and shoved him against the tile wall, jamming my forearm in the back of his neck.

Then I saw a tattooed hand on my arm and the cooks were pulling me off. Scotty just huddled there, still facing the wall, his shoulders shaking and the back of his neck red and splotchy. There was blood smeared against the tiles where I crushed his nose into the wall. Genny

40

Glimmer Train Stories

the hostess was crying and trying to hold the scraps of Scotty's shirt up to his bleeding face. I'd never done anything like it before in my life.

I'd come back to Staunton for my father. He died almost six months ago and somehow I was still here. My ex-wife is an actress, still living in West Hollywood. She had a penchant for getting drunk and chain-smoking a UCLA frat house. My modeling career had dried up pretty quick, and my HBO drama pilot didn't go past testing.

Perhaps the only consistent thing in my life up to that point was that I had been operating a short-wave radio on an Advanced Class A license for eleven years. I was a satellite-radio operations airman in the Air Force before I went to L.A., but my father is the one who got me into short wave. I had 1,500 watts of output, an ICOM 735 HF two-way that could reach around the globe and back. But at the time I had my radio equipment put up at Billy's Gun and Pawn, almost four grand worth of electronics. The divorce wiped me out, and since I hadn't been getting much work in the last six months of our marriage, I left L.A. with nothing but debts. Billy set up a payment plan for me; I just had to get him four hundred up front to get my set back. I had to get that money together quick.

Billy knew my dad from way back, and so he gave me a .357 Ruger, a massive black pistol, to borrow for the duration that my radio was in hock.

Gotta protect youself, Billy said. Every man needs his own piece nowadays.

I didn't believe that, but Billy was giving me a break on my set. He let me keep my recording instruments on-line in the back of his shop, so I could keep tabs on the short-wave number and tone stations, the stations I'd been tracking for almost ten years. So I kept the pistol in the glove box in my Volkswagen.

After the incident with Scotty Marin, I thought I'd be fired for sure. I kept waiting for Mahoney to call me in to can me. But it didn't happen.

In fact, it seemed to make me more popular than ever. After that night the cooks started shooting me my entrees across the shelf when I walked in the door, everything hot and looking nice. Even Sebastian, the head line cook with just about every exposed inch of skin covered with tattoos, the sinister kind—even Sebastian hooked me up with an extra plate of meatballs plus a cup of seafood bisque on my break.

Big mother, Sebastian was, at least six-six and a rangy two thirty or so, with a shaved head and a heavy Teutonic profile. But that wasn't his most remarkable feature. A few months ago Sebastian got all lit up on cheap weed and booze and laid his motorcycle down on a stretch of Interstate 81 going about ninety. The guardrail caught him by the head as he went skidding by, and he had to wear one of those halo immobilizer things fastened onto his head and shoulders. There was a frame set up on his wide collarbones, with four vertical iron bars surrounding his head, and more rods circling his forehead. It was all screwed into the bone, eight rods into his neck and shoulder bones, and four bolts threaded into his skull. Sebastian had to wear it for another six months. In his dingy cook smock he looked like a sauce-splattered golem with a chandelier on his head.

A week or so after the Scotty Marin incident I gave Sebastian a ride home after work. It was near midnight and Sebastian stunk like Italian sausage and old cheese. I was driving my Volkswagen a bit more carefully than usual because of all the ice on the roads. It must have been about ten degrees out and the sky full of stars as we headed through the eight blocks that make up this town.

As we crossed Bluestone Drive by the Walker feed plant a vanload of Mexicans cut me off. It was a bunch of guys from the poultry factory, just getting off the second shift and probably high already. I didn't pay them much mind, but at the next light we pulled up next to them and Sebastian looked over, turning his whole body because of his halo-head, and the next thing I knew they were yelling and flicking us off, and Sebastian had his tattooed arms out the window giving them both of his long, bony middle fingers. So the next light they stopped in front of us and four little guys tumbled out of the van and started strutting over, thumping their chests and shouting in Spanish.

I was thinking it was a little funny, because they still had on their hairnets from the plant. Then Sebastian said, Oh shit, real quiet like, and locked his door. I couldn't believe it. I reached across him and pulled the .357 out of the glove and when the first Mexican came to my window I rolled it down and jabbed the barrel right in his fat cheek.

Amigos, I said, get back in the fucking van. *Vosotros no quieres este.* And they went rolling ass-over-teakettle to get back in that van, and that was that. I could feel Sebastian looking at me kinda sideways, as best as he could without moving his whole body, as I drove him out to his place.

A few days later Mahoney called me up and asked me to come see him.

So, Mahoney said. He was sitting behind a massive desk in the back of the restaurant. He was wearing a peach cashmere sweater and his hands sparkled with rings.

I heard about the thing with Scotty Marin.

My stomach made an audible groan. The algae was turning my colon over like a cement mixer.

His mother wants to press charges, Mahoney said, but I've fixed that.

Here it comes, I thought. I knew Mahoney wanted to get into my pants.

I've heard some things, Mahoney said. I was wondering if you'd like to make some extra money. I was thinking, if I had some problems I wanted taken care of, maybe you could help me out?

You would be surprised how many small Southern towns are being bought from underneath by a growing cartel of ambitious young gay men. Staunton was a small, old-style agricultural/industrial burg crisscrossed with train tracks and feed lots that moved cattle, feed, and lumber out across the Shenandoah Valley, and it was starting to spread, outward, in the awkward, ugly way that all small Southern towns do. It was ripe for a guy like Mahoney. Suited me fine, made things interesting when these hicks found out their local convenience store or restaurant or city block was owned by the Pink Mafia. Besides, the gay guys had class and style; they opened up a California-style brew pub, a couple of nightclubs, a few nice restaurants, a designer-clothes shop, coffee shops, and restored the old downtown theater where they now showed classic films and art movies. They held the weekly meetings of the Shenandoah Valley Gay and Lesbian Association at Mahoney's downtown art-deco coffee shop, a place I liked to hang out.

Most of Mahoney's money was tied up in real estate. You could say he was the biggest slumlord in Rockingham County, with run-down college-kid houses, decrepit downtown apartments, and a multitude of trailers spread across the valley. Some of these people didn't pay their rent, and they owed Mahoney big money. The Pink Mafia needed someone to collect, and that's where I came in.

I met my hippie-chick college girl at Mahoney's downtown coffee shop, the Artful Dodger. Anne was what my father would have called a "flaming liberal." She was also real into natural organic foods and stuff like that, and I first met her when she sold me some organically grown blue-green algae.

I was reading Cassinni's book on satellites and nuclear propulsion theories and drinking the Hard Times Special, which was a small cup of black coffee, no cream or sugar allowed, for twenty-five cents. Anne came walking over wearing one of those Deadhead halter-top dresses with no bra, and I couldn't take my eyes off the fine, broad bones of her shoulders and her graceful neck. At first I thought the algae was for smoking, but she laughed at that and then proceeded to explain the various health benefits of blue-green algae. She was long and slim and after an hour I had bought a case of Running Water Blue-Green Algae supplements. It was a foolish thing to do—I couldn't even afford a latte, and here I went and bought forty bucks worth of algae. To refuse a woman's request takes a real act of will. That comes from my father.

The algae pills were mammoth green-blue capsules that took quite a bit to get down. Reminded me of the ear-and-hoof-rot doses we used to give the Holsteins back on the farm when I was a kid. Anne kept asking me about them, how I felt, so I figured I might as well start taking them. I went through four cycles—almost eight weeks' worth, and they actually did some interesting things. I had trouble sleeping at night sometimes, which was fine because I usually hung out at the Gun and Pawn and listened to my set. I thought I knew why they called it Running Water, because I spent a lot more time on the thunderbox than usual. And there was also a strange sort of energy, like my muscles were coiled and ready to spring, like an acute sensation of the moment before taking flight, or falling.

I tried to figure out why Mahoney picked me for this job. I assumed he heard the bit about Scotty Marin, and maybe Seb told him about the vanload of Mexicans. I do have a look that a lot of gay men like, thin through the waist and hips and broad shoulders. The same look that got me modeling work in L.A. after the Air Force. I wear a forty-two-long jacket and have a twenty-nine waist. I got a lot of fitting work, mostly pants and underwear. I had a brief run of good fortune in 1990, when I got several full magazine layouts. Then it sort of dried up. I still got some beefcake stuff, but that meant I had to wax my chest every other week. But I wasn't a tough guy. Back in the Air Force they used to call me Pretty Boy, and things like that. I always avoided confrontations; at least I used to. I understood electronics and astrophysics; that's what I related to.

I sort of felt like coming back here would be a good thing for my father after his heart operation. As part of his surgery he got a pig valve put in his chest. Afterward he used to come into the kitchen in the morning and say, Man, I'd love a big slab of bacon right now, rubbing his hands and grinning. Then he'd lean against the sink and drink his decaf with his arms folded, just like he did every morning when I was growing up, when my brothers and I were tumbling our way off to school, and then off into marriages and divorces and other lives, all far, far away from home. It's true I was devastated by my divorce, even though it was none of my doing. My ex-wife's career blew up after her breast augmentation—which I paid for—and her cocaine habit increased exponentially as well. But in L.A. people are much more willing to give up on things and just move on, so I did. But I lost everything and then some. I still had legal fees and equity to pay toward our Seal Beach condo.

One day soon after his surgery I caught my father out back blasting away at some crows in the trees with a double-barreled shotgun, with his chest staples only a week old. He set the gun against a tree and unbuttoned his shirt. He was split open, the staples loosened by the concussion of shooting, and a gap about a half-inch wide ran from his sternum to his collarbone. For a brief moment I saw the inside, the deep, slick redness of the organs and heart. He started to laugh, and then the pain hit him, and he went to his knees, then crumpled on the grass. He was dead a few days later.

Nothing really illegal, Mahoney said. He pulled a bottle of scotch off a shelf and offered me a glass. It was twelve-year single malt, so I took it. He said he'd have something for me to do tomorrow—Don't worry about showing up at the restaurant anymore. He'd call me from now on, no more than ten hours and a guaranteed five hundred cash a week. He counted out five hundred in twenties on his desk and slid them over to me.

How about I call you, Wednesday morning, two days from now? Okay?

I just nodded. I wasn't sure I knew what was happening.

Oh, Kaiser? One more thing. I got some things I want you to wear.

I went right to Billy's Gun and Pawn and put down four hundred to get my set out of hock. I put another fifty down on the .357 and a box of shells since I figured I might be needing it. Billy hooked me up with a holster and a concealed-weapons permit application, an easy thing to get in Virginia, and in twenty-four hours I was licensed to carry that puppy in a shoulder holster under my jacket. The jacket was one of the things Mahoney gave me to wear, and I was already starting to like it. It was a black-leather Givenchy with high lapels, and

TELEMETRY

it fit me tight like a glove. I was also wearing a black DKNY crew-neck and pleated charcoal wool pants by Valentino. I had to hand it to Mahoney—this was pricey stuff.

Billy watched me as I practiced loading up the pistol. I know he wanted to say something about the new threads, but you normally don't make those kinds of cracks to a man loading up a .357.

I went over to Anne's place to see if she wanted to have dinner together. She lived in a giant old Victorian house across the street from the college with about ten other people. Anne was studying in her room, and I'm sure glad I left the .357 in the car because the first thing she did was jump up off her bed and leap at me, a textbook tackle with her forehead buried in my chest. She squeezed me and rubbed her face into my stomach, something she liked to do, while I stroked her hair.

I have a new job, I said.

Anne screeched and began pummeling my stomach with her tiny fists. Anne was always overly enthusiastic. But she didn't even ask what the job was, which was good, because I hadn't really thought about how I would explain it. We ended up snuggled up on her bed for the next couple of hours until she had to get back to studying. I suppose I should have also been surprised that she didn't notice my new clothes, but that wasn't the sort of thing that Anne would notice. She seemed to have her eye on the internal picture of people, a way of seeing inside of you, some sort of elemental empathy unclouded by the surface matters of life. She seemed to know just what I wanted at any given time without even asking. We arranged to get together the next afternoon for a picnic on my dad's old farm.

I spent most of the night setting up my radio in my downtown apartment and getting it calibrated. I was renting the studio from Mahoney, a few blocks from the coffee shop and above a second-hand-tire shop. All I had in it was my bed, two armchairs, a lamp, and a few bookshelves, and the extra books and magazines stacked in piles. Of course now I also had a closet full of designer outfits, lots of Italian and mostly black, as well as a few pairs of shoes, belts, even an excellent Fendi overcoat and muffler. I spent very little time there, especially when my radio was in hock, and in the evenings, if I wasn't out drinking, I would read scientific texts: mostly astrophysics, mathematics, or wave theory; anything from Stephen Hawking to Alan Turning. Now that my set was back, I had it set up on the kitchen table and a few extra crates. Fat power cords snaked across the room from three different outlets.

I had to use my headphones, because the Wetsel Seed Company train yard lay directly behind my building, and throughout the night trains steamed in to clash their boxcars against the loading chutes and other engines. The lights of the car-men flashed across my window as they crept between the cars swinging their lanterns and cursing. They came in at night to load the cattle carcasses into the giant hoppers that ground them up to use for feed. In the dim light you could see the stiff hooves of steers sticking out of the tops of the cars, hundreds of them. I got used to the noise, but some nights the stench was so bad it made me sit bolt upright in bed.

It only took me about ten minutes to get all my finders locked in and the presets humming. They were still out there, dutifully transmitting, a few dozen stations that have been broadcasting odd, often repetitive signals for many years, and nobody knows why. Places like the Gong Station from somewhere in Germany, producing a constant series of gong sounds that only varied twice in the nine years I'd been tracking it. Or the Buzz Station, channel S1 at 436.006, playing a constant buzz that only varied twice in over fifty years; once in 1945, and the other when the Berlin Wall came down. Coming from somewhere from South America. I'll be damned if I wanted to miss out when it changed tone again.

But my favorite is the Taiwanese Number Lady, coming out of S2 at 123.004, wishing us a good morning and then giving out a series of random numbers, every Monday for over thirty years. She ended each broadcast with an enigmatic goodbye, different every time, something like: I hope these numbers were of use to you, or Please help these numbers find their way home. Sort of like a bad fortune cookie. The numbers were impossible to crack, seeing as they were probably matched to some sort of scheduled key, only in the hands of the few people who the numbers were intended for. But the messages were the thing that intrigued me the most; they seemed to be something she was making up herself, the message that she was trying to deliver to the world.

People call her Taiwanese because that is the best approximation of her accent—obviously Chinese, Mandarin, but not mainland. She somehow managed to bounce her signal off several satellite receptors, which made her location impossible to pinpoint. The CIA used the timing of her broadcasts and the principles of telemetry to determine that the signal was in fact originating out of the South China Sea, or at least using satellites that routinely tasked through that area, but the apparent origin was too random to be sure. My theory is that she's transmitting from a ship, skirting around the coast and foraying occasionally into the Pacific, tactics to hide her location. I sometimes think of her at the rail of some rusted trawler, or maybe even an old junk, staring out into the gray waves, the sound of the teletype chattering out a new set of numbers down in the cabin.

These stations were hooked into something serious; they were communicating with someone about something. Most people guessed undercover operatives in foreign countries. Whatever they were, I admired their tenacity, their refusal to quit. They couldn't know if anyone was out there listening, but they kept at it, transmitting into the vast darkness of radio subspace.

My father taught me how to set up a station and work the dials. He got into it during the war. There was always a pile of radio equipment in the basement when I was growing up. I learned to swap out a twelve-point crystal tube before I could throw a baseball. I helped him hook up the antenna wires to the rain gutters, giving us a wider broadcast area. We spent hours "chasing DX," seeking out remote broadcasts from all over the world. I still have his list of famous call signs, which he kept nailed to a small board on a rafter above the set: Juan Carlos, King of Spain—EAOJC; Barry Goldwater—K7UGA; Walter Cronkite—KBC6SD.

But mostly I remember my father, late at night, down in the basement, spinning the dials, monitoring various stations, looking for some change or message. Sometimes he would be down there all night, and I would get up and pad through the kitchen in my pajamas and listen to him through the crack in the basement door, calling, waiting for a response.

Dad introduced me to monitoring—how to log onto stations and search for variables in signal and tone. He's the one who got me hooked on it. But it carries such a true sense of satisfaction if you do it right. There is a sense of commitment to monitoring; you have to remain extremely diligent or the moment of change might slip by.

When Mom died he packed up the set for good. I think he was proud of me when I went into the Air Force as a satellite-radio airman, and when I came home on leave we'd go into the basement and dust off the old set and get it humming again. I wish he could have had a chance to use my new stuff; it's far more advanced technology now, though the basic principle hasn't changed in fifty years. Low wavelength signals, traveling slowly for long, long distances, bouncing signals off repeater stations and low-level satellite links. He never got the chance to see how diligently I've been tracking my stations, how careful I've been.

The next day I took Anne out to the farm to see the RUDACK satellite intersection. I picked her up around four and she jumped into my car with a picnic dinner she'd made. I didn't tell her about the intersection; it was a surprise.

My cousin owned the farm now, annexed into his growing spread, but he didn't mind if I came down there to hang out around the old house. Anne loved the narrow river in the back and kicked around in the gray-white rocks in the shallows in her sandals, even though it was November and the water was sluggish with ice crystals. I built a fire on the bank and we had some red wine with grilled tofu and eggplant, no cheese, because Anne is vegan. She wriggled her pink, wet toes at the fire and grinned into my neck, holding me close.

Satellite intersections like these rarely happen. I've only seen a few myself, and I spent almost every night out in California, out by the airstrip when I was at March AFB, or even in L.A. I'd head up into the Hollywood hills where the light pollution wasn't so strong. I spent many nights laying out my charts and calculating trajectories, sitting on the top of my car, watching all the satellites that came through my area. I explained to Anne the principles of telemetry, how with the exact Keplerian elements, which is the mathematical model of a spacecraft in orbit, along with the correct time and viewing location, we can calculate exactly when the satellite will be in view, where it will appear on the horizon, which direction it will be moving, and even the speed of travel across the sky.

The RUDAK intersection was a rare event when two satellites, in this case RUDAK phase-communication satellites, which are the standard link for short-wave radio, enter the evening sky and intersect at an exact point. Of course they are at different orbital altitudes, so they don't collide or anything like that. But considering the magnitude of the open expanse of sky, it is a remarkable occurrence.

As it got toward six o'clock, I let the fire burn down. The riverbank had a nice, high, wide, grassy spot with a clear view of where the satellites would cross. I spent a couple hours out there last week calculating it exactly. RUDAK AO-30 would enter from the line of oaks just over the river directly in front of us. Thirteen seconds later, RUDAK AO-65, traveling a bit faster, would enter from our right, over the line of hills that bordered this open end of the valley. The forecast was for clear skies, and sunset at 6:03 p.m. I didn't tell Anne exactly what was happening. I don't know what she was expecting, but I think she was just enjoying lying back on the slope, snuggling under the heavy wool blanket, and staring up at the purpling sky.

Are you happy? I said.

Yes, she said. All I need is to hold on to you like this. This is the best surprise.

That's all it took. When I was with her I sometimes felt that I was the same way, that maybe I just hadn't given it enough of a chance. But then other times it wasn't enough.

I pointed out RUDAK AO-30 as it came out over the trees. Then I pointed out RUDAK AO-65, and Anne gasped as they came into focus and their trajectory was clear. A satellite is most visible at dusk, and at first it looks like a slow-moving star. As we continued to watch them, our eyes began to focus for distance, and we could begin to make out the actual shapes. As they crossed more directly overhead and caught more of the fading sunlight, we could see the true artificiality of the things as the light played over the various protrusions and antennas. I always think that it's amazing that it doesn't just fall out of the sky. A man-made object, hurtling around the earth, propelled purely by gravity and initial momentum. Put into motion with an initial push, then something else, something elemental takes over, something that would go on forever.

Anne squeezed me tighter, giggling, her fingers digging into my ribs, as the satellites arced their way across the sky. At the moment of intersection she stiffened and fell silent. We watched them continue on, back down again around the curve of the earth.

We lay still and silent until the purple sky turned to legions of black, and the pinpricks of stars burned their way through as the river gurgled darkly at our feet.

Around noon the next day Mahoney called me up and told me to come down to his antique shop for my first collection gig. I was wearing black Dolce & Gabbana pants and Doc Martens boots, with a black Hugo Boss turtleneck and my black leather blazer over that. The .357 was so heavy and bulky it stuck out real obvious. Mahoney wanted me to do a few collections from some tenants who owed. He said I should take something that looked valuable if I couldn't get money out of them, like televisions or VCRs, jewelry if I could find it, and it'd all hold up legal-wise, he assured me, if things got rough. He gave me a paper with three addresses. Then Mahoney said that he'd sent other people out there before, and they had a bit of trouble.

Do whatever you need to do to get that money, Mahoney said.

I looked at the paper and it had sums written down next to each address. The smallest amount was twelve hundred bucks.

Those pants fit well, don't they? Mahoney says.

I was a little concerned. Mahoney may have been a certified Nancy-boy, but with a flick of his jeweled pinky he could have had me rolled in one of his Indonesian hand-made carpets and dropped in the landfill that he owned before I could say homophobia. The fact is Scotty Marin could have had me in jail for assault, and somehow Mahoney fixed it so he couldn't.

Don't you worry your pretty little self, Mahoney said, and at that moment there was something to the cadence of his words that reminded me of the Taiwanese Number Lady. Something purposely soothing, pleasant, grateful to be of service, and yet the voice of someone lost, someone drifting out on a cold sea, watching the lights on the horizon.

Easy money, Mahoney said, easy money.

The first place was this old farmhouse in Broadway, just outside of Staunton. The heat in my Volkswagen was shot so I was freezing my ass off and thinking I should have brought my heavier jacket. *Walter Showker, 348 Collicello Street.* There was a bunch of junk in the front yard like oil drums, rusted tricycles, and car parts. A haggard young woman answered the door. She seemed a little surprised by my clothes, at least until I told her who sent me and why I was there.

Then she sighed, and like she'd said it a thousand times before, she said, You'll have to talk to my *husband* about that and *he* ain't here.

She went to close the door but I got my boot in and then jacked it open with the other hand. She staggered back into the house and I stepped in, and immediately I gagged, because the place stunk like crap and old food.

You better get on out of here, she stammered. My husband'll be back soon and you'll have to deal with him.

We need that money now, I said, and started walking into the kitchen because it seemed like a good thing to do. The place was a wreck: dinner plates full of cigarette butts, crushed beer cans, pots of rotting noodles on the stove, newspapers stacked on the floor.

You owe twelve hundred, I said. Either you give me cash or I can take something else.

But I started looking around and realized quickly that there wasn't anything there worth anything. I walked into the living room and there was a small boy watching a TV set. He sat up real close, and he didn't seem to notice me.

I heard nails scratching on the floor, the unmistakable sound of a large dog gearing up to take flight, so I pulled out the .357 and turned around as she let in a large rottweiler from the backyard. As it leapt for my throat I pistol-whipped its head with an angled overhead swing. I felt its skull crunch, and the dog crouched there and shook its head from side to side, over and over.

Oh my God! the woman screamed.

What the hell'd you do that for? I yelled.

The rottweiler staggered back a few steps, careened into the kitchen table, and knocked over the trash can, spilling cans and styrofoam cartons onto the floor. The kid wasn't watching the TV anymore, but didn't seem too concerned, either. The dog, blood pouring from its head, started greedily chomping on the spilled trash, and the boy got up to try and pull him away, dragging the gagging dog by his collar. The woman cried and rifled through a drawer, looking for her checkbook. I held up the .357 to the kitchen light. There was blood and bone flecks on the barrel.

The next couple of houses were much easier. But I did have to hold down a half-naked drunk until his girlfriend got out her purse, and scare an old man into digging under his mattress, something I didn't like doing at all.

I headed back to Mahoney's an hour later with about two grand in my pockets in wadded-up bills, personal checks, a bag full of antique coins, and one television. Mahoney was having a small cocktail party back there with a few of his buddies. I handed over the cash and told him what happened at each place. Mahoney grinned and nodded, and his friends snickered as they sat on an antique velvet couch. The room was full of fine paintings, and all the furniture was extremely rare. I took a seat on an eighteenth-century straight-backed chair carved with delicate whorls of chocolate wood and gold-stitched backing. Mahoney was top shelf all the way. He straightened out a fifty and handed it to me.

A tip. For a great job on the first day. I'll be calling you later this week. Want a drink?

I took my martini straight up, dry. A man in full denim made it with Mahoney's spectacular, all-silver bar set. Another guy in a net singlet looked at me, rubbing his hands together. He looked sixteen.

You're fabulous! he said, and touched my wrist. He had a half-dozen rings on each hand. I could see something in his eyes that frightened me for the first time, something I hadn't seen since L.A. It was the intoxication of the scene, the dreamland.

It's a bit hard to explain. These guys were right off the farm, feeding cattle one day and biting a pillow in Mahoney's downtown gothic pad the next. They were loving it. Mahoney and his boys were the way out. There's a sort of desperation that hangs over rural towns like these, all over the country. Growing up gay in Staunton or anywhere in southern Virginia can't be much fun. It's hard to hide differences of desire in towns like these.

I was thinking that I may want a partner. That thing with the rottweiler back at the first house was just way too close, and really just plain lucky. It wasn't the kind of thing I wanted to do again. I figured most of the work could be done with just pure intimidation. I needed someone big and scary, who would take maybe a fifty or so a day for it.

I fended off the boys for a few more free drinks and then beat it when the dancing started. I had an extra fifty in my pocket, and I was feeling good. I called up Anne and got her to meet me at the new fancy California-style brew pub.

We took a couple of stools at the bar and I stayed with the gin, Bombay Sapphire gimlets, while Anne started in on the Bacardi and Cokes. I was still buzzed from the collections, and being with Anne started to calm me down again. I didn't tell her about my day; it didn't seem like something she would like to hear about. Especially the bit about the dog.

Later on I called the restaurant and got Sebastian on the horn, and he agreed to come by. Anne was getting a little sauced. She was jabbering with the long-haired bartender about last summer's Dead tour. Sebastian came by the bar about midnight, struggling for a moment to get his halo-head through the door, and I bought him a few drinks before I put my proposal to him.

Don't worry, Seb, I said. Just look scary.

I showed him the .357. I got you covered if it gets nasty, I said.

The hippie bartender saw me flash the piece.

Jesus, man! You can't have that thing in here!

Relax. I got a permit.

What? Anne said. She didn't see it, and I was glad. I made a small sign to the bartender with my eyebrows, the kind of sign that only a man can make to another man, and that you couldn't refuse: *Let's keep this to ourselves, please? Thank you.*

A few minutes later she leaned over and asked me if I minded if she went out back and got stoned with her bartender friend. I knew she was real fond of the stuff, so I said sure. She always said I should smoke pot, that it would relax me, but I couldn't imagine a world without tension, or a world without the clear linear processes, like electronics. I wouldn't know what to do. It wasn't that I didn't want to enjoy that other world, like Anne was able to, just that I felt like I would be relinquishing my duties here, that I would be letting someone down if I didn't pay attention.

Then this guy Phil Herring came in.

Hey, Kaiser, he said, nice clothes.

Phil Herring went to high school with me way back at Broadway High in eighty-two. We played football together. I couldn't stand him.

He had a few other guys with him, and one of them was Scotty Marin. Seb came back from the bathroom with his freakish halo-head and sat down next to me, and started back in on his plate of nachos.

What are you doing, Phil? I said. Hanging out with these kids? That's sad.

Not as sad as your ex-wife, Scotty Marin said. I heard she's trying to blow the whole state of California.

At this Sebastian rotated his body on the stool to look at me.

I was wondering when you'd start paying attention, I said to Sebastian.

Jesus, Phil Herring said, who's the android?

My uncle is looking for you, Scotty Marin said. Watch your back.

Can't be much of a sheriff's deputy if he can't find me in this town, I said.

I felt the algae singing in my veins. Or maybe it was the gin. Either way I felt the rise of the wild, hilarious type of rage, boiling my nerve to a fine, high key.

You don't need to provoke me, I said. In fact, I'm going to walk outside, and if you fellas come along, I'll break your asses, one at a time, while my android friend here holds my drink. Starting with you, Scotty.

I pointed right at his throat.

I'd never said anything like that before. It wasn't the job, or the gun jabbing into my hip, or at least I don't think so. Maybe it was all that algae I'd been taking. Maybe I had reached that point, the edge of things, the place that my father searched for in the black space, the vast emptiness of radio.

Whatever, Kaiser, Phil said, fuck you.

And then they all walked over to a table by the window and tried to signal a waitress. I got my next drink and Seb and I walked out the front door. I handed my drink to Seb and walked over to the window where they were sitting. I stood there and looked at them, with a look on my face that said: Well? Well? They pretended to ignore me. I wanted them to come out real bad. My head thrummed with rage and I felt quick and brutal and ready to give in to that glorious spasm of violence that comes from desperation.

Then Seb tapped me and I looked over and I saw Anne and the bartender in the alley behind the bar. They were leaning against the wall and sharing a joint. She was wearing her sandals, like always, and I thought her feet must have been freezing. I could tell right then and there, just by the way she held her body, the way she shifted her legs, the way she leaned into him, that I didn't have a chance in the world with that girl. Maybe if there were a satellite intersection every night of the week. But that was it. I knew that she would never fall in love with me. It was the clearest thing I had ever known in my life.

And then I wasn't mad anymore. But I felt a bit sick. Seb seemed to understand this and started to head off to the car. I stood there a few more moments, thinking maybe I'd like to see her look over or something, but she didn't. As she leaned against the wall, her head tilted back with a slight smile, the alley light made the crown of her head, the top of all that beautiful hair, glow like something wonderful and strange.

In the car Seb said, You okay?

All this damn algae I've been taking, I said. It's doing weird things to my system.

Seb nodded his halo-head ever so slightly, because that was all he could do.

That night I dreamt of my father in a field pointing a shotgun at the sky. What are you aiming at? I said. Can't you see them? he said. But he never fired. He just kept pointing the gun at the darkening sky, deep blue and cloudless, rotating the barrel, pivoting his body, as if he was trying to cover the entire horizon. Stop, I said. Please.

Three days later I was trying to kick in the door of a farmhouse off 64 outside of town, and Sebastian was standing there with his halo-head smoking a cigarette and picking something out of his eye. The guy inside was yelling: I'm a preacher! I'm a minister, Baptist! You can't do this to me!

The door was stronger than it looked and I was getting tired, so I turned to Seb and said, You want to fucking *do* something here?

Sebastian just shrugged. He wore wool Prada pants about three inches short in the inseam and an old T-shirt that said *Catch and Release All Finless Brown Trout*. He couldn't wear most of Mahoney's clothes because of his halo-head. But he liked the pants.

Useless, I said. What the hell.

So Sebastian put his giant motorcycle boot through the middle of the door.

That's the way, I said. Now we're cooking.

Then the next thing I knew I was on my knees by the side of the trailer with my hands over my ears. There was a horrible blast, and a shattering of wood. Seb lay about ten feet from the door. Something was wrong with his halo-head, because he lay on his back, but his head was turned to the side, facing me. Things moved with a slight blur, small trails coming off the points of Seb's halo and the tips of my fingers. I got to my feet and pulled the pistol out of my shoulder holster. I ran around to the back of the trailer and I saw the backside of the preacher running full sprint for the woods. I sighted him with the pistol, the hammer lying right in the center of his back. I couldn't do it. In a few seconds he was gone, leaping like a fat, bloated deer in boxer shorts through the high grass, then disappearing into the trees.

I ripped some sheets off the preacher's bed and wrapped up Seb's middle. He caught a small spread of quail-load that peppered his torso like a slab of prime rib. He was real lucky the preacher hadn't changed the load in his shotgun since dove season. Seb looked real confused, trying to look at the broad stain on his stomach, his head wrenched at an odd angle, the bolt points in his skull twisted and bleeding. I knelt down by his head, afraid to touch anything. To do anything might just make it worse.

They got Seb off okay and I spent the next couple hours in hand-cuffs talking with the police. Then most of the cops left and there was this last sheriff's deputy who wanted to talk to me alone. I didn't even bother to look at the name on his badge. He led me around to the back of the trailer. The sun was going down, and the long field of grass and alfalfa smelled fresh and clean.

When the taser dart hit me in the chest, the electric surge locked my head back and buckled my knees. I closed my eyes as my vision went white and hot. Then it relaxed and my body sagged, and for a moment I thought it was over. Then the nightstick caught me across the ear, and my face was in the grass, and through the tickling blades I could see the fading crimson spreading over the valley. I thought of Anne and the smooth bones of her neck, the way she wrapped herself around me, the sweet smell of her hair. I thought of how after all it came down to something as simple as a blow to the head, a falling satellite, a missed signal, a momentary failure.

The introduction was always just a set of three tones, and then: Good Morning! Ready?

It was three-thirty in the morning, Eastern Standard Time. I brought a tape of the Taiwanese Number Lady's latest broadcast into Seb's room in the hospital. They re-drilled Seb's skull, and he'd have it on for another eight months now. I punched the play button and the Number Lady began to read her numbers. There was an upward lilt in her voice, and she seemed like she was having a great time:

Seven. Four. Eight. Twelve. Sixteen.

She sounded as if she were reading the numbers that would save the world. Sebastian didn't ask why I brought the tape here, why we were up at three-thirty in the morning to listen to some Taiwanese woman say some numbers, and I was grateful for it. I scratched at my swollen and crusty ear. Through the window the streetlights glimmered on the frosted panes. Her voice came out of the speakers with a crystal stillness that was almost frightening.

Seven. Fourteen. Eleven. Three.

Seb's eyes were shining, motionless, his hands folded on his stomach. There was a pause, and something seemed to contract and gather itself in the room.

The principles of telemetry can pinpoint the locations and trajectories of satellites. But those are just mathematical models, the theory of how things move and find one another. It didn't help locate the transmitters, the initial parts of the equation, those of us who beam our signals into the sky to be caught by satellites and dropped down upon the earth like electronic snowfall.

Please enjoy today's numbers with a full heart. Goodbye.

Sebastian grinned, a loose, wide, toothy smile, and I had to laugh. She would never be found. It would take a miracle to find any of us.

INTERVIEW WITH
FREDERICK REIKEN

by Eric Wasserman

Photo credit: Nancy Crampton

Frederick Reiken

In his remarks to the McSwee-ney's Mammoth Treasury of Thrilling Tales, editor Michael Chabon asserts that the contempo-rary short story has become "plotless and sparkling with epiphanic dew." The current backlash against tradi-tionalist stories presenting the quiet power of hope is part of a growing contempt for MFA programs and the type of fiction graduate students often produce. Ironically, some of the most vocal opponents to such works are prominent MFA graduates.

It is true that modern fiction on domestic themes—much of it produced by MFA graduates—has occa-sionally degraded into over-stylized intellectualization that abandons the emotional engagement of the genre's masters, ranging from canonized mini-malist staples like Raymond Carver to free-form naturalists better known within literary circles such as Alistair Macleod. Yet writing programs are attracting greater numbers of applicants than ever, and the domestic story remains a vital presence in the American literature that has been defined by everyday magic for more than the past two decades.

In the face of the current debate stands a fresh generation of writers who continue to build nurturing academic communities where aspiring writers are encouraged to develop their own stories rather than conform to the current trend of slick, narcissistic sensibilities dominating the literary market. Students who are still drawn to the transformation of the individual rather than the revelation of plot can look to these writers for assurance that there is no illegitimacy in the longstanding impulse to explore human connection, and that doing so within the temporary environment of academia has benefits.

Frederick Reiken, who teaches at Emerson College, is among the many writers who still believe in stories that emphasize the struggles of ordinary people placed in extraordinary situations, and who uphold the merits of writing programs. Likewise, he has not been adversely affected by or compelled to respond to the recent criticism of work like his own with defensiveness, but acknowledges that the new wave of literary domestic fiction must accept that pop culture inevitably influences the identity of contemporary characters, whether it be the music they cherish or the sports teams they hold allegiance to.

The tradition of depicting characters that do not necessarily find definitive answers to life's complications, but are instead left with the acquisition of hope when they come out the other end of adversity, is still held sacred by Reiken. His characters continually face an imperfect world on their own terms, just as the most memorable voices in American fiction—from Tom Sawyer to Nathan Zuckerman—have always done. Whether it be a young boy discovering more about himself than he ever expected when the details of his brother's disappearance never materialize, or a woman having the chance to say one last goodbye to the great love of her life whom she could never tell a soul about, Reiken has set himself among the documenters of everyday life with the conviction that perseverance produces hope in the most surprising and often most meaningful ways. It is a sensibility that is not isolated to the written page but is carried into his classroom, where the difficulty of defining oneself as a writer is as crucial as the process of coming to know who we are as people. While the MFA critics banter about the state of modern fiction with indignation, Reiken and others politely strive for the positive choice, fostering writing programs to assist students in exploring how we relate to each other, where we come from, and where we're going as writers and individuals.

A Princeton Legacy and University of California at Irvine MFA recipient, Reiken published his first novel, The Odd Sea *(Harcourt), in 1998. It won the Hackney Literary Award for first fiction and was selected by both* Booklist *and* Library Journal *as one of the best first novels of the year. This was followed by the publication of his more ambitious second novel,* The Lost Legends of New Jersey *(Harcourt), which became a bestseller and is described by Charles Baxter as "a miraculous balancing of tone and theme." Reiken's choice to stay true to his own particular Garden State vision appears sound, even when musing in the* New York Times *op-ed section about the anti-mystique of the New Jersey Nets.*

When we spoke, his recent story, "The Ocean," was appearing in the New Yorker, *and was being received with similar praise to his lengthier fiction. He expressed that he was "madly" working to complete his newest novel, due for publication in 2006, and, not surprisingly, he wasn't flinching in his chosen course of literary outlook.*

Cynthia Ozick once said that while Michael Chabon is Jewish and also a writer, that he isn't a "Jewish writer." Have you been witness or victim to this bantering over ethnic literary legitimacy?

So far I haven't, but to me it seems a moot point. While it's clear that there are some brilliant specialists—Cynthia Ozick, for instance—who have built important bodies of excellent work on the basis of writing about Jewish themes, the notion that such a path is more legitimate than the writing of someone like Michael Chabon is in my mind like saying that an Olympic athlete who specializes in, say, the high jump is more legitimate than someone who does the high jump and the long jump and the hurdles. I don't know the context in which Cynthia Ozick made this statement, so it's unfair to guess at what she was insinuating, but so far as my own path as a writer goes, I don't foresee myself being considered a "Jewish writer" so much as simply a writer who is Jewish, and my own particular sensibility is much more suited to the range and flexibility that comes with the latter.

Regardless of specific ethnicity, people tend to hold their cultural icons up on pedestals, but parents are not exactly known for being enthusiastic about their children pursuing careers in the arts.

Actually, my father's opposition to my choice of becoming a writer was something I grappled with for a long time. And it was not as if he was a tyrant about it, nor did he do anything to stop me. But he has always been a very persuasive man, and he simply could not fathom why, when I announced at the age of twenty-two that instead of applying to medical school I was going to pursue becoming a fiction writer, I would choose something that would not guarantee me a predictable income. In all earnestness, he would say things to me like, "Most doctors play golf on Wednesdays. You could write on Wednesdays." The day I graduated from my MFA program, we were talking on the phone, and he asked me what I was going to do now. I said I had applied for several teaching positions and was also considering a work-exchange position at an artist's colony in western Massachusetts. He said, "Why don't you think about getting an MBA?" and I said, "Hello, Dad. It's me on the phone—Rick, your son."

If you think about his perspective, however, it isn't that illogical. He was that classic second-generation American. He grew up in Jersey City, a poor Jewish kid who won a scholarship to Princeton. He went on to law school and, as they say, made good. As the classic third-generation American, I grew up in the suburbs, lived a comfortable upper middle-class life, which, even if fraught with domestic dramas, was one in which I was always provided for monetarily. I simply did not grow up with the fear of being poor, and so even as I followed in my father's footsteps and went to Princeton, I was never fixated on monetary wealth as an objective.

It was only after I finished my MFA program that I began to understand just what it felt like not to have enough money to fix my car or afford health insurance. It was during that period, circa 1993, that I had my last real crisis of faith with regard to being a writer. I had written a novel as my MFA thesis and thought it was, of course, the best book in the history of Western letters, and around that time it became clear that it was never going to get published. Surprisingly enough, my father read it and loved it—though he still thought I should get an MBA. In late winter of 1993, I took a little trip, motivated by a desperate romantic impulse, and went to find a woman I had known during the year I'd lived in Israel, right after college, and had worked as a wildlife biologist in the Negev Desert. There had been a lot of attraction between us, but I never acted on it due to the fact that at the time I was intending to marry my girlfriend from college—only to find, upon returning, that she didn't share the intention. So three years later I went back to Israel, quickly learned that my attempt to execute a romantic fairy tale was deluded, briefly considered hanging around and trying out for the soon-to-be-formed Israeli national ice-hockey team, but ultimately decided to return after a month and "make good."

The month I returned, and without telling my father, I registered to take the MCATs, visited the UMass medical school in Worcester, and began an intensive review of chemistry, biology, and physics. I had taken the MCATs as a college senior, but the five-year expiration had just passed, and so I had to take them again. I've always done well on standardized tests, and on the practice tests I was pretty much nailing the scores I needed, so I figured it was just a matter of getting through this ordeal, applying to UMass, and then I could call up my father and surprise him.

About two weeks before the test date, I started having a sort of existential crack-up. I did most of my studying in the Forbes Library in Northampton, and one day I happened to lay eyes on the *New York Times Book Review*, picked it up and, for the first and only time in my life, read it from cover to cover. Then I walked down to a nearby bookstore, purchased two of the books that had been reviewed, and started reading them in a cafe, whereupon I woke from this little trance and went back to studying organic chemistry. More of the same continued over the next two weeks, and every day I would have moments of asking myself, "What am I doing? I'm a writer. I've spent the last five years apprenticing myself to this art. Now I'm going to just chuck the very essence of who I am, the identity it took me so many years to discover?" But I kept going. I covered all the material, all the while knowing that if I simply got through the MCATs I would have defeated my crazy notion of becoming a novelist, defeated the thing that was making me so miserable. That once I got those scores back in the mail, once I had been offered validation by my MCAT scores that I really was meant to be a doctor, the die would have been cast. I'd be off and running and the rest of my life would make sense.

As it turned out, I didn't sleep a minute the night before the MCATs. All night I tossed and turned and worried and thought and questioned. Around five I got up, drank coffee, and decided that, sleep or no sleep, I was going to get through it. I'd operated many times on no sleep, and while I'd never taken an eight-hour test without having slept a minute, I told myself I would do it.

So I drove to Westfield State College, aced the first of the four sections—reading aptitude and comprehension, which was the easi-est—and began to feel pretty confident. The second section was the organic-chemistry/physics section, and of the two science sections this was the one on which I tended to score higher, so I knew I had to nail it. I got about halfway through the section without a hitch, but then I came to a set of problems that I couldn't figure out. That is, I didn't see what concept it was addressing, and had no idea how to calculate the answers to the next seven or eight questions. I stared at it for five minutes and suddenly the words were rising off the page. I closed my eyes, took a breath, and reluctantly went on to the next set of questions, only to find that I had lost my ability to read words. Whether some divine protective spirit or mischievous imp had cast a spell on me, or whether I was just having a sleep-deprivation-induced anxiety attack, I'll never know. But after trying unsuccessfully for another ten or fifteen minutes to just read through and comprehend a single problem, I gave up, put my pencil down, waited in a state of shock until time was called, then got up and had my scores cancelled. I walked out of Westfield State College feeling a deep sense of failure, but on the drive home I started to have an idea for a novel, which I began six months later, and which became *The Odd Sea*.

One uncanny little addendum to this story is that a committee at Westfield State College chose *The Odd Sea* as their "campus book"—intended to promote a campus-wide dialogue regarding the novel's various issues, and required reading for all faculty and students—for the 2000–2001 academic year, and then called to invite me to come give a ninety-minute talk, for which they paid me a nice amount. So just about seven years after my MCAT fiasco, I returned to Westfield State College for the first time since then and told this story to a filled auditorium. Afterward, someone asked me the obvious question—Was I now certain that I had made the right choice in becoming a writer? And I said that no, I still had lingering doubts. It's only now, at the age of thirty-seven, that I'm starting to understand that I never wanted to be a doctor at all. When I finished writing "The Ocean," though, I began to have the nagging sense that I should have become a marine biologist.

You are direct about the ethnic identities of the characters in Lost Legends. *One thing that separates it from the majority of Jewish-American novels is that you frame the religious identities with an equal attachment to specific geography. Was this important when you initially began the project, or did it evolve?*

Place is where everything seems to start for me as a novelist. Before I can even begin to think about my characters, they usually have to be attached to a specific place, which is the first step in activating my imagination. In fact, a strong sense of place is crucial to my writing process, precisely because it gives me something to attach imaginatively to long before I know all the quirks and habits of my characters. One of the biggest discoveries I made while writing *Lost Legends* was that with New Jersey I had more archetypal places to choose from than I could even make use of. You can't get any more archetypal than the Meadowlands, and even without Bruce Springsteen, the Jersey Shore has a mythology all its own. As the book evolved I became conscious that I was carving out a landscape that for me was as resonant as Arthurian Camelot, and in most cases a lot more interesting, since I had lived there.

A sense of place certainly crosses over ethnic boundaries and even different artistic forms of expression. Bruce Springsteen says that he felt a great sense of accountability to the people he had grown up alongside when writing Darkness on the Edge of Town. *Did you experience anything similar when writing* Lost Legends?

Absolutely. I felt it throughout the writing process. I would go so far as to say that what I felt was far more than accountability. I grew up in Livingston, New Jersey, where the book is set. All through grade school I was part of a very close group of friends, but after my parents separated, I began attending a private school and then moved away in eighth grade. Over the next six years I would live in the towns of Summit, Short Hills, West Orange, and South Orange. Since I was, of course, preoccupied with simply trying to succeed in my adolescence, I didn't think about how much I'd lost when I left that town and that group of friends behind.

While I was writing the book, it was as if I was going back to that lost world, where all of my life's "legends" seem to have sprung from. In my imagination I would visit those streets, see all those places, and I did feel a strong compulsion to get every last detail correct—not only street names and landmarks, but even stores that have not existed for twenty years. It seemed imperative that I double-check everything, though I rarely found that I'd made any sort of mistake. In fact, the only mistake I know of is that the yak cage is apparently not next to the penguin cage at the Turtle Back Zoo, and I learned this from someone I'd never met who wrote to suggest that I check my facts next time.

Why do these things matter so much? Well, this was our world, and this book was very much written for all those guys I grew up with. One of my grade-school friends who read *Lost Legends* commented to me that he loved reading the scene that takes place at the Little League field, had forgotten that the main field was called the Treat Field, and wondered how I had remembered that since they renamed it sometime in the eighties. In general, all of my friends from Livingston were amazed by how much of that landscape I remembered. As I explained, though, this world was etched inside my brain and body in a way that it would never have to be for someone who had continued living there, gone through high school with the same people they'd always known, and experienced the kind of continuity I did not have.

When *Lost Legends* came out, I did a reading at a bookstore in Livingston. A lot of those guys were there, as well as other people I'd gone to grade school with. My former next-door neighbor was there with her parents, and asked if I'd based the character of Juliette Dimiglio on her—I hadn't. My fifth-grade teacher was there. My first girlfriend's parents were there. It struck me then that writing *Lost Legends* was very much my way of going back to that lost world, of telling a story that would represent all these people, as well as a story that would—in some oblique, metaphorical way—apologize for having left. Without devolving into sentimentality, I'll tell you honestly that I feel a great loss from having fallen out of that context and losing the immediacy of those friendships. Almost amazingly, many of those guys I grew up with continued to stay the best of friends through college and beyond. They've all been the groomsmen at each other's weddings. Two of them live on the same block in Short Hills now, and put each others' kids to bed. Although I get together with them all once or twice a year now, it's not the same as if our lives had continued to be intertwined.

Youth is a continual theme in all of your work. "The Ocean" revisits your interest in the complications of adolescent romance. There is always the danger of portraying first love as idealized. How do you avoid the cliché?

Most adolescent romances are very self-centered and overblown, which may be natural and feel true for a thirteen year old, but tends to make for trite fiction. I initially considered letting Jordan and Dara begin experimenting sexually—as a response, in a sense, to what's going on with their parents—but I realized that the power of the story rests with Jordan's innocence and naivete, and his everpresent but unacknowledged reality—that his life is about to get, as his soon-to-be-adoptive mother Beverly states, "very, very hard." Dara is much more worldly, and much more angry than Jordan. I think the differences between them made for nicely counterpointed characterization, and a lot of the story's energy arises out of their differing views on things, which also had the effect of making their relationship seem very singular and distinct. My sense is that in avoiding the cliché of idealized first love, the key is creating characters who are distinct enough, in themselves, and whose particular relationship is specific enough to avoid those clichés, regardless of what's happening.

In "The Ocean" you implied the sexual content, but with The Odd Sea *you made the choice to graphically depict sexuality. Has your sensibility changed since your first novel?*

While writing *The Odd Sea*, my standpoint was that I was dealing with adolescent boys and that naturally adolescent boys think about sex a lot, and hence a very frank—I certainly wouldn't call it graphic—exploration of sexuality seemed a legitimate approach. Looking at it now, I still don't think there are any gratuitous scenes. But in hindsight there are definitely some things I would cut, one or two images that to me now seem excessive—that is, moments where the novel itself lapses into a bit of adolescent behavior. So, yes, I'm now trying to deal with sexuality in a more subtle way, and that will probably continue.

Many contemporary writers have a tendency to justify infidelity. You simply present the situation. For example, in "The Ocean," Dara knows that her mother is promiscuous and says so almost factually. How then do you construct the reality that these betrayals still hurt people emotionally?

I try not to make judgments in my novels, because I think a well-told story will leave a reader with a very clear sense of the consequences of any action, from which they can make judgments for themselves. In the case of the story "The Ocean," I was intentionally presenting certain loaded questions such as, What are a person's moral obligations in the face of life-threatening illness? If you happen to be in remission from leukemia, does that make infidelity okay? But in asking these questions, it was not my intention to propose answers. I think some readers will come away from that story thinking that the protagonist's father's behavior was abominable, while others will find it perfectly acceptable. What interested me was that it seemed such a complicated situation, and such a complex question.

I'll tell you a secret about that story, though. I started writing it simply because I was attracted to the idea of writing about coral reefs and that particularly wondrous Caribbean landscape, where, at age twenty,

I spent a summer taking a course in marine biology. This is a case of my attaching imaginatively to the landscape before I even knew what the story was. I think the reason that the story ultimately worked was that I happened to come up with an external situation—a young boy's last summer spent with his marine biologist father who is in remission from leukemia—that meshed well with the whole undersea world that the protagonist, Jordan, spends so much time elucidating. In my mind, this was very much a story about a soon-to-be-orphaned boy who turns literally to the ocean for refuge, and in this sense it was for me a very spiritual story.

A lot of the new plot-driven, pop-culture-saturated fiction today tends to avoid spirituality. Aren't all memorable stories spiritual on some level? One can't help but think that even a blatantly political novel like J.M. Coetzee's Disgrace *hinges on redemption.*

I think *Disgrace* is a great book, and it's because Coetzee is willing to make his protagonist Lurie, in the end, a human being. Obviously, it's a book with large political dimensions, but what I remember most are those euthanized dogs that he takes such care with as he's loading them onto the conveyer belt. To me, that really was a redemptive moment, and I agree with you that most, if not all, memorable stories hinge on such moments. Perhaps this is where my writing will always seem "unhip" to a certain type of reader, but I personally could not even sustain the interest necessary to complete a short story if it didn't incorporate deeply emotional and/or transcendent moments. For me, however, the spiritual is usually not tied to religion or anything of that sort. Often it's tied to nature, but sometimes it's tied to a rotting clarinet found in a landfill in the Meadowlands, as was the case in one chapter of *Lost Legends.*

You teach at Emerson College now. Have writing programs become institutionalized, the antithesis of art?

I think a common mistake that young would-be writers make is the belief that an MFA program is going to be like law school, that you can go through your two or three years and come out a "writer." Many find out the hard way that this isn't true, that unlike law school, there is no cause-effect relationship between going to an MFA program and getting a book contract, though it certainly can help. I also think that because of this misperception, writing programs now have a certain marketability, and so naturally they'll play into this idea—that by getting an MFA you'll legitimize yourself as a writer. That's the biggest problem, that the perception exists and is reinforced by the institutions, and that many students are surprised or alarmed to find that one's evolution as a writer to the point where you're creating truly artistic fiction that is also publishable generally takes a lot longer than two or three years. Some writers do land book contracts after three years of an MFA program, but they're usually the ones who had been at it for years already when they began the program.

Still, I would say that writing programs are not the antithesis of art. In any group of fifty people who call themselves writers, there might be two you can consider genuine artists. Those writers are probably not going to be adversely affected by spending three years in a stimulating academic environment, getting feedback from established authors as well as peers, and being part of that particular school's writing milieu. In fact, they're probably going to gain a lot from it.

A lot of instructors at such programs refrain from brutal criticism. Students aren't always told what they need to hear, even when it's the painful truth. Do you feel that writing programs should weed people out, as is done at medical programs, put commitment to the test?

My sense is that writers need to hear straight and honest criticism, in a respectful, nurturing atmosphere. I personally see no reason for a teacher to look a student in the eye and tell them their story is a piece of shit, even if it is. Most writers who I've seen go on to succeed have done so because they are intelligent enough to learn from the feedback they receive, smart enough not to listen to most of it, and determined enough to keep writing.

In fact, most successful writers are successful because—through some mix of talent, perseverance, self-reflectiveness, and egomania—they are capable of continuing even though many people have suggested they do otherwise. My first fiction workshop was with Paul Auster during the fall of my senior year at Princeton. He was a very hands-off teacher, who gave us an assignment each week, and then would offer five or ten minutes or so of feedback to each student. It was exactly what I needed, and in that semester I went from writing work that was basic undergraduate drivel to work that was promising undergraduate drivel. At the end of the year, when I was trying to decide whether to go to med school or apply to MFA programs, I dropped by Paul's office and asked him what he thought. He said, "You know I admire your writing, but you should probably go to med school. You'll have a much nicer life."

I reminded him of this when I ran into him at the Miami Book Fair last year, and he noted that although in my case it may have been the wrong advice, it was good advice—and I agree. Anyone who would respond to that advice by going to med school probably should go to med school. But I'll point out that what Paul gave me was not brutal advice. Brutal advice would be more along the lines of "Your writing stinks. Don't waste your time." The fact was, my writing was quite unformed at the time, and the odds of my succeeding as a writer would have seemed slim to anyone. But thankfully no one gave me any brutal advice. It probably wouldn't have deterred me in the long run, but in the short run I would have felt that much more embarrassment and shame.

You've mentioned that you see only twenty percent of MFA students continue to write after earning a degree and that eighty percent who enter a program romantically committed will not be by the end. Publications such as McSweeney's *have an open disdain for writing programs. What is the argument in favor of sustaining them?*

It's hard to be a writer. Unless you happen to have a trust fund, you have to wait tables or work some tedious day job in order to make your rent, and finding quality time to write is very difficult. The best contribution of writing programs to any writer or would-be writer is that they provide a focused time in which you've put aside everything for two years because you've made the decision to write. It also gives you a community of support, which is again why I'm not a fan of the brutal-criticism school. In a predatory environment, it's hard to feel supported.

In my case, an MFA program gave me a sort of jumpstart since I'd been so focused on the sciences. UC Irvine provided me with structure and taught me what I'd eventually need to do on my own—i.e., when I no longer had the luxury of workshops and fellow writers all around me. And frankly, I had no need for workshops after two years. I'd pretty much internalized all the workshop ideas and was ready to move on.

It's true that only twenty percent or less will continue writing once the program ends, but for that eighty percent who quit, at least they gave it the old college try and hopefully had a decent social life while doing so. *McSweeney's* hates writing programs because most writing programs are traditional and *McSweeney's* stated objective is, more or less, to undermine anything traditional. I think it's great that *McSweeney's* has created another niche—a sort of hip anti-niche, aspects of which are quite brilliant—but it's just a different position and perception.

So I think the whole thing should be taken with a grain of salt. Writing programs won't make you into a writer, but they're useful as a stepping stone for people who have, in one way or another, been writers and/or potential writers their whole lives, and who feel like such an environment would be productive. But there are also people for whom writing programs will be a waste of time. Unfortunately, some of those people come to writing programs anyway, and perhaps that's one bad aspect of the establishment part of MFA programs—that people think they can't become a legitimate writer without having an MFA.

I'd also say for anyone who attends a writing program, it's important not to hang around in that MFA environment for too long. Once you're done, get out and figure out who you are. In the end, writing is a self-starting, solitary endeavor, and to continue as a writer you need to find a way to build this into your real life. MFA programs provide structure and can be helpful, but they are not real life. In terms of real-life credentials, the only thing an MFA degree will do is help you get a teaching job, assuming you've already published a book or two.

A criticism of writing programs is that students are quite impressionable and are in danger of imitating a certain type of story. Many students are drawn to imitating domestic writers such as Raymond Carver and Alice Munro. Isn't there a risk of promoting a specific kind of literature if instructors refuse to challenge students?

I recently saw folk singer/guitar virtuoso Leo Kottke play in Northampton, Massachusetts. He told a little story about his mentor, John Fahey, and how at one point he said to Fahey something like, "You know, I have this fear that I'm going to sound a lot like you." Fahey's response was, "Well, everybody has to go through someone."

My sense is that this is true for all artists, and is particularly applicable to writing. That is, I think most if not all writers must go through a phase of assimilating and emulating their favorite writers if they're to have any chance of finding their own voice. Simply put, all writers need models of form and technique, and any writer worth his or her salt will go through various authors and come out the other side.

It's true that Raymond Carver and Alice Munro tend to be MFA-program staples everywhere, and this is because they're two of the most important North American writers of the late twentieth century. In the thirties you had Hemingway, Steinbeck, Fitzgerald, and Faulkner. In the fifties and sixties you had Cheever, Roth, Bellow, Salinger, O'Connor, Welty. Who do you have of that caliber to come out of the seventies and eighties? Carver and Munro. They've both, in certain ways, modernized the tenets of Anton Chekhov. And whereas Carver might be thought of as the heir to Hemingway, Munro might be thought of in some ways as an heir to Faulkner. No matter how you look at it, and whatever labels you try to put on them, their work has affected our modern literary tradition. To be a contemporary American literary writer, you need to understand the understatement and scene-by-scene movement of a Carver story, just as you need to understand the elliptical expository methods of Munro. That's not to say one should try to write like Carver or Munro—in fact, Carver and Munro imitations have the same parody-like quality as an emulation of Hemingway or Faulkner, simply because their voices are so distinct. From what I can see in the programs I've been part of, most MFA students are going to be exposed to a wide range of contemporary fiction, ranging from formalists like Jhumpa Lahiri to satirists like George Saunders, so it's not as if there's really a risk involved in focusing on these two masters of the form for a short while, particularly since their stories become a good and useful model for so many people. And whether or not Lahiri or Saunders gets assigned in your grad class, those books exist, and it's any writer or would-be writer's job to read and read and read.

As far as influences go in general, I've always held the belief that a writer can be influenced for the wrong reasons or the right ones. The wrong reasons are that, as you've suggested, they feel pressure to conform with the thing that is being celebrated at the present moment—and such impressionability typically comes with a lack of emotional maturity. Being influenced for what I'm calling the right reasons means being influenced by a writer whose work resonates with you because you share some aspect of that writer's sensibility. In finding a book that speaks to you, you've usually found a writer who in some way shares your own sensibility, and who has already taken ideas and impressions about form or content that are still inchoate for you, and transmuted them into something tangible and fully realized. In reading a work that influences you, you're essentially reading a work by someone who has mastered some aspect of what you hope to master, and so by reading that work you are embarking on the process of going through a mentor.

Like most writers, I went through a period of impressionability in which I was unconsciously emulating writers for precisely the wrong reasons. Just after I graduated from college, I took a night course at the New School and had a teacher who despised everything I wrote, and perhaps me personally. He was a big fan of Carver, and "What We Talk About When We Talk About Love" was one of his favorite stories. Toward the end of the semester I finally wrote a story he liked. I included it with my MFA applications, and when I got to UC Irvine and sat down the first week with my advisor there, he pulled out the story and said, "Now here's an interesting little piece. I think you should change the title to 'What We Talk About When We Talk About Hockey.'" This is the kind of risk I think you're talking about, but I would say that it was ultimately my responsibility to recognize what I was doing. Thankfully, I did.

That was the same fall I had what I think of as my one and only prophetic dream, which I'll be so bold as to relate, since I think it relates to this discussion. In the dream I came to a bookstore window and found that the entire window was displaying copies of what was apparently my first book. But the book, instead of being pages bound by a cardboard cover with dust jacket, was, in each little wooden bookstand, a bunch of celery, complete with leaves and stalks. When I awoke, I likened the dream to a Magritte painting, said to myself something like, "Neat," and didn't think much of it. But later, the dream's meaning hit me full force. What I was writing was the equivalent of celery. I didn't care what it was so long as it would be published, and so it really was interchangeable with celery or radishes or whatever. I would say it took me almost two years after that realization to start writing fiction that I could honestly say was not the equivalent of celery. And I would say to any would-be writer of literary fiction that there are thousands of much easier ways to achieve notoriety and/or make money than by being a writer. So if you're going to do it, you have to give over to what is meaningful and authentic, for both your readership and for yourself. And that means letting go of your need to be like any other writer. The best writers' writing does not remind you of anyone else.

Since you don't think much about what readers are comfortable with, would you also say that the author's original intention doesn't matter once a book is placed into the public arena? Philip Roth, Nikos Kazantzakis, and Salman Rushdie all had to deal with this in unpleasant ways. Likewise, J.D. Salinger certainly had no intention of speaking for generations of young people.

We've all heard of the "intentional fallacy," and as you point out, intention certainly didn't matter much for Salman Rushdie with regard to the public response to *The Satanic Verses*. But I would say, and strongly, that while it will often be disregarded or prove irrelevant in the public arena, an author's intention is of the utmost importance. That's what I was talking about, to some extent, when I mentioned my celery dream. In deciding not to write celery, you're deciding to write something that you can stand by, whether or not it's a bestseller, and whether or not someone wants to kill you as a result of it. Many people, including authors themselves, seem to forget that an author is a person who has to live with whatever he or she has created, and in the extreme case in which someone issues a *fatwa* after reading your book, it seems to me important to be clear that what you wrote possesses both aesthetic and moral integrity—which is not to say one shouldn't, if so inclined and for legitimate reasons, write a book about an amoral protagonist. If a book gets wrongly interpreted by the public, well, that's always been one of the risks of the profession. Usually such misinterpretation will just result in the book being dismissed, but occasionally there will be a backlash of the type Rushdie experienced, as has been the case throughout history.

There's one more tricky part of this, though, and something that I don't want to believe, but find that I do. That is, I think writers have a responsibility to be smarter and more aware than the average person. Anything you write is going to have political or psychological implications, and it is necessary to be aware, at least intuitively, of those implications, and, to some extent, to be able to anticipate the reaction to what you're doing—because if you don't think you'll be able to stand by your own work in the face of an unfavorable reaction, you're probably writing celery. I'd say that the worst writers I know are invariably those who are completely unconscious of their subtexts, often to the point that the subtexts themselves conflict with what's ostensibly being said. That's something you see all the time in movies. But this type of thing is more acceptable in movies, as movies, with some exceptions, tend not to be high art and tend to be put together by a committee. A literary writer, who is the sole author of his own book, simply can't afford such a gaffe, because it undermines his or her credibility.

Of course, some reactions are impossible to anticipate, and there is a point where you just have to let go. But if you're going to write, say, *Lolita*, you have to know that there are going to be people who won't appreciate it, may want to ban it, and may attempt to discredit you as an author. And in knowing that, you need to be doubly clear about what you're doing, so that if those unappreciative people dismiss your book, you can still feel at least a modicum of peace about what you've written.

Likewise, it's important to get beyond or at least compensate for one's own narcissistic impulses. Surely, most writers or artists of any kind possess a strain of narcissism, even if a polite one. I recently read a book in which John Berger was discussing the life of Rembrandt. As Berger points out, the difference between his early work, which is largely a celebration of his own talent and good fortune, and his last self-portrait, in which his expression seems only to hold unanswerable questions, is the difference between a young virtuoso and a master. If you look at the work of Philip Roth, you'll see a similar pattern. His work through the 1960s and '70s, good as it was, did not approach the richness and resonance of his recent work.

Roth has become a master of portraying the character as writer. Both of your own novels possess characters who have blatant writer personalities: Philip finds a bit of a writer in himself, Anthony sees everything around him as a legend, and his cousin Timmy expresses a desire to write books someday. However, you are fairly rigid in drawing boundaries between author, character, and narrator. Are there lines that shouldn't be crossed without good reason?

I think it all depends on your sensibility, your aesthetic, and what it is you're trying to do. Philip Roth, for instance, has invented Nathan Zuckerman as an alter ego, and at times is so merged with Zuckerman's identity that there's an odd flatness to his prose, in which it does not feel imaginatively projected, and hence doesn't feel like fiction at all. The first hundred pages of *American Pastoral* are like that, but Roth is such a good storyteller that it doesn't matter. Even if Zuckerman gets self-indulgent at times, Roth is always looking outward, at the big story. That's his secret and it generally works.

Many other writers who play with the boundary between author and character are doing so simply out of authorial narcissism, and I have read many books in which the subtext is simply: Here's how I see it and I'm right, so please adore me. Most young writers simply don't know any better, which is why as a teacher of writing I'm always stressing the need to see your protagonist as an "other," even if the protagonist is in fact based on yourself. Some people have the capacity to do this naturally; others don't. Another strategy, and one that Roth makes use all the time, is to focus the story on some larger-than-life character who is rendered through the point-of-view of the authorial stand-in. For instance, the place where *American Pastoral* starts to come alive is precisely the place where Zuckerman stops talking about himself and begins to project instead the story of Swede Levov. This is more or less the same strategy used by F. Scott Fitzgerald in *The Great Gatsby*. As a narrator, Nick Carroway is a cipher because he's basically a stand-in for Fitzgerald, and hence Fitzgerald never really envisions him. But the book works because its focus becomes the larger-than-life, if enigmatic, Gatsby. I'd say the same thing about Conrad's *Heart of Darkness*. Marlowe is a cipher, but the book works because Marlowe mostly stays focused on Kurtz.

At the other end of the spectrum, a book like Nabokov's *Lolita* demonstrates a very clear separation between author Nabokov and narrator-protagonist Humbert Humbert, as is made apparent by the fact that Humbert fails to recognize the point at which he's lost the reader's sympathy, even as author Nabokov seems to have crafted it this way with very conscious intention. I'd go so far as to say that this is why, in my mind, *Lolita* is in no way pornographic, whereas many attempts to emulate it are nothing but pornography. This occurs for the same reason that writers trying to emulate Nick Hornby usually wind up with pretentious displays of their knowledge of pop culture. That is, the author hasn't envisioned the protagonist as an "other," and so what you get is an author acting out perverse sexual fantasies, or an author simply demonstrating his encyclopedic knowledge of the history of rock and roll.

One of the problems, as I see it, is that crossing the line and having a protagonist act essentially as a stand-in for the author is that the reader often winds up being asked to become complicit with whatever the character is involved in. Occasionally this approach works—for example I would point to the racial issues raised by Roth's technique in *The Human Stain*. In not knowing for the first eighty-eight pages that Coleman Silk is really an African-American, Roth essentially tricks us into becoming complicit with the same racial stereotyping that becomes the thematic focus of the book. But Roth is so acutely aware of what he's doing and hence maintains such a balanced perspective on the matter—placing us alternately on either side of the argument—that it never feels as if he is asking us to share his own beliefs, but rather is asking us to explore various perceptions by looking at the situation through the eyes of various characters.

More often—and usually due to a lack of conscious intention—an approach that asks the reader to become complicit fails because the writer starts to use his characters as mouthpieces for his or her own myopic arguments or beliefs. A common and generally uncomfortable occurrence in undergraduate workshops is a situation where a student accidentally turns in a blatantly sexist story in which we are asked to be complicit with the sexism, rather than simply observing a sexist character. It is certainly possible to write a compelling story about a sexist person, but often what I see is a sexist author, unconsciously merged with his or her protagonist, who is asking the reader to join in. What results ranges from a clunky, disturbing psychological stance to elegant pornography along the lines of *The Story of O*—a book that is endlessly adored by those who find in it validation for their own misogynistic and sadomasochistic fantasies.

The thing about *Lolita* is that Nabokov never asks us to become complicit in the actions of Humbert Humbert, and in fact sets it up so that while at times we are in fact charmed by Humbert, we also recognize him for the pedophile that he is.

Pop culture has been given a prominent position in literature over the past few years. It used to be taboo to admit these influences unless they were artists such as Bob Dylan who possess intellectual credibility. One thing that Irvine graduates have in common is incorporating non-literary influences. Did Irvine encourage this, or is it a generational departure?

I wasn't aware of anything like that going on at Irvine, but I'm very much of the opinion anyway that it is a generational departure. As much as I was profoundly influenced by Joyce, Woolf, Faulkner, Munro, Chekhov, García Márquez, and many other writers, I can equally say that I was profoundly influenced by the Beatles, Pink Floyd, Yes, the Grateful Dead, the Doors, Simon & Garfunkel, Bruce Springsteen, Rush, CSN, Neil Young, Led Zeppelin, and many other rock groups that I would consider literary, or at least of having literary pretensions.

I would say the same is true for most writers of my era, and the reason seems pretty obvious to me. Literary rock music—which now tends to fall under the heading classic rock—more or less started in 1967, when the Beatles put out *Sgt. Pepper's Lonely Hearts Club Band*, and it was only when groups like Pink Floyd and Yes followed suit in the late sixties that this kind of literary influence started to become available. I was not the kind of kid who sat home and read *Moby Dick* for fun, and so the books I read were only those that were assigned for English classes—and I was usually speed-reading them on the bus. Now and then, I would have strong reactions to a book—as was the case with *Huckleberry Finn*, which I recall having vivid dreams about, *The Catcher in the Rye*, *The Sun Also Rises*, *The Great Gatsby*, and even *Wuthering Heights*—but equally as important to my understanding of literature were those Saturday night parties where we'd sit around analyzing the dark metaphors lurking in Pink Floyd lyrics, or feel the mystical elevation that comes from listening to an exalted, grandiose Yes song such as "And You and I" or "Siberian Khatru."

Music is such a dominant definition of generation identity, but it's often used ineffectively in literature. What would be your advice in avoiding some of those problems?

I think music is, as you say, a dominant definition of generational identity, because music has the capacity to represent aesthetically the emotions of a particular era in a way that writing or any other art form simply can't. It's a visceral response that has been proven scientifically. And when a recording artist gets it right, the fusion of music and the lyrics it's been united with becomes a medium into which we can sublimate or channel ourselves. That's why the explosive indignation of a song like "Ohio" can stand for so much in the Vietnam era, why more escapist/romantic songs like "Born to Run" and "Thunder Road" hold the post-war mid-seventies, why the cryptic and resonant ambiguity of REM takes over in the eighties, and why moody, explosive angst-driven groups like Smashing Pumpkins and Nirvana rule the nineties. Like most people, there are certain songs I have trouble listening to because it feels like half of me is in there. Somehow or other we sublimate parts of ourselves into music, whether it's Frank Sinatra or Queen.

Naturally, writers are going to want to bring that same kind of channeled emotion into their writing, but it's a mistake to think that throwing down references like "It took me four days to hitchhike from Saginaw" is going to do anything more than invoke nostalgia, for those who do get the reference, and it's certainly not going to convey all the involuntary memories that come with it and make it meaningful to you in that nonverbal, musical sense. It can be fun to throw in cryptic little things. For instance, the phrase "Sit you down, father; rest you" shows up a few times in my new novel, and for that one out of five hundred readers who knows instantly what I'm referring to, it should be a fun little revelation.

But it seems to me that ineffective use of music references usually results when writers try to give a particular line from a song or reference to a band too much weight. Likewise, basing a story's mood around, say, the trippy atmosphere at a Grateful Dead concert often becomes a cliché or an unintentional parody. We have a whole set of associations with the Dead, and because the writing usually can't hold the multidimensional effects of actual music, a writer is reduced to those hackneyed associations. My advice to writers would be to use music references with a light touch and not to depend too much on them for weight and meaning, in the same way you don't want to depend on dream sequences for causality, though they can be quite nice when they're dropped in to provide texture.

So many writers say they wish they had been in a band, and so many musicians say they really wanted to be writers. A lot of writers have a secondary artistic outlet. You play hockey. The writers I know who had at one time been athletes tend to be the most disciplined. How has your love of hockey found its way into your writing process?

It's true that often former athletes are among the most self-disciplined writers. Athletes learn a certain level of discipline at a young age, and most who have any success at all do so in part because they are coachable, meaning that they can assimilate suggestion and criticisms, and in the process even learn to tolerate a lot of judgment and, at times, verbal abuse. I think a lot of athletes also have an understanding that just as developing a decent slapshot takes years, learning to write a decent short story may take years, and former athletes often seem more willing to practice writing in the form of apprenticing themselves to it in the same way they'd give over to the demands of being on a team. That was certainly the case for me. I attribute a lot of my drive and focus to the hardwired skills I developed as a very young boy on the ice rink or soccer field. I learned that everyone begins as a novice, and that if you stick with something long enough, your level of talent and potentiality will start to become clear. The trouble with sports, however, is that the maniacal focus many kids give to it—which is supported and deeply encouraged by our cul-ture—often becomes problematic, since unless you're truly a super-star and can make the pros, your sports career typically ends at the end of college, if not sooner. And yet, for all those years of dedica-tion, it's been almost a vocation. Had you put that kind of time into the violin or oboe, you'd probably have a very good chance at going pro. This is due in part to the fact that our culture is not as support-ive of and enthusiastic about the violin or oboe, so those who stay with it typically do so because it's clear they possess substantial talent and hopefully they enjoy it. Meanwhile, it's very possible to dedicate your whole childhood to soccer or basketball or hockey or competi-tive swimming and then find yourself at a dead end due to talent limitations and very often physical/genetic limitations.

I played hockey and soccer through high school and, following a serious knee injury, I played a couple years of college soccer. But the knee injury had slowed me down a lot, and after my junior year, I made the decision to quit the team. Not surprisingly that's when I started writing. I needed some place to put all that focus and obsession and day-to-day intensity, and even then I realized that my mindset, when I sat down to write, was very much the mindset I had each time I got on the ice or on the soccer field. However, I will say this. All the published books in the world would not compare to ten seconds on the ice during, for instance, my high-school hockey team's run when we won the state prep-school championship during my sophomore year. I've heard Bill Bradley say something similar—that his whole political career didn't compare to one game with the Knicks. There's something about sports that is so immediate, so instantly gratifying, and so euphoric, that it really is like a drug.

One last thought on this. It seems to me that the most naturally gifted athletes may not in fact make good writers. The most naturally gifted athletes do not always develop that level of self-reflection that is so crucial for someone like me, who, despite whatever gifts I had, was always considered very good but not a truly great player. Players like me learned that getting ice time meant, at least to some extent, following our instructions, whereas Wayne Gretzky, at least until he went pro, probably never had much need to think about instructions. Nor did he ever have any need to become a writer.

Hemingway was not a very talented athlete but he did love sports, and for all the stories of his alcoholism, he was known to write sober with incredible discipline. Steinbeck said that Hemingway saw other writers as competitors. Is the athlete within a writer a mixed blessing?

I think it's true that being an athlete naturally leads to a sense of competitiveness as a writer, and in many ways this is a good thing. I know that at times it certainly motivated me. The older I get, though, the more I've let go of it.

Without asking you to give away a surprise, is "The Ocean" a sign of the direction you intend to pursue with this new novel you have almost completed?

I don't know. So far in this book, I'm mostly thinking about bears.

Eric Wasserman was born and raised in Portland, Oregon. He is the author of a collection of short fiction, *The Temporary Life: Stories* (La Questa Press, 2005). He currently lives and teaches in Los Angeles, where he is working on a novel set during the height of McCarthyism.

"Wormwood" was written in longhand on a rooftop in Santo Domingo around 1973, and forgotten until the winter of 1989. It then began a shadowy life in various computers, eventually revised and taken seriously by my eldest daughter, Christy, who managed somehow to glean from it a certain pathos relative to her Dominican childhood. We are pictured here, my daughter and I, outside one of the four homes we inhabited during our Caribbean years.

Jimmy Olsen is a native of Hoffman, Minnesota, and has degrees from St. Cloud State University and the University of Alabama. He's worked as a newspaper reporter, editor, and photographer. A life-long scuba diver (instructor since 1974), he lived five years in the Dominican Republic where he taught English and owned a dive shop. His first novel, *Things in Ditches*, was published in 2000, to be followed soon by *The Poison Makers*. More information about the author is available at www.jimmyolsen.net.

WORMWOOD

Jimmy Olsen

That year we lived upstairs in the house of an elderly doctor and his wife on Avenida Independencia. It was on a corner, Independencia and Calle del Mar, two blocks from the ocean. Across Independencia was an elementary school and playground surrounded by a high, dirty concrete wall, and across the other way a home where the people kept a large hog, some chickens, and two goats they finally ate.

The doctor and his wife were small, him especially, and they owned a small car for which they had a chauffeur named Julio. There was a maid too, Luz, which is *light* in Spanish. I don't remember the first name of either the doctor or his wife, but the last name was Abranté. They'd always rented to North Americans, they said, and spoke some English, though I don't think they liked Americans much.

Patricia was pregnant about six months with Melanie then, and extremely uncomfortable in the heat. There was no air conditioning, but we caught an ocean breeze in the daytime and a cooler breeze from the forested mountains at night. The fresh air and two balconies, one leading off the parlor and another a step down from the kitchen, widened the small apartment quite a lot, and we felt very much the adventurous expatriates with so many balconies. Later, when the baby was born, Patricia rocked her in an iron rocker on the parlor balcony and watched the hog overturn the neighbor's garbage drum.

Late one afternoon we were rocking there, just the two of us, and Patricia said sharply, "Do you have any interest in what happened here today?"

"Sorry," I said. "Didn't mean to talk so long."

"We've been getting robbed."

"Robbed?"

"Burgled."

"Antonia?" I said, immediately suspecting the young girl we'd hired.

"You'll never believe it," she said, shaking her head so her brown hair slapped her cheeks. "Sneaks up the back stairs to the kitchen balcony, sees if the coast is clear, and makes her move."

"Who sneaks up?"

"Mrs. Abranté."

"The daring old bitch," I said. "What does she steal?"

"Used coffee grounds."

A tall woman in plastic sandals passed in the street below, balancing a laundry basket on her head. Her simple dress was stretched tight across a swollen belly. "Why would anyone do that?" I asked.

"I snuck down the stairs after her and watched through the window. Her and Luz made coffee. Dr. Abranté was called in from his little office and he drank the coffee too. Coffee from our stolen grounds. Have you ever heard anything so demented in your life?"

"No," I said.

"They won't let me use their phone. Mrs. Abranté laughed at me. She's so superior. We can't use her telephone, but she thinks nothing of stealing our coffee grounds."

During the day the cotton curtains stood almost straight out from the windows, but early in the evenings the breeze grew listless, allowing the supper cooking smells and goat dung to mix with whatever had washed ashore. "If there's an emergency," I said, "we'll just go down there and use the phone. We don't need permission in an emergency."

"If I wasn't so pregnant and fat and tired, I'd find a job."

"You know there's no jobs." Across the rooftops toward the sea, it seemed like the sun rested on the Hispañola Hotel. "Not for a *gringa*, anyway."

"Guess what else," she said, pouring two fresh rums. "They're all laughing at your legs because you keep wearing shorts after I've told you *how many times* men here don't wear short pants."

"You saw them laughing?"

"Luz told Julio and he likes Antonia so he told her and she told me." She placed her drink on the balcony ledge and gazed past me toward the green hills. "They call you *Patas de Gallina*. Chicken legs."

"Suppose they think it's funny."

"I do."

The hog house across Calle del Mar was square and boxy and flat-roofed, made of concrete like ours, but ours was all rounded corners and tall. The house across reminded me of a rooftop pigeon cage where different birds fly in and out, and you watch, but can't distinguish one from another. The same was true of the people who lived there, and we discussed the look-alike people quite a lot.

I wanted to discuss them now, instead of talking about my legs. "Who's that guy?" I pointed. "Have we seen him before?"

Patricia liked talking about them, too; she was a great people watcher. "Sure," she said. "He's the husband or boyfriend of the old lady's fat daughter. Not the short fat one, but the fat one with long hair."

"I don't think so."

"I'm telling you. That's who he is."

"No. I think he's a new one, and we've never seen him before."

"You've been seeing new ones every day since they got robbed."

"Not every day."

"Almost."

We'd watched a robber—we thought he lived there—walk in one afternoon and take cash from two of the bedrooms, and help himself to a plate of *chicharron de pollo* from the dining table and walk out and down the street munching away. Some of the people inside finally chased him and we watched that, too. We didn't catch on, and it got around that the *Norte Americanos* just sat on their balcony drinking rums while their neighbors were being robbed. What can you expect of foreigners?

"I don't think we should do anything about the coffee grounds," I said. "You'd just throw them out anyway."

"I didn't say we should *do* anything. I just told you about it."

"Dr. Abranté said last week that Julio would drive me to a used-car lot on Saturday and he'd come along to translate. We've got to get a car."

All that happened before Christmas and other things happened, too, which I forgot. I bought the car that Saturday for one thousand, six hundred pesos; a lot of money for a ten-year-old car in those days. But hardly anybody there had cars then.

It was the only foreign car I ever owned. A British Morris, gray and shaped like a Volkswagen Beetle, but with the engine where it should be and a trunk with a hump. In the floor of the backseat there was a hole big enough to stick both feet through. No door on the glove compartment and it got forty miles to the gallon. James A. Michener rode in that car once and didn't say much, but that was a year later, before Patricia had her accident and wrecked it.

The new year didn't start out very well for us and the Abrantés. It was because of a book. I went down to beg a phone call. Standing in their darkened parlor heavy with black furniture, I shifted from one foot to another to avoid the clouds of tiny mosquitoes hovering under the tables, chairs, and lamp stands. They refused to install screens. Upstairs we burned green coils that gave off a toxic yellow smoke and left a gray ash. Mrs. Abranté led me to the phone and saw I was carrying a copy of a novel I was using in class then, *The Ugly American*. She called the doctor in, and he read the title, and they discussed it in both Spanish and English and then told me how funny it was that I was an American reading *The Ugly American*. I never saw the humor in that, and when I didn't, it made it all the more funny for them. They never got over it, and the more they thought about it, I guess, the better it sounded.

They laughed at me unexpectedly sometimes after that. Mrs. Abranté's saggy black eyes mocked me, flicking along my pale skin to settle on the perpetual sweat of my forehead. "You sweat," she used to say, suggesting that I came from an inferior race that couldn't hold in its sweat. I was young then, not ugly, but sweat-ugly to her, and if so, maybe to anyone there. White men seldom entertain thoughts of racial inferiority, and I was puzzled by it until I understood it.

In April when it really got hot again we ate our suppers on the balcony. Melanie was four months old by then and Patricia doted on her.

"Now she's telling me I can't play cards with Antonia," Patricia said between spoonfuls of plantain and chicken-liver soup.

"Mrs. Abranté?"

She nodded, catching the dribbles with her napkin.

"Why can't you?"

"Some kind of no-fraternization policy."

This made me laugh. "And all the time her and Luz gossip about every move we make up here. Talk about fraternization!"

I leaned over to be sure they weren't listening. The house had a small yard they called a garden, and it was L-shaped with the long part on Independencia hidden behind a wall. The garden had one tree, a palm, ringed with croton and some kind of vine that climbed straight up almost to the coconuts. They had some green grass there, too. Julio and Mrs. Abranté watered it three or four times a day. Julio cut it twice a week with a machete that had a broken tip.

"Are they listening?" she asked.

"No."

"I don't care what they say. Antonia's the only friend I've got, and we like to play casino in the afternoon. She wins every time."

I finished eating and had to wipe the sweat from my face, even though the sun had gone completely and it was very dark. The city had poor street lighting, but the nights were alive with music and laughter, and though it was all foreign to us, we'd come to like it because we could hide in the dark of the balcony and watch and listen. We talked softly and I smoked sometimes.

"She's your maid," I said. "You can play cards with her if you want to."

"She's more like a friend. It's a nice break for us when the baby takes her afternoon nap."

"If you say so I'll take my ugly face and go down there tomorrow and tell them both to quit pestering you about it."

"You'd really do that?"

"Well, I don't want to, since they let me put the car inside the wall." They had an extra iron gate on the Independencia side, and let me bring the car in there so it wouldn't be stolen or stripped. Anything left out at night was gone in the morning. We got rid of a laundry basket full of termites that way once. "I'll do it, though," I said.

"Never mind."

"Remember how long we looked for this place? Two months in that hotel without a car. That's what took almost all our money—but that doesn't mean they should pester you about the maid."

"I said never mind."

That was the night before Patricia lost her temper.

I came home around four. The house had an outside stairs straight from the ground to the kitchen balcony, and around front an enclosed granite stairs spiraling up from the main door. That day I entered by the main door and the fight was already in progress out back. Can't say I was too surprised about it. That fight had been coming a long time.

Patricia has a deep voice, and when she raises it, it can be heard for some distance. Inside the concrete walls her voice had a fine acoustical quality and reminded me of that Pentecostal preacher who works El Conde in the afternoons.

"This is disgusting, sickening!" she thundered. "You expect us to live like pigs?"

"What do I care how you live?" I recognized Mrs. Abranté's heavily accented voice. She spoke English very precisely because she'd learned it from a book.

"Why won't you come up here and look for yourself? Maybe you'd like to eat off my cupboard. I'll make you a sandwich. Come on! I dare you!"

I entered the kitchen and Antonia was standing near the door, well back, hand clamping her mouth. She did this whenever she laughed, to cover the gap where her front teeth were missing. Mrs. Abranté was not in the room. Patricia's broad back was to me, and she was shouting at the open balcony door.

"No one likes your food," Mrs. Abranté told her from somewhere below.

"Come and see why, then," Patricia said. "Come on up. I dare you! Come on."

"What's the matter?" I asked.

Patricia spun around, surprised to see me. She pounded the kitchen cupboard with her fist. She has big hands, and the force of her blow overturned some cups and the salt and pepper shakers. "Look at this," she ordered.

The cupboard was old, worn, like everything there. Most of the white paint had peeled, leaving brown wood heavily grained and soggy, almost like something waterlogged. "Needs paint," I said.

"Look closer."

She scared me a little the way her eyes darted, unfocused, so I examined the cupboard carefully. It was ripe with narrow white worms—bone white and corpulent, with hard golden heads. "Pretty bad," I said. "Lucky we didn't get sick."

"Not that that old bitch cares! How many maggots do you think got mixed in the baby's formula? How many?" Her face was very red, and spittle had collected at the corners of her mouth. "Now! I want it replaced now!"

Mrs. Abranté was gone when I looked down the stairs. "She wouldn't listen?"

"She left?"

"Yes."

"She better not leave."

"She's gone."

She looked for herself, and when she came back I thought she seemed more composed. "Fine," she said. "But she forgot to take her maggots with her." There was a small iron pan on the stove, and she swung it up against the rotting wood, splintering the corner. Antonia gasped and ran away.

"Honey," I said.

"Help me."

"This won't solve anything."

"Help me!"

Together we battered the wormy wood until it loosened pretty much in one piece. We threw it down the back stairs so it landed hard against Mrs. Abranté's back door. "My baby doesn't eat maggots!" Patricia shouted.

There was no answer.

We moved out of that house in June and I never saw the Abrantés again or heard anything about them.

I never thought much about them, either, because so many more memorable things happened there during those years, and it wasn't until today, a lifetime and thousands of miles away, that for no reason I thought about them. I was tired of trolling, and the motor sounded rough, so I anchored and slipped my shoes off to see if I could tan the tops of my feet, which seemed to stay white all summer, and the Abrantés popped into my head. They appeared with such clarity that I heard their voices and smelled the hot peanut oil Luz used in nearly all their cooking. They must be long dead now, but I remember everything exactly. The memory, though, unlike the truth, has lost its bitterness.

VERY SHORT FICTION AWARD WINNERS

1ST PLACE
Sallie Bingham receives $1200 for
"Oh Beautiful City of Dreams."

Bingham's bio is on page 96, preceding her story.

2ND PLACE
Belle Boggs receives $500 for "Youngest Daughter."

*On the passenger seat beside him are three dozen eggs, trembling in their cartons
with the engine's rattle, and a letter from his youngest daughter, which he had
opened and read in the post office.*

Belle Boggs received her MFA from the University of California at Irvine in 2002.
Her fiction has appeared in *Best New American Voices*. She was the 2002/2003 recipient of the Glenn Schaeffer Award for Writing from the International Institute
for Modern Letters. She is working on a novel and a collection of short stories
while teaching first grade in Brooklyn, New York.

3RD PLACE
Kristin Faletic receives $300 for "Southbound."

*During the summer, younger brothers become tagalongs. They follow you through
Old Packard's field riding their scraped-and-dented bottle-green bikes. As they
coast through furrows, they whoop like cowboys and ride clumsily over molehills
like girls or headless chickens.*

Kristin Faletic lives in Herrin, Illinois with her husband, Jason, and dog, Emmy.
She received a BA in English and Psychology from Ball State University in 2000.
Her fiction has appeared in the *MT Cup Review*.

---

*We invite you to visit **www.glimmertrain.com** to see a list of the top twenty-five winners
and finalists. We thank all entrants for sending in their work.*

Cape Cod: I learned that summer how to ride the big North Atlantic waves.

Sallie Bingham started writing as a child. After she graduated from Radcliffe, Houghton-Mifflin published her first novel, and subsequent novels and short-story collections were published by Viking, Permanent Press, Zoland Books, and Sarabande. Her latest collection is called *Transgressions* (Sarabande Books). She has won several literary awards, as well as fellowships at the MacDowell Colony, Yaddo, the Virginia Center for the Creative Arts, and Blue Mountain.

OH BEAUTIFUL CITY OF DREAMS

Sallie Bingham

In those days something floated at the edge of her mind and then
moved off for a while.

She and her new husband had moved to the city right after college.
To her the city was a gold edge along the West Side Highway during
a winter sunset, the Hudson oily with color. It was the grim hotel in
the West Fifties where they stayed because they didn't know any better. Later it was Central Park, suffused with summer light, seen from
the high windows of their first apartment, which was too expensive,
but somehow right.

There were many parties that first summer. Someone would call, and
they'd meet at a restaurant—all these people who'd been at college
together. These dinners would go on and on, with lots of wine. Once
she walked home alone, at dawn, all the way up Lexington Avenue, past
closed shops where her reflection shone among the things displayed.

One evening at a German place in Yorkville, a photographer took
their picture: six friends, forks and glasses poised, blinded by the flash.
She was wearing a green sundress with white polka dots, one of her
favorites.

A year later she gave birth to a little boy, whom she adored. Ronnie, her husband, also loved him without stint, but Ronnie was often

away, and, in spite of the baby, she was lonely. She began going out to lunch with a curly-headed poet who was about to publish his first book; she stopped calling her parents in Georgia, and began crying nearly every day.

That first fall in the city, the poet said, "I can't do anything for you. You ought to see someone," and he copied out a name and a telephone number from his address book.

That first winter, she came to know the drugstore near the analyst's office and the cafe where in good weather a few tables were set out on the sidewalk, as well as the florist where tiny pots of African violets were sold, and sprays of forced forsythia in the spring.

During her second summer in the city, she left Ronnie and moved further east with the little boy and a nanny Ronnie's mother had hired.

There were more parties. Often she came home at dawn to find the little boy asleep in her bed. Once she woke up in a bedroom in an unfamiliar neighborhood and remembered that the nanny was away, and the little boy was alone. She ran all the way home and found him eating cornflakes with his fingers, out of the box.

Just wait, her mother said when they finally talked. It was a threat out of her childhood.

She married again during her third summer in the city, and moved to the close-in suburbs. There was another child, a girl. Now she rode the train two days a week to read manuscripts in a musty office belonging to a literary review. She wasn't paid, but the work gave her day a shape, as the analyst's appointments had. I didn't know you were psychotic, he'd said when she wanted to stop seeing him because she was in love again and there were no problems.

In her sixth year, she moved back to the city with the two children, leaving her second husband behind. The lake in the park turned gold on winter afternoons when she hurried along, holding her children's hands. She was working at a small publisher and coming home at night to cook dinner and read to the children from an illustrated book of Greek myths.

Once she met a well-known author at a literary party and he looked straight through her. She never wore that beige shantung sheath again.

Most of the manuscripts she read at the publishing house were quite hopeless, yet she continued to believe in the possibility of good writing, and finally she found one novel that was published and made a splash. It was a simple story, set in a simple time, and she loved it, as did its readers.

She married a man who wrote popular books about science, and had another child, a girl.

Then the city went through a troubled period, with strikes and a power failure that gave people stories to tell about being stranded in elevators in tall buildings. After that the city seemed to darken, as though the failure of power had been general.

Now she went to friends' apartments for dinner and entered into enthusiastic discussions about change. At home, she made soup from scratch and helped her older children with their homework. After her third husband left, a man would sometimes spend the night, but she always made him get up and go before dawn, for the sake of the children.

Time began to pass more quickly. She became aware of that as she marked the children's heights on the kitchen doorway. Sometimes the city still flashed gold when the children were away and she stood alone at her window; park trees shrouded the high bristling lights of the West Side, and she would hear uniformed doormen on the street below, whistling for cabs.

The thought that had hovered at the edge of her mind for so many years moved a little closer.

As she worked her way up in the publishing company, she found ways of devoting most of her time to the endeavor. Her friends now were writers, agents, and editors, their wives and husbands, their former wives and husbands (she insisted on remaining on good terms with both sides), and, eventually, their grown children. Some of the men in this group became her lovers; most did not. Her children traversed adolescence and began to talk about living on their own.

Now the city at twilight seemed pale and soft. Her ex-husbands paled, too, until she could no longer remember how they had disappointed her. She thought perhaps they'd forgotten the tears and recriminations, too; they looked at her now with affectionate curiosity.

Spaces opened around her as her children left home, small spaces, at first, like empty pockets holding crumbs of their former contents, then spaces long and wide as empty rooms. The struggles and griefs of the early years dried up, and she wondered why it had all mattered so much. Her children, her marriages, and other relationships seemed to have developed independently; only her work, in its small way, was responsive to her desires. The grid of her life was becoming visible, as bones rise through aging flesh.

And she understood, finally, what she had guessed at and feared all along.

In the middle of the hottest part of her life—passion, childbirth, the despair of abandonment—she had, she realized now, been utterly solitary, and her screams and cries had echoed in her ears alone, as though she had spent her young life at the bottom of a well. Faces had peered down at her, from above: her husbands, her lovers, her children. But her cries and screams had been silent, like the noise of a tree crashing deep in the woods. Perhaps those others had noticed the shape of her mouth, but the noise itself had not been heard.

The aim of her life—her expression of herself—had in this way been missed, and only now, when the walls of the well seemed to be lowering, was she able to wonder whether she had ever actually wanted to be heard.

Her apartment was now much too large, but she did not seriously consider moving. In the long, tan corridor set with the closed doors of what had been her children's bedrooms, she walked lightly, becoming invisible even to herself.

The need to exist—to speak, and to be heard—shrank until it seemed eccentric, like an appetite for artichokes. She looked out now from her silence like the Lady of Shalott, seeing the world reflected in a mirror, but the world, she realized now, had always been reflected in a mirror—the mirror of her own large, pale blue eyes.

She spent a great deal of time alone, reviewing the past.

And the city—the beautiful city of dreams, with its gold edge and its river of intense, oily colors—where had it gone? The hum of traffic below her window was the only reminder that it had existed and existed somewhere still, like the memory of a summer long past, part prophesy, part delusion, that never was and yet may someday be.

This is a photograph of my mother with me and my baby sister.

Alice Mattison's novel *In Case We're Separated* was published in 2005 by William Morrow, preceded by *The Wedding of the Two-Headed Woman* in 2004. She is the author of three other novels, three collections of short stories, and a collection of poems. Her stories, essays, and poems have appeared in *Best American Short Stories*, *The Pushcart Prize*, the *New Yorker*, *Ploughshares*, *Threepenny Review*, and many other magazaines. She lives in New Haven and teaches in the Bennington MFA program.

THE BAD JEW

Alice Mattison

Alice Mattison

I'll eat on a fast day, a bad Jew, exultant,
happy beyond fear of my maker, my God.

from "A Bad Jew" by Joyce Peseroff

For one year, at fourteen, I went to synagogue. I liked a ceremony during which the rabbi carried the Torah up and down the aisles, but on the whole I was restless, vocal with objections. My parents had joined the temple at my request, but didn't go there; presently their membership lapsed. To them religion was a simple matter: we were Jewish, we should always say we were Jewish, we should eat traditional Jewish foods along with our ham and shellfish, and that was enough. Years later my mother told me that her immigrant parents dressed up on the High Holy Days and went to the movies, letting the neighbors think they were in *shul*. I imagine my grandparents serene as they carried out this deception, but as I grew up, still defiantly irreligious, I never became serene about anything.

"The entire content of Jewish services is 'God's good, we're Jewish, God's good, we're Jewish,'" I'd say to one of my more observant cousins. "And I'm not so sure God's good."

But envy complicated my impatience when, invariably, the cousin would reply, "I follow the laws that make sense and ignore the rest. I just want the children to know they're Jewish." When I married, it was not to a Jew. Children of a Jewish mother are Jewish, but even after my marriage broke up and I was alone with my son and daughter, taking

Alice Mattison

lovers as wild-eyed as possible while soberly working as an editor, I didn't know how to make my Jewish children know what they were.

Eric Teak, a flamboyant man who was not a Jew and not my lover, was the publisher of the Boston environmental magazine *Aqua* when I was its editor. When I worked for him, Eric was in his sixties—ten or fifteen years older than I—with messy gray hair, a belly, and the smooth-speaking voice of a younger man. He belonged to the rich Boston family whose foundation paid *Aqua*'s bills. He wasn't married, not then. While interviewing me for the job, Eric offered coffee. I declined, then wondered as he abruptly left the room and returned, hurrying, to set down a glass of water. Confused, I took a sip.

He shook his head, and into the water stuck a long middle finger, which seemed to swell as I stared. He flicked droplets at me. The gesture was all but obscene, but I guess it also resembled baptism, because I heard myself say, "I'm Jewish."

"I'm not," he said. Then he said, "Water." The magazine dealt with water pollution, endangered aquatic mammals, depleted fishing grounds, rivers restored to cleanliness. "Can you take water seriously?"

I said I could, and tried to make sense of him.

Nobody worked at *Aqua* but Eric and me. "How's your sex life, Ruth?" he said, passing through the open space in the middle of the office on my third or fourth day.

"None of your business," I replied pleasantly, trying to decide just how much I minded him. (My sex life was all right. For a few years I'd had a lover who lived in New York.) Another time, Eric asked, "Ruth, do you still menstruate?"

One day, downtown, I stopped to look at posters and photographs mounted on a kiosk: students were protesting foreign sweatshops run by American companies. That night I had a dream. Eric stood near me as I proofread galleys at our metal table. The story was about monthly self-examination of the breasts, and I asked him, "What has this to do with water?"

"How often do you examine your breasts, Ruth?" Eric said in the dream, as he might have in life. He stretched an arm across the table and squeezed my left breast through my sweater. "You have cancer," he said, "but it's a good kind of cancer. I'll just cut it out." He took a Swiss army knife from his pocket and opened the blade.

"I'd rather have my doctor do it," I said, and awoke. As I opened my eyes I remembered, from the protest wall I'd glanced at the day before, a photograph of a young woman. Its caption was a quote: "My boss touches my breasts."

A few months after I took that job, Eric and I hired a young man named Tibby to type, answer the phone, and help out. My children's age, Tibby had left college to train dolphins in Florida, then returned home to Boston because his grandmother was dying. Though it was late fall, Tibby wore no coat to his interview at our office; a long green woolen scarf was twisted around his neck. While we spoke, as the three of us sat around the metal table in the office's central room, Tibby seemed to play with something, and then he dropped it and had to scramble to retrieve it: a red wooden yo-yo. Unselfconsciously, he wound the long cord tightly while Eric stared, and only then put the yo-yo into his pocket.

Tibby looked fragile in appearance, like a man on stilts who might fall. He didn't seem impressively efficient, but he was the only applicant we cared to remember after a series of interviews. "How do they capture those dolphins?" Eric demanded of me, as we sat alone, making the decision. "Are they allowed to mate?"

"We need someone *good* here," I said. I admired Tibby's interest in the dolphins and the grandmother.

"Moral or competent?"

"Moral."

"Are we bad?" said Eric. We hired Tibby, who might or might not have been moral but continued to be noticeable, untwisting that green scarf as he arrived, talking, every day. Like my children, Tibby had grown up calling adults by their first names, and sometimes I wished he was slightly in awe of us. He and Eric argued about those dolphins, and the morality of confining any animal. Aging, untrammeled Eric hated zoos and aquariums, however well run, but Tibby believed in the capacity of right-thinking people to do anything right. He did his work, but slowly. His friends visited him at the office, silently watching us or interjecting opinions of their own. Tibby was learning to do tricks with the yo-yo, which looked tiny hanging from his outstretched bony hand, held high above the ground. Occasionally I had to interrupt him with a task as the thing swooped and wobbled. When he wasn't learning tricks, he kept the yo-yo on his lap or on the table, twisting its string on his fingers, or rolling it until it clattered to the floor.

When the three of us were alone one day, Eric paused before entering his office to ask me, "Do Jews believe in original sin?"

"How should I know?" I said. I had an office of my own, but I preferred the light at the metal table, and I was proofreading there.

He said, "You've expressed interest in morality. I'm a Christian, and I believe in original sin. The first thing you ever said to me was 'I'm Jewish'—not that I overhear you praying in Hebrew. Not that a Star of David bounces on your breasts."

"My breasts are my own business," I said. "In what sense are you a Christian? Do you go to church?"

"Yes." He brought his big face close to mine.

"Why haven't they thrown you out for thinking about sex all day long?"

"Sex is part of God's creation," said Eric.

Tibby turned from the copying machine and said, "I'm half Jewish."

"Do Jews believe in original sin?" said Eric, now turning the other way.

"I was raised Episcopalian. My mother's Episcopalian."

It turned out that Tibby's mother went to Eric's church. "Anglo-Catholic," Eric explained to me. "High church. Bells and smells."

"Do they know life is complicated?" I said. "I never found a synagogue where they knew life is complicated."

"That's the main thing Jews know," said Eric. "How hard did you look?"

"I'm not respectable enough for organized religion," I said.

"What an angry lady," said Eric. "Not enough sex. That guy from New York doesn't show up often enough. Or you're resisting him."

"That's a boring assumption," I said. "I'm angry, so it must be sex. Isn't that a Christian idea? Sex is evil? Jews don't think like that."

"Oh, everyone thinks like that," said Eric, disappearing into his office. Then he stuck his head out and called, "Except me." The door closed again.

"Hey, Ruth," Tibby said, pausing at my desk, his arms laden with light, hot pages from the copier, his eyes bright. "Did your parents think sex is evil?"

"No," I said. "They thought it was foolish. But what are we doing to your young mind, sonny?"

"Don't worry about me," said Tibby, and carried off his pile of copies. When Eric next emerged, Tibby hurried to stand just opposite him, raised an index finger, and in the dazzled tone in which Eric himself proposed story ideas, said, " 'What Do Walruses Think about Sex?' " He paused. " 'What Do Fish Think of Sex?' " Another pause. " 'What Do Algae Think about Sex?' "

"Write 'em up, I'll print 'em," said Eric, and clapped Tibby's thin shoulder.

Tibby took that opportunity to ask for a week off without pay. His grandmother had not died after all, and he wanted to visit his friends in Florida, to see the dolphins. "I'll find out everything you want to know, Eric," he said. "If I write a story about dolphins, will you pay my plane fare?"

"You're always talking about writing stories. How do I know you'll even come back?"

"I'll come back."

The office was quiet without Tibby, and though I had to do my own filing and copying, I could concentrate more easily without his ebullience and his yo-yo. The day he was to return I came to work a little late. Eric was sitting at the metal table, his head down, and he pointed wordlessly at the answering machine, then stood up, making a strange, alarmed noise, and took me in his arms as I stepped toward it. Tibby had drowned in Florida, swimming in calm water off the end of a friend's boat. The message, which I finally made myself listen to, was from his sister.

Eric and I did slipshod work that week. We hugged often, stopped making jokes and talking about sex. I dreamed about Eric and Tibby and me as if we were a family—the three of us in a car, the three of

Alice Mattison

us walking on a windy sidewalk. Tibby's funeral, in Eric's church, was
attended by heartbreaking crowds of young people who looked as
if they hardly ever got that dressed up or entered such a building. I
looked for the ones who'd come to the office. It turned out Tibby's
real name was Theobald.

I didn't like the funeral. I felt rage at the priest who seemed to think
that putting on brightly colored vestments and executing stylized
movements made a difference, rage at the young people who'd missed
seeing Tibby disappear, rage at myself. I could have protested when
he asked to go. Our gathering, miles from the scene of Tibby's death,
behind closed doors, felt misguided, irrelevant, maybe heartless—as if
our presence on the shore might have saved him, as if staring out at
Eric's complicated ocean could have rescued Tibby.

Eric and I sat close to the front of the church, in a side section.
When it was time for communion, he squeezed my shoulder and
stood to join the slow procession toward the altar. Suddenly alone, I
watched him advance. He looked dignified because he seemed to let
himself look foolish—or, rather, unprotected. He let himself be seen
doing what he wanted to do. I was reminded of something, and then
realized, with a smile I couldn't suppress, that this was the way a good,
serious, middle-aged man—like my New York lover—moves toward
you when he's decided to take off his clothes and make love to you:
dignified in the acknowledgment of the self.

Eric reached the front of the line and knelt to receive the bread. A
moment before he had to, he opened his mouth, and I saw his lips
and tongue. I watched him receive comfort from the priest, a man
his own age. They were like two businessmen conferring, except for
one man's clothing, except for their postures, except for what they
did with their bodies, one feeding the other like a parent and a baby,
like a bird and a baby.

Without discussion we walked a block or two in the cold. I thought
we were venting emotion through aimless roaming, but Eric steered
me into a Starbucks. Maybe he always went there after church. "Or we
could keep going and find a synagogue," he said, as we sat down.

"A synagogue?"

108

Glimmer Train Stories

"Tibby was half Jewish. We should pray at a synagogue, too. Would that help?"

"Help Tibby? Or help me?"

"Tibby's dead, and I don't see any Jews but you around. The man at the counter doesn't look Jewish."

"It wouldn't help me," I said. Without further remarks, Eric went to the counter and returned with two cups of coffee and a handful of sugar packets and cream containers. We both drank the coffee black, without sugar, and I arranged and rearranged the containers of sugar and cream as we sat in silence.

"Do you believe in heaven?" Eric asked then.

"No."

"That would make it harder."

"Do *you*? Do you believe in heaven?" I didn't know anybody believed in heaven. The optimism of it stunned me.

"Of course, it's impossible to imagine heaven," he said. "I think of clean water, but what does that mean? I would like to believe in heaven."

He spoke so quietly and seriously that I didn't say, "Like to! Well, *like* to!"

And indeed he continued, "And maybe I do."

I believed not in heaven, but in the poems I'd read and written in college, in my love for my children—not that I found anything, that long winter, to comfort me for the loss of somebody else's child. I planned to visit his parents, but only sent a note, not just out of cowardice. With a magazine to put out and without Tibby's help—we didn't replace him—I worked late most nights.

I didn't go near a synagogue as an adult, I didn't do anything identifiably Jewish, but on every holy day I knew just when sundown decreed candle lighting and the end of work. I knew what I would have been doing if I had been observant. The religion I didn't practice was not my cousins' comfortable, up-to-date compromise, but some unforgiving orthodoxy, the Jewishness that takes over life: defiantly, I did not follow law after law. I so thoroughly didn't follow them that my son grew up apparently unmindful of religion, but somehow my daughter,

Laura, learned how to be slightly Jewish, and, unlike me, was serenely comfortable as she cheerfully lit the odd Hanukkah candle, attended services now and then, or sent Jewish New Year and Passover cards to my parents, who received them happily. My mother steadfastly cooked on holidays, my daughter was grateful, and both would ignore me when I'd demand, "How could God allow Hitler?" looking left and right over my matzo-ball soup. But my mother was getting old, and even the matzo-ball soup had been omitted lately. The year Tibby died, Laura phoned me early in March to ask, "Is Grandma making a Seder?"

"When did Grandma ever make a Seder?" Soup wasn't a Seder.

"Once, she did." Once, when Laura was about eight, she had. An uncle had read the prayers and the long Exodus story. Other years, the children and I had sometimes been invited to Seders at the houses of the cousins. We took turns reading aloud, we swallowed bits of matzo spread with this and that.

That March I wasn't doing well. Grief for Tibby had dulled but not lessened. I hadn't known him well enough to mourn properly. I didn't miss him, in truth. He'd been in my life so briefly; he was gone and things were as before. I knew no one else who knew him, except Eric, who didn't speak of him. But I didn't feel better. Sometimes I didn't remember why I felt bad. I rarely saw my lover, but had no inclination to spend more time with him, or break up. Later we lived together, then did break up—but that was all to come.

"Do you think you could put on a Seder?" Laura now wanted to know.

"Good God, no."

"I mean the two of us, but in your apartment." Laura was a junior at Brandeis, outside Boston, living in an apartment with several roommates. Brandeis was founded by Jews, and it closes for a week at Passover. "I don't want to feel abandoned," she said. Some of her friends were traveling home to Seders. "I don't want to go out for pizza that night."

"I'm sorry, honey," I said.

I hung up the phone and looked at the calendar. Passover was in three weeks. I'd heard from no cousins. I couldn't be expected to think about Passover because I was grieving for Tibby, the boy with the yo-yo. Then, of course, I called Laura back—my own child, the child who was safe—and agreed to put on a Seder. The next time we spoke, I asked her, "But who'll conduct it? Who'll be the uncle? Who'll be the Jew?"

"I've been to Seders, and so have some of my friends."

"Doesn't someone have to take charge?" I had already invited my friend Annie, but she wasn't Jewish and didn't believe in anything. So I invited Eric. "You're the Jew," I told him. "The believer."

"I'm the Jew."

"I'll meet the bad man," said Annie on the phone.

"Oh, he's not bad."

The Seder was work. Laura had papers to write and no car, so I bought Haggadahs, the books we had to read. I bought what had to go on the Seder plate. I bought matzo and lots of parsley. I bought groceries to Laura's specifications: this was also a dinner party. She promised to cook, along with her friends, and when I came home from work the day of the Seder, three girls were in the apartment, and potfuls of food had been prepared: chicken, rice.

Laura followed me into my bedroom and closed the door. One friend had told her that rice wasn't allowed on Passover, while the other had brought a cake—not a Passover cake, just a chocolate cake.

"If you're going to worry about rules, I'm leaving now," I said. I had brought plenty of wine—not Passover wine, just wine—and in my socks I went back to the kitchen and poured a glass for myself. Laura clutched at her light curls, a habit since babyhood, as she tried to organize my inadequate plates and silverware while her friends washed vegetables. "You're right, the food will be fine," she said then, smiling at me.

Eric, in jacket and tie, was the only man at the Seder. Laura had invited her flute teacher, who met Annie on the front porch. They came upstairs together, looking pleased and expectant, which made me feel like a fraud. As we gathered around the table, I imagined Eric looking at this roomful of women. He'd picture us bare-breasted, I decided. The image in my mind—our varied breasts (and Annie had had a mastectomy) above the mismatched plates—was wholesome, not erotic. Laura lit the candles. She knew the prayer in English.

Crowded around the table, we looked in the book and explained to one another what to do. Laura was bossy but happy. She began the reading, and then we all took turns, joining in for the responses in earnest chorus. I kept forgetting to start at the back of the book and proceed forwards. Some of the Jewishness felt odd, some surprisingly familiar, and I tried to count up just how many Seders the cousins had lured me to. Eric participated loudly and confidently. We blessed the wine and he drained his first glass, while the rest of us sipped. We ate parsley, we broke matzo. The flute teacher—a black woman with long hair coiled behind her head and elegant pewter jewelry—beamed, saying she'd always hoped to attend a Seder. "This is great," said Annie more than once. She, Eric, and the flute teacher seemed like benevolent parents at a school play.

One of Laura's friends wanted to ask the four questions. She knew the beginning in Hebrew. I could see my quick-moving, hair-clutching daughter mind that, and mind the fact that she didn't know a word of Hebrew, which made me briefly regret my life. "Sorry, Jen, it's my house," Laura said then, though it wasn't her house, and she asked the questions in English.

Seders like ours were apparently not unforeseen by whoever thought up the idea. The ceremony itself was in part about not understanding it. "Why is this night different from all other nights?" asked Laura, who might well ask. It turned out there were no more questions, just elaborations of the first question. "On all other nights we eat vegetables and herbs of all kinds, while on this night we must eat bitter herbs." Children were supposed to ask these questions, though at Seders I'd attended, self-satisfied children knew more than anyone else present.

Before long the book described more questioning children, the wise son and the wicked son, the good Jew and the bad. The wicked son asked, "What is the meaning of this Passover service which God commanded you?" It was my turn to read, and I read that the wicked son was to be abandoned to his wickedness. "You," he says, not "us." The others were to tell him that God had led them out of Egypt. Presumably the wicked son had been elsewhere when this happened, leading his interesting secular life.

"I want to defend the wicked son," Eric announced. "The wicked son's failure is a failure of imagination, nothing more."

"What's worse than a failure of imagination?" I asked. I would never change—I would always be the wicked son—but I would not deny my wickedness. We continued with the simple son and the naive son, and then came the story itself: the Israelites in Egypt, Moses, God. The ten plagues.

"The ten plagues are barbarous," I said. "I don't like God."

"A nice God wouldn't last a week in *this* universe," Eric said from across the table. "That's why the wicked son belongs in the family." He was sitting right at the corner, straddling a leg, and the corner poked into his belly. His napkin was stuck into his belt though we weren't going to get our dinner for several more pages. He smiled benevolently as if he were God's consultant in the matter of hardening Pharaoh's heart so as to require the ten plagues.

"But it's his universe," said the flute teacher. "Couldn't he provide any universe he wanted?"

Eric said, "We picked this one, and we go on preferring it."

"I don't prefer it," I said, thinking of Tibby.

"You wouldn't like a namby-pamby universe," Eric said. "Eve tells the snake, 'No thanks,'—we get a boring world."

"Hasn't our taste just been spoiled by the world we've got?" said the flutist, but her question was unanswered. Laura and her friends were shouting the ten plagues.

To express our moderate sorrow over the sufferings of the Egyptians, we were to dip a finger in our glasses of wine at the mention of each plague—blood, frogs, lice, boils—and shake a drop on our plates. Eric stuck all his fingers in, one after another, and flicked extravagant drops, then licked wine off his fingers. "I *extend* my pleasure over the sufferings of the Egyptians."

"You're a character, aren't you?" said the flute teacher.

The Hebrews fled in a hurry, with unleavened bread, and the Egyptians followed. The Red Sea parted for the Israelites, but drowned the pursuing Egyptians, and we offered thanks for several pages, then finally ate our dinner, with normal conversation. Then, just when I began to think we wouldn't return to the final prayers, Laura proclaimed with good-humored fake surprise, "The *afikomen* is missing!" Half a piece of matzo had been wrapped in a napkin sometime earlier. Laura had hidden it, and the rest of us were supposed to search.

More ritual felt tedious, not just, I think, to me, but we stood and followed Eric, who joyfully flung open closet doors and even pulled out drawers and peeked ostentatiously into them. On our third trip through the living room, I noticed a book at an unaccustomed angle, and withdrew the blue-and-white checked napkin, which was folded around the piece of matzo.

"You took so long!" Laura exulted, like a little girl. "May I have the *afikomen*, please?"

"No," I said, as the others returned to their places. I was surprised to hear myself. "No, I want something in return." I suppose I'd half-consciously remembered part of another Seder, because the young people assured us that, indeed, the *afikomen* is always redeemed.

"I forgot," said Laura. "I didn't plan a reward. Does anyone have a reward for my mother?"

"You won't give me the reward I want," I blurted out, angry now with the entire evening.

Laura said, "We can't bring Tibby back!" His name hadn't been mentioned, but backs straightened and breath was drawn in; everyone knew the story.

"What made that kid an Egyptian?" I said, in tears. "Why didn't the sea open for him?" I heard myself give a low cry, then lowered the wrapped matzo and crushed it in my folded hands.

The *afikomen* remained unredeemed. After a while I sat down, feeling foolish, and handed the lumpy package to Laura, who distributed bits of matzo around the table. Now we spoke more quickly, thanking God yet again. Then it was time to fill a glass of wine for the prophet Elijah, and to open the house door so as to let him enter.

"The apartment door will do," Laura said. I lived in a second-floor apartment in a two-family house. But I wanted cold air on my face, and a moment alone. I opened the apartment door, then walked down the stairs. Halfway down, I heard a heavy tread and turned to see Eric following me. "We still haven't redeemed the *afikomen*," he said. "I thought what to give you."

"Forget it." The house was old, and tattered rubber mats were nailed to the stairs. Eric tripped and scrambled, recovering himself, and I took his arm. We made our way down the stairs like an elderly couple, the old parents banished from the happy table for bitterness and sorrow. I opened the front door and we stepped onto the little wooden porch. The air was cold and pleasant. Elijah was visiting at the house across the street, too—or else those people just didn't bother to keep their front door closed.

"You can close it now," came a voice from upstairs. "Come back!"

But Eric withdrew something from his jacket pocket: Tibby's red yo-yo.

I gave a cry, then said, "Where did you get it?" I grasped it as if it were holy, an object sacred to my people—as if Eric didn't know what he had—and closed my hand around it.

"He left it in the office. I found it, weeks later, under a pile of papers."

"And you kept it? You carry it around? And you'd give it to me?" I slowly understood that if Eric had it at that moment, he had it all the time.

"Yes."

I kissed him on the lips. Across the street, the house door was still open. I wanted to see someone come and close it. Waiting, in my mind I found a rough map of Greater Boston, with house doors open here and there. Beyond Boston, all through New England, some people opened a door for Elijah. It was an intrinsically good act, I decided, to open a door, now and then, to Elijah. "Everywhere are Jewish people," my grandmother used to say. In New York and New Jersey—my mind moved down the coast, omitting and then restoring Long Island—more open doors. If Elijah or anyone else cared to enter, that was temporarily possible. Eric, who stood behind me, flung an arm over my shoulder and across my body, so his elbow collided with my breast and his hand grasped my arm. "Come on," he said, turning me around. We lingered a moment longer, while the door still stood open to the cold spring air, then climbed the stairs to the noisy dining room, where illicit cake had been served. Eric and I sat down to eat cake and praise God some more—God who could move the ocean aside, but mostly didn't.

*The doll was a gift from Grandma Leah. In Grandma Leah's house,
which is gone now, stood a buffet holding hundreds of frilled wooden
toothpicks, cocktail umbrellas, and tiny plastic swords. There was a
black-tiled bathroom, flocked wallpapers in the living room, a secret
door behind a mirror, and moss on the windowsills. The only thing we
weren't allowed to touch were the poker chips ... but we did, anyway.*

Abby Frucht's short-story collection, *Fruit of the Month*, won the Iowa Short Fic-
tion Prize for 1987. Since then she has published five novels, and has received two
National Endowment for the Arts Fellowships and a Quality Paperback Book Club
New Voices Award. She has raised two sons, lives in Wisconsin, and teaches at the
Vermont College MFA in Writing Program.

FRANKIE D

Abby Frucht

Kenneth Martin Mueller, who had just turned fourteen, and his grandmother, Gayle Pilsbury, were eating lunch in Gayle's new husband's screened-in porch when a tennis ball thumped down the short flight of concrete steps and rolled past the TV stand. The TV wasn't on. Gayle forbade it. She also forbade Kenneth calling her new husband Grandpa, which was okay with Kenneth, even though he had never met his real grandpa, who had died before Kenneth was born. The resemblance was striking, people said. Both Kenneth and his Grandpa James had sand-colored hair and a compact build. They were furtive, industrious, neat, and self-sufficient, but given to private manias, peculiar fits of reverie. James had had no favorite color in particular, Gayle remembered, but his creased eyes and keen posture gave him a romantic, seafaring air.

Kenneth's favorite color was Halloween Orange, which projected his air of being unencumbered, like something the progress of which might be squinted at from shore. He wore no other color, these days. She told Kenneth that secretly, she thought all of that orange made him look like a jailhouse inmate. Kenneth knew that what she meant by *secretly* was that she wouldn't gang up against him by taking her high-strung daughter's side. She went on to say that, once, when she was walking the dog in Oberlin, Ohio, where she and James used to live, she had come upon some jailhouse inmates out for a stroll. Dressed in orange jump suits, they were gathered at the corner of Cedar and Morgan Streets, waiting to cross to the mulberry-spotted trail that led past the reservoir into the woods. One of the inmates Gayle knew socially, for he had once been James's colleague, a professor at the college. He had had too much to drink one night, stolen a car belonging to one of his students, and traded it for sexual favors in an alleyway in Cleveland. The two of them, the tall professor and the diminutive Gayle, had tipped their hats to each other there on the frowsy, shaded corner of Cedar and Morgan, which is to say they exchanged polite, even gallant, hellos.

The funny thing was that this couldn't possibly have happened, not even in liberal, progressive-thinking Oberlin. No matter how gallant or well behaved, no inmates were allowed on strolls through town, and definitely never on outings past the verdant wooded reservoir into the arboretum, with its tagged but untended botany experiments, its footpaths twisting between curtains of grass and willow.

The episode went hand in hand, she confided to her grandson, with Gayle's foot-in-mouth blunders about the finality of death. Years after anybody had died, her first impulse upon finding herself face to face with a surviving relative was to ask how the dead person was, just as she would were they still alive.

"How's Ellie?" she had asked a friend whose sister had recently passed away.

"How *is* Tipper?" she had needed to stop herself from asking someone whose freckled daughter had been dead two decades.

"I wonder how James is doing," she often caught herself speculating, and imagined his faint voice answering, *Not much going on in these parts, I'm afraid. And that's official, my darling Darling.*

It wasn't that she thought of James as being in some Heaven or some afterlife, or still walking the face of the earth without her. She just wanted to know how the dead people felt about being dead, whether they were restless and discontented or were all right with it. Most of them got used to it, she imagined. They politely accepted no longer being around, and wore their shapeless, pointless clothing gladly enough.

The tennis ball was Frankie D's signal that he wanted to play. He knew better than to step into the porch while meals were being served, but that didn't stop him from speaking his mind. Frankie D was a whopping seventeen years old. Kenneth's parents, who lived in Wisconsin, had bought him to keep Gayle company in Ohio after James had died, and to nuzzle her into some semblance of having a normal day when all she wanted to do was lie there. Frankie D, the puppy, had lapped up her tears, Gayle liked to exclaim. And he had been at her side whenever she found herself dressing for James's departmental picnics, to which Gayle was still invited even after James was dead and would since have retired, the two of them gallivanting into old age.

At one of these picnics, she had met George, who lived, of all places, in Wisconsin, just several hours north of where Kenneth lived in his parents' house in Milwaukee. George was in Ohio visiting his sister and brother-in-law. His long-distance courtship lasted only a month or two before he asked Gayle to marry, to which she insisted he drive to Ohio to get her so she wouldn't need to put Frankie D on a plane. Gayle couldn't drive, because of her hands, but she could still sightsee. Unluckily, not long after the drive to Wisconsin, George lost his license, the result of spells of dizziness caused by years and years of trap shooting.

The house he had built for retirement sat atop a grassy slope ending at a creek. Across the creek was pasture for a small herd of buffalo belonging to a game farm, which was why George had chosen that lot for his house—because he wanted to grow old looking at something that had been around longer than he had. The animals stayed all together in a wooly cloud. If the cloud wasn't in sight, you were supposed to be waiting for it to crest into view, and if it was in sight, you were expected to take in the sight of it—watch the breeze comb the dark locks, watch the grass get cropped beneath, and watch the buffalo lift their massive heads and suddenly thunder away, spooked.

"You play with him and I'll clear up," said Gayle when she and Kenneth had finished their sandwiches.

Gingerly she stacked the dishes onto the tray, while Kenneth scooted for the tennis ball and whistled for the dog. The idea was to throw the ball far enough away to give Frankie D a run for his money, but not so far he would have to pull himself back up the slope. Kenneth simply rolled the ball sideways along the ridge. Frankie D didn't actually run anymore. He just sort of loped along, showing off his new green collar. His real name, Franklin Delano, was etched onto the tag. He couldn't seem to see or smell the creek or the buffalo, and he didn't hear the dishes clatter in the sink, and when he'd finally reached the ball, he didn't pick it up. Instead he spent a long time nosing it back to Kenneth's grandmother in the kitchen, one fetch being enough for a Saturday afternoon.

Since Kenneth's last visit around two months ago, his grandmother's hands had grown noticeably more crooked, and more, as she put it, patriotic—the knobs whiter, the fingertips bluer. The rest of her was still pixieish (also her word), dressed in the usual slender sweater, the trim capri pants that always came to mind when Kenneth was on his way to see her, and the flat, doll-like shoes.

And she still wore all four of her rings—the engagement ring, the wedding band, the square topaz, all from George, and on her right hand, Kenneth's favorite, the delicately curled lizard with the onyx eyes, from James. And though George had heated the porch and ar-ranged for storm windows to be installed, she was never without a hand-warmer, passing the teabag-looking thing from one claw-like hand to the other even as she ate lunch or turned the pages of a book. George's house had included no bookshelves before Gayle moved in, but now, a year later, there were two respectable sets, along with some cubbies George had hammered up in the back of a closet. James's books had all been donated to the Oberlin College Library, and Gayle kept the rest of hers in boxes on plastic sheeting in Kenneth's parents' basement in Milwaukee.

Her books were all biographies, and when Kenneth was visiting, she and Kenneth liked to start out Sunday mornings looking at the captioned black-and-white photographs in the middle of them. Every time he came to visit, he brought a fresh book over from his parents' basement, exchanging it with one from his grandmother's limited shelves. That way, all of the books had a chance to be looked at, instead of staying unread in the basement boxes. You weren't supposed to choose the book, exactly; you were supposed to let it choose you. This morning's selection included snapshot-like photos of an embarrassed-looking person scrunched in a sled; a woman wearing a man's shirt while hunkered over a desk surrounded by "as many as a thousand books," the caption read; and some children playing musical instruments.

There was the requisite wedding-feast photo, and a close-up of the woman in winged glasses, one eye in "haunting" darkness and the other peering out.

A tall fur hat, a snowy railroad, a girl suspended from the wing of an airplane, a small figure seated on top of a camel, somebody playing a saxophone.

The Life and Times…

The Life and Work…

A Life…

But George had mixed feelings about fourteen-year-old boys sitting around looking at pictures of dead people in books. What Kenneth's mother and father didn't know wouldn't hurt their college-educated sensibilities, he decided, and that was that Kenneth was going out pheasant hunting for the afternoon. George was going to make a proper Male-Chauvinist Gun-Toting Republican Swine out of him, he teased, leading Kenneth to the closet with the book cubbies in it.

"Or at least make a regular Joe of you," he added, and unknotted the top of a Hefty bag, pulling out a pair of black rubber boots that had been made for fighting the Korean War.

"Were they yours?" Kenneth asked.

"Of course they were mine. They *are* mine. Here they are in *my* hand," George answered, holding up the heavy boots. The U.S. army would never make a warmer pair. "You know india-rubber balls?" George asked. Kenneth didn't. That was the kind of rubber the boots were made of. Someone standing in a supermarket checkout line had offered George a hundred fifty dollars for the boots, which were so enormous that Kenneth could fit his orange sneakers inside them. They had steely grommets as big as fish eyes, and tied just below Kenneth's knees. The boots looked impressive on him in the mirror, but funny when he peered at them from above, as if he were made of the top and bottom halves of two separate bodies, neither of which was his own. Plus, the boots weighed more than he did. No hawk would swoop down from a telephone wire and pluck Kenneth off the ground when he was wearing those boots, George said, and if he got lost, he could use them for shelter.

"But did you fight in them?" Kenneth insisted.

"Yes, he fought in them," Gayle called from the porch. "But you don't want to get him going."

"Yes, he does," said George. "Don't you," he added.

"If I want you to, I'll ask you," Kenneth compromised.

Gayle, who had been trying to pour some lotion into a special gadget George had bought her at the drug store, dropped the bottle, needed both hands to pick it back up, dropped it a second time, and let Kenneth pick it up and set up the gadget. You poured in the lotion, flipped a switch, waited ten minutes, and when you pressed the nozzle, the lotion came out warm.

Frankie D was much too old to hunt, and had never been a field dog in the first place, but George's friend had a trained retriever, a pro, George said. The friend came to get them in an old but immaculate Buick with stiff plastic seat covers. The leggy old men folded themselves into the front seat while Kenneth slid in back with the piles of Blaze Orange vests and hats. Kenneth wore his blond hair long, in a ponytail, and if he slipped the ponytail through the hole at the back of the hat, the hat stayed on. The vest tied at the sides and had a bright vinyl pocket. In the pocket he discovered a hand-warmer, still wrapped in its colorful package and not yet activated.

George's friend drove under twenty miles an hour the whole way. The farmhouses went by so slowly that George joked he could run into the kitchen, fix a bag lunch, and be back in the car before it reached the next mailbox. When finally they turned onto a dirt road leading to the hunting ground, Kenneth reached out the window and caught a dangling inchworm in the palm of his hand. One of the roads they had passed on the way was where Kenneth's parents turned to get to their marriage retreats after dropping him off at Gayle's. George had pointed the road out to him—the exempt railroad crossing and a distant overpass. The retreats were for couples with children only, so there were always at least seven children whose parents were now gathered on the same big exercise mat as Kenneth's were, his mother often reminded him by way of apology as they were setting out to deposit him at her mother's. Often she added, "Like the quitting-smoking group I went to," her signal for Kenneth's father to exhale out the window.

Kenneth had planned on threading the inchworm onto a new tree when they got out of the car, but they parked on a road with cornfields on both sides, the stalks not yet mowed down, the fields struck with glittering, straw-colored sunlight. The men put on their vests and hats and circled around to the trunk, which they fumbled with a minute, not having the correct key. Finally they popped the solid lid open. Out jumped a golden retriever. Kenneth was both relieved and disappointed to see only two guns in there. He wasn't going to shoot, it turned out. The old men pulled on leather gloves, then took them off again to load the guns. The retriever bounded around, thrilled. When Kenneth reached to pet it, it ate the inchworm off his hand. Then it darted in zigzags back and forth across the road until the men started off, without taking a minute to explain to Kenneth what was going on. He seemed to be just supposed to know. George went tromping off in one direction along the side of the road while his friend tromped off in the other direction along the same side, leaving Kenneth just standing next to the car. Because it was a dry, sunny day, not muddy at all, he bent to unlace the boots and stepped out of them.

"Stay where you are!" George called over his shoulder to Kenneth.

"Here!" the friend called a little later. At what was by now a sizable distance away from each other, the two old men turned sharply from the road, marched across the ditch, and disappeared into the cornfield, not even their bright caps showing.

Kenneth followed. He took the ditch in one leap and stepped into the dark space between stalks.

It was a different world in there. The only thing ahead and to the sides of him were corn stalks, and pretty soon corn stalks were the only thing behind him as well. The ground was clean dirt and the sky was gone, hidden by the papery crowns of the plants and all the fanned-out husks and tassels. Kenneth needed to do a breaststroke in order to keep his hat on. Otherwise the stiffly arching leaves kept knocking it off his head, slapping his face, and strangling him with every step forward. Every once in a while, the straight, even rows switched orientation, the stalks growing right where his feet should be.

He couldn't have been much happier. The only sound was a rustling at his ears as the big leaves parted to let him through, and the swish of his shorts. He couldn't hear a thing from the old men, and the sure knowledge that they had forgotten about him was deeply satisfying. So was the retriever, who kept crashing into Kenneth from out of nowhere and then veering away, nose to the ground, tail spinning like a propeller. The retriever's name was Louie, but it responded with the same delirious unconcern whatever Kenneth called him.

"Hey, Thoughtful! Hey, Index! Hey, Pistol! Hey, Third Eye!" Kenneth said each time the dog came crashing into him, but the dog only kicked up all the more air before dashing out of sight.

Then all at once the cornrows came to an end, and Kenneth found himself on a ribbon of bristly grass, the old men conferring under a stand of trees. In the distance stood a silo and a red barn the size of Kenneth's thumbnail.

"You want to step back in that corn again and march in that direction," one of them instructed Kenneth. "I'll take these trees and he'll take the strip. And if you hear shots, quit walking until it's over. The dog gets crazy when he's birdy, and he sure is birdy now."

That's official, my darling Darling, Kenneth heard his grandmother saying in his head, in the imagined, lusty voice of James.

Over the next hour the sky turned pearly, the dry husks no longer flaming in sunlight like paper lanterns. Although the silo somehow failed to appear again after that first glimpse, Kenneth gradually acquired an understanding of what was expected of him. Namely, he was supposed to be doing exactly what he was doing, just walking along, not even trying to be quiet. If a bird got flushed into the air, one or both men would shoot it. Ground swatting wasn't admirable. It wasn't until they ended up back at the car and trooped off into the adjacent field that Kenneth jumped at a loud sudden squawking and a flapping of wings that seemed to be all around him.

No shot went off. It turned out George's gun had jammed, though why his friend hadn't fired, George didn't know. After waiting at the edge of the corn with Kenneth a couple of minutes, George reloaded and took an inquiring shot at the sky before calling his friend's name and Louie's.

Neither dog nor man emerged, and no answering shot was fired.

"You stay here and I'll go in and look for him. Or I stay here and you go in," George strategized, looking exhausted himself, his mouth slackening.

So Kenneth marched back into the corn and made a couple of sharp turns, peering down one corridor and then another, like someone in search of the drawing room. "Come, Jeeves!" he called. When he stepped back out of the field empty handed, George too was gone. Kenneth recognized the trees, the giant ravens reestablishing themselves among the same yellow branches. He adored the idea that he knew where he was, that he had his own landmarks, his own code, the birds like footballs balanced in the trees. And he adored being the lone orange speck on that serrated grass, the miles stretching every which way, the usual points of the compass obsolete.

But once he started heading back it seemed necessary to do so with a certain deliberation. So he kept to the mown swath, taking stock when it turned. He could be a fast walker when he wanted to be, but he could take his time, too. He knew he cut a nice figure just gliding, unperturbed, the way he sauntered the halls at school, everyone banging their lockers around him, their coats and backpacks flying, the bell going off just as Kenneth leisurely dialed his combination, the hall clearing out. A plane drew a broad arc across the sky, moving more slowly the farther away it got. He could have sworn he smelled cinnamon toast. Close by were some voices, and soon he came to the road, the two old men rummaging in the open trunk of the car.

"Wanted a Coke," George explained, and he brought out a third Coke for Kenneth and zipped shut the cooler. His friend gave a sharp whistle. Louie scrambled up into the trunk, scooting into the dark end before the lid came down.

Kenneth chose the trip home past the farmhouses for breaking open the packet and activating the hand-warmer in his front vest pocket.

Quickly the mixture of iron and carbon turned hot, and it was this phenomenon that exerted the strongest hold on Kenneth as the rest of that day spun out of control. The house empty on the ridge, Gayle's wailing and panic down in the creek, her sodden sweater spread-eagled empty on the ground like a chalk outline of a murdered person, the ambulance sirens, the police, his parents' tardy response because the rule of the marriage retreats was that cell phones weren't to be answered during role-playing sessions—all of this happened as if miles away from the small parchment sack of constant heat, like the Korean War boots that Kenneth had forgotten at the side of the road, and that nobody ever mentioned to him again. His parents had been playing *themselves* at the role-playing session, his mother explained to one of her friends by phone on the midnight drive back home to Milwaukee—their own selves re-enacting their very first date, and then the second date had to be cancelled, the two of them having to rush off into the thick and thin, she sighed, of things.

But all along there was the pouch of fire blazing in the pocket of the vest, and Kenneth finally falling asleep underneath it. His dream was of two buffalo. As in real life, Frankie D was drowned, his body a clot of fur trapped against a sandbar in the middle of the creek where Gayle had tried so very hard to reach him. The two buffalo were Kenneth's parents on their first date. His mother wore a dress of midnight blue, a bracelet dangling just under her tapered hoof where it rested against his father's lapel. His father's dreadlocked tail kept time to the music. The floor was a scuffed, church-basement linoleum, the exercise mats pushed off to the side for sitting on, in case anybody got tired of dancing.

Around the corner and several blocks from Kenneth's parents' house in Milwaukee stood a small, gabled house with evergreen trees and gauzy curtains, crowded by other houses. A girl lived there, named Cicely. When he was seven and eight, Kenneth had had a fierce crush on Cicely, because she was smart, and because of the way her humorous eyes turned instantly, deeply serious the second she was called on in class. Her house itself was feminine, cinched and triangular, a dress with a bow. After school, if he took the long way home and the curtains were parted, which they usually weren't, he sometimes got a glimpse of her practicing piano. Since she was taller than he was, her feet likely reached the pedals. She sat with her back to the window, and though her posture remained entirely straight and the notes barely made it as far as the sidewalk, her hair jumped and swung as if with the intensity of her playing. He didn't dare pause as he walked along, but nonetheless his look was brazen enough that had she swiveled on the bench he might have caught her eye.

Before starting third grade, Cicely had been switched to the Lutheran school, and a short while later, Kenneth stopped taking her street. Now and then he heard somebody mention her or her parents, and once he thought he caught sight of her riding her bike, her hair fluttering in a way that bore no relationship to the breeze. Though he took it on faith he would run into her again someday, he didn't exactly care if this happened or not. So he was only mildly interested to learn, sometime over the weeks following the midnight drive back home to Milwaukee, that Cicely was to be a student in the youth strength-training class in which his mother had agreed to enroll him at the YMCA. Under-sixteen-year-olds weren't allowed to use the equipment until they had passed the course.

He missed the first meeting, because he was grounded. Some kid had waved a knife at him on the way home from school, and Kenneth hadn't told his mother. The kid was decent enough, overweight, not too bright, and jealous of Kenneth the way a lot of boys were, simply for being himself. Just a day earlier, Kenneth had stopped wearing orange. With as little fanfare as when he had started, he had gotten out of bed and put on a pair of silvery basketball pants and a turtleneck. No one commented to him up front about it, but there was a kind of a buzz in the air, in the midst of which Kenneth's friends, who called him Ken, became the objects of a renewed vicarious popularity. The small band of them—Kenneth, Sally, Ingrid, and Mohammed—had just been passing the construction site for a new office building when Brian Hoorst appeared from around a corner, pulled out the knife, and waved the blade inches from Kenneth's throat.

The other kids just stood there, mortified for Brian, who despite being overweight was runty looking, and endured the reputation of having a father who wore bowling shoes to parent-teacher conferences.

"I don't swing that way, Brian. Nothing personal," said Kenneth, at which they all started walking away, Ingrid in her inside-out Moosehead Beer sweatshirt bringing up the rear. Brian ducked through a gap in the so-called security fence to be camouflaged by grayness, dimness, undone-ness. It was one of the girls' mothers who called Kenneth's mother to tell her what had happened, and then Kenneth's mother who called police. On further reflection she turned on Kenneth, as angry at him for not telling her that he had been "assaulted" as she was worried Brian might come back and really slash at him, next time.

"He's more likely to come back now that the police are after him, than if you had just let me leave the poor kid alone," said Kenneth, regretting saying so at once.

He knew his mother's winces, their stages of profundity. According to his father, Meredith was always seeking out the rationale behind her feelings and sorting them according to some system of classification that reconfigured itself whenever anyone else got close to keying it out. Not long ago, she had completed seven weeks of radiation therapy for breast cancer. The hospital was spired, arched, gargoyled. Walking into it each day, she would be led beneath vast ceilings to the locker room, where other patients stood tying on gowns, their bare skin chalky in locker-room light, their voices commingling. After her final beaming, when her treatments were done, it was like she'd been exiled from the kingdom. Nothing mattered down here among earthlings anymore. No one called out, "Good morning, Ms. Martin Mueller!" when she walked in the door, until Kenneth and his dad began doing so at breakfast. "G'morning, Ms. Martin Mueller, how are you feeling today!" they called, amusing her for a day or two, but then forgoing their Cream of Wheat unless they cooked it themselves, because she wouldn't anymore.

If she hadn't been so attentive to her feelings, she wouldn't have been forced to experience, so vehemently, the paradoxical twists and turns of all the bad things that might have happened, all the humorous things that might yet come of them, and everything in between. She imagined bringing flowers, chocolates, to her new friends still undergoing treatment at the hospital, or, at some later date, her own illness returning, and finding herself tying on gowns again. Then what would she say? She imagined Brian bloodying Kenneth in retaliation for her having phoned the cops, and then, in his exalted, oxygen-depleted reverie, Kenneth's heroic pardon of the boy.

"You have the power…," she said earnestly to Kenneth, suddenly chewing on a fresh, invigorated worry. The "Notice to Victims of Juvenile's Acts," which the cops had brought over for them to sign, jumped in a blast of air when she opened the oven door. Tonight was early dinner, and then she would be on her way to the university with her blotted mascara, her self-blacking eyes.

"I can handle him. Don't get so worked up," Kenneth told her a day or two later. "Brian's cool with it now. We talked about it."

"You talked about it!?" His mother was amazed. "He didn't come after you!?"

Immediately she was at the telephone calling the District Attorney. Meredith was more like her mother than her father, Gayle had once remarked, but mostly she was like something they'd smuggled home from their honeymoon along with the fruit James had hidden away in their luggage, which was silky and tart but got its revenge in a big way.

"I'm Kenneth Martin Mueller's mom. Meredith Martin Mueller. I have here a 'Notice to.'" She knocked around on the desk a minute in search of the afternoon's mail. "'A Notice to Victim of Case Processing, Intake Case Number 7958,' that says, hmmm, the case is being forwarded to the District Attorney's office for their review. But I have to say that Brian, the kid, the boy who pulled the knife…no, it's a disorderly conduct charge…he's no longer behaving in disorderly fashion. In fact he's…yes. I was afraid he would retaliate on Kenneth for us calling the police! But…no. Right! So I feel that to continue with these charges would be a mistake all around, because he, Brian Hoorst, is…exactly. Thank you very much."

"But Brian doesn't know *we're* the ones who called police. He and I didn't talk about *that*," Kenneth corrected, the second the phone was back in the cradle.

His mother turned stock-still, her hand in the air. All possible misunderstandings and their potential consequences scrolled behind her expression like oranges and bananas in a slot machine. You couldn't tell which she was going to bite into. It was exhilarating, teasing his mother when it was so easy to be on the level with everyone else. A bewildered Meredith sent Kenneth to his room, banning him from strength-training class, the ironic consequences of *that* decision already whipping past her eyes.

So he was the first to show up at the Y fitness center for the next week's class, his mother being in such a guilty hurry to get him there. It was while he was looking in the wall of mirrors, at somebody performing a series of grueling mid-air push-ups from what looked like a giant rubber band, that the door next to the Gatorade machine swung open, which Kenneth had been preparing himself for.

"Show up, pay attention, speak the truth, and don't be attached to results." A quote from one of Gayle's biographies passed through his mind, and then there was Cicely, her hair as all over the place as in the second grade, but tamed by a rubber band today, as was required.

Kenneth drew himself up. At fourteen, Cicely was a dismaying sight. Her neck was too long, her face too thin, her nose too pointed, and her ears too big. And the rest of her was...*flat. Just flat. The narrows...* Kenneth heard the voice of his Grandpa James, who shouted, *Throw her a rope!* even though he had never actually been a seafarer; had only smelled like one—bracing, stinging, deep.

Cicely took her place near the water fountain, which was where you were supposed to line up, without appearing to notice Kenneth. Maybe just a flicker of the eyes, as if to say, So there. When a safe number of other classmates had lined up beside her, Kenneth got in line, too. He was beginning to show a hint of mustache. In the wall of mirrors, he stopped his eyes from straying to it. Considering the kind of person he intended to be, it would be wrong to condemn Cicely for his new mustache being beside the point, so he was glad there were none of his friends around to watch him force down his disdain of her. Too long for what? he scolded himself, while the class took turns with the various weights and pulleys. Her neck was too long for what? Her nose was too pointy for what?

During break, the class was sent to where some mats lay stacked in an alcove, reminding Kenneth of the dream he had had in the car, of his parents slow dancing. As if he were part of the dream himself, he purchased two bottles of Gatorade out of the machine and gave the orange one to Cicely, keeping the blue for himself.

"So what are people praying for at Sacred Heart these days?" he asked.

Cicely had rabbit teeth. "Oh, you know," she said.

Across her face was that same pallor Kenneth remembered from grade school, her eyes like black ice with small fissures splintering under the surface. *It must be hell to be a girl at fourteen still looking like you're eight*, Kenneth imagined himself coming out with, and took a rebukeful sip of his drink.

"Why does it quench your thirst?" he asked. "What's different about it than water?"

"Ions," she answered menacingly. "It's radioactive!" she screeched, flopping backward on one of the mats so her shirt hiked up to reveal an outie bellybutton, and grabbing an exercise ball for abdominals, the next part of class. She was always the leader. He found his own ball, carried a mat to the glass divide overlooking the swimming pool, tipped back, and delivered his gaze into the high, fluorescent space. He wedged the ball beneath the small of his back and simply levitated a moment on what felt like the flickering hum of the lights—too much Gatorade.

It was May, and George's eightieth birthday celebration, before Kenneth saw his grandmother again.

Big-band music was playing on the stereo, the speakers arrayed on the flat ridge of lawn amid tables of catered food. A row of stout new evergreens had been planted at the bottom of the slope, not exactly obscuring the view of the creek but fringing the banks, softening their appearance and breaking the sandbar into ragged, bubbly splashes. For months, while George and Gayle were wintering in Phoenix, the buffalo had also been away, in whatever clime game burgers get trucked to in winter, George said, and George had begun to resign himself to their not returning in time for his party.

But early that morning the barest glimpse of the herd could be seen from over the distant hill, just a ripple of brown, like the tops of some grasses ruffling in a breeze. And now there they all were, where the guests could admire them and drink to George's vigorous repose, knowing how fortunate he was to have earned the right to live on such a corner of earth and have no one begrudge him it, at least no one who could see him, and no one he could see. For he was a generous man. His solicitousness toward Gayle was an unmistakable aspect of every minute of their life together. The frigid creek waters had done Gayle lasting harm, visible in a stiffness of her bearing that looked alternately like fortitude or as if a key had jammed. Even so, she was pixieish in baggy-kneed tights, her ribcage bulging under a V-neck tunic, her four rings too big on her fingers. She and George would never have made the trip to Phoenix had Frankie D been around and had to get on the airplane, which she never tired of reminding everybody, not wistfully, but with a fresh enthusiasm, as if saying it startled her anew, jolting her into a state of wonder and sad surprise.

Kenneth wasn't the youngest at the party, by far, for there were all sorts of cousins from Texas, and other kids his grandmother didn't even know the names of. Generally, other kids didn't come near Kenneth unless he made some welcoming gesture, after which they wouldn't leave him alone. Some time soon he would get out the four-wheel and organize rides, but for now he was at his usual guard, mainly keeping an appropriate distance from his parents—his mother pregnant in a clingy dress, his father loading her plate with all the fattening things they wouldn't dare keep at home. Fried chicken pieces, potato salad, even cake crowded the plate, because George believed in cutting into the sheet cake right away instead of waiting for people to be too stuffed to enjoy it.

On the cake was an icing photo of George in which George was James's age, Kenneth found himself thinking; James's age in Gayle's photos of James, which Kenneth would someday turn out looking like. It made him uneasy, all of a sudden, to harbor an inside view of things. Not only was George's portrait really a portrait of James and Kenneth disguised as a portrait of George, but there was something else he knew about the cake, and that was that Gayle disliked icing photos, period.

For one thing, they were in color.

Color photos cheapened things, she had explained to Kenneth earlier that day, before the caterers had arrived.

Her least favorite books were the ones that people who didn't know her very well tended to give her as gifts, knowing only she enjoyed biographies. Most likely if photos were in color, the human subjects had divorced by the time the book came out, or had by some other method—legal suits, letters to editors—disqualified themselves from joining that throng of people living on as crosses between ghosts and memories. The college professor in the jailhouse jumpsuit, whose name was Hendy Jones, made an especially commendable example of such a cross. For years, Gayle had pictured him strolling past the reservoir in Oberlin, biting ripe mulberries off dangling branches. She had known this wasn't possible, because he was in the commons room in jail, playing cards with the inmates, or maybe he'd been released, not teaching anymore but enrolled in hotel school or something.

Then, just recently, thumbing through an old alumni magazine, Gayle had learned that Hendy Jones was dead. He had died in prison years ago, not long after she had run into him, or hadn't run into him, as the case may be, on the crossroads of Cedar and Morgan Streets. The whole thing cast Hendy front-row center in that sepia crowd of people tilting their faces into the air. He was dead but not gone, gone but still eagerly making an appearance.

Plus, Gayle had confided in Kenneth, photos on cakes made cakes look like tombstones. Just like photos on tombstones made tombstones look like cakes.

Kenneth's mother had been napping when they had this conversation, while George and Kenneth's dad were setting up for the party, pulling stacks of fresh hand towels out of the upper reaches of the linen closet, and raking the lawn. Some bottles of brandy had wound up out on the porch on the wheeled cart Gayle used for lunches, so she had asked Kenneth to pour her a little. What did Kenneth remember of the afternoon Frankie D had drowned, she suddenly wondered?

"Your wet sweater and my mom saying hand-warmers are poison," he had answered without hesitation.

"They are if you eat them," Gayle said through a welling of tears, telling him how she had thrown the ball sideways on the ridge, just like George and Kenneth did, only it hadn't gone sideways, it had rolled down the hill. The ball had been stopped by a tassel of grass, way short of the creek, so why the dog had kept going, she didn't know.

It was awful to watch her cry, yet impossible for Kenneth to stroke or embrace her. Goodnight kisses were all that had been in their repertoire before, and besides, she was too crushable looking. She kept saying she was sorry, lifting her hands in a puzzled way, sorry for letting Frankie D go. She meant "letting him go" as in down to the creek, and "letting him go" as in die, and "letting him go" as in carried away by the muddy, cold water. She meant "sorry" as in regret, and as in sorrow.

"But I got what I deserved, at least," she claimed, "having to go on living without him."

"But you have George," Kenneth had ventured, there in the breezy, cement-smelling air of the porch. It was what an adult might say, and he knew that it was woefully inadequate when what she wanted was James.

"I'm glad to have met George," Gayle agreed, turning the lizard ring on her finger, the onyx eyes spotting. "But Frankie D was the love of my life, you know," and then she had said it again, more wrenchingly, in a way he could hear in his mind even after the party was underway, as if her sobbing were still going on. "Frankie D. Frankie D was the love of my life!"

Aware now of his hands in his pockets, his ponytail meeting the fold of his shirt collar, Kenneth waited for his grandmother to make her way through the party over to where he was standing. Her illness was the kind that was said to turn people into statues of themselves, and now he saw she did look like a statue bumping along between one group of guests and another, and into whose curled hand someone had fitted a drink. The less she let herself drink, the more liquid sloshed over the lip of the glass as she carried it along. By the time she reached Kenneth—which actually turned out to be much, much later, after the four-wheel rides and the trek with the cousins into the woods—she was practically sober again.

"Still, I should be sitting right down," she said, when he had fitted a Styrofoam cup of coffee into her hand, as into a car cup-holder. He set up two folding chairs in a remaining pool of sunlight, then trotted indoors for her sweater, assuring the cousins, who were watching videos up in the bedroom, that he would join them soon.

"So, Kenneth," Gayle began when he had settled the cardigan like a cape on her shoulders, "are you interested yet in girls?"

He told her he was.

"And do you have a girlfriend?"

"I don't know," Kenneth answered.

She gave him a doubtful look, reading the way he'd put a finger to his hint of a mustache, which felt like a shadow might feel—a tactile blur—if you touched where it wavered beside you. From over the ridge a breeze was blowing, carrying a musky fragrance of dung and having the effect that George had predicted—loosening people up. The music was turned a notch higher, and people started shimmying around.

"I mean, I do sort of have one, only she hasn't figured it out yet," Kenneth explained.

An image came to him, as it did many times, of Cicely's bellybutton—like a bald, baby bird in a nest. With it came the fact that he didn't agree with Gayle, after all, that people were all right with being dead. They might pretend to be all right, but they'd be going totally insane, stampeding around in their minds while stuck in quiet, polite little poses. He couldn't stand the thought, poor clueless Cicely turning the pages, her socks slipping into the heels of her shoes. His grandmother nodded when Kenneth blushed, and savored another swallow of coffee. Eventually she pulled herself out of her chair, gliding off like a statue on rickety wheels.

But the statue wasn't headed for the rest of the party. Flapping its hand in the direction of the revelers, instead it swerved demurely toward the screen door leading into the porch, which opened from within as Gayle approached, and was held there as she passed through it. Somebody, Kenneth couldn't tell who, must have seen her coming. There was a glint of indiscernible color. Then the door shut, and the somebody stayed on the other side.

SILENCED VOICES:
MAMADALI MAKMUDOV

by Siobhan Dowd

According to international human-rights groups, the former Soviet Republic of Uzbekistan is today a state of fear. The government of President Karimov apparently brooks no opposition. Those who seek to express their opinions freely are likely to find themselves threatened, beaten, or behind bars. Followers of Islam must practice their religion within recognized limits or face prosecution. Writers must espouse the

Mamadali Makmudov

official doctrine or be silenced. This year, the country's human-rights record is under close scrutiny by the United Nations Human Rights Committee. There is grave concern that, while the authorities have signed up to such agreements as the International Covenant on Civil and Political Rights, a yawning gulf exists between their stated intentions and actual practice. Amnesty International, Human Rights Watch, and International PEN are among those highlighting the discrepancy and urging the UN to bring all its influence to bear on President Karimov to implement urgently needed reforms.

In this context, it is small surprise to find Uzbekistan's premier writer, Mamadali Makmudov, languishing in jail, serving a fourteen-year prison term on charges of "threatening the president" and the "constitutional order." His arrest in 1999 followed a series of bombings in the capital, Tashkent, but there is no evidence at all connecting him to these crimes. The case against him instead rests on his writings for *Erk*, the magazine of a banned opposition party of the same name. Indeed, his close connection to Muhammed Salih, the leader of Erk—now in exile—seems to be the main cause of his detention, coupled with his pre-eminent status as a writer who has famously explored the theme of repression in his work.

The Karimov regime is a past master of throwing allegations at Makmudov that simply fail to stick. In 1994, he was arrested and accused of illegal possession of a firearm. When the charge was greeted with general disbelief, the authorities quickly dropped the charge, but pressed against him a new and equally unfounded accusation of embezzlement and abuse of office, based on his role as a member of the Uzbek Writers' Union and the Uzbek Cultural Foundation. Again, human-rights groups, including the United Nations Working Group on Arbitrary Detentions, discounted these charges as fabricated. Makmudov was deemed to be one of thousands of dissidents jailed for crimes they did not commit. On this occasion, he was released in 1996 in an amnesty. However, he must have remained a thorn in Karimov's side. After the 1999 bombings, Karimov announced that he held the Islamic Movement of Uzbekistan responsible, but the ensuing wave of arrests went much further afield. Prominent dissidents from a range of backgrounds were targeted, including Makmudov.

The Erk Party has for years been a major challenger to Karimov's hold on power. It was defeated in the presidential elections of 1991, then banned in 1993, after which its leader, Salih, fled abroad. Today

Salih lives in Norway. In 1999, he was tried in absentia for allegedly orchestrating an assassination attempt on President Karimov; he would face a long prison term if he returned, and any associate of his is automatically a *persona non grata*.

Makmudov's marginalization stems also from his charismatic status as a national poet. Uzbekistan enjoys a rich Turkic-language literary heritage in which the traditional form is the *dastan*, an ornate form of verse. The *dastan* typically contains distinctive narrative motifs, celebrating heroes known as *alps*. An *alp* might speak when only a few days old, or have other magical qualities. He will normally emerge glorious in battle. He might fall in love, face treachery, but will surmount all obstacles. The form was frowned upon as "reactionary" by the Soviet authorities. Back in 1952, the official *Literaturnaia Gazeta* dismissed the *dastan* as being "impregnated with the poison of feudalism."

Makmudov wrote short stories, but his chief accomplishment was his modernizing of the *dastan*. His 114-page poem *The Immortal Cliffs* was four years in the making. In it, he created an *alp* named Buranbek. Inspired by his ancestors, Buranbek seeks to unite the Turkic peoples in the late 1800s. He fights the invading Russian army and is captured and tortured. At one point, he falls prey to the treachery of his own kinspeople, in line with traditional *dastans*. Although Makmudov tried to present the piece as an example of permitted "social realism," the Soviet authorities disapproved of the work and forced him to repudiate it. When the Soviet Union collapsed, Makmudov's status as a major writer was quickly restored by the newly independent republic. He was granted the prestigious Cholpan Prize, a national award. However, his decision to support the Erk Party and the fact that his work was a ringing condemnation of repression rendered his time in favor short.

Makmudov's current sentence was handed down in a closed trial. It seems that Makmudov was given scant access to legal counsel, and his claims that he was tortured during his interrogation were disregarded. Now in his sixth year of detention, Makmudov has been transferred between the Navoi, Jaslyk, and Chirchik prisons. In 2003, he smuggled out a letter detailing appalling maltreatment of inmates while in Navoi Prison. "From early morning to evening they made us crawl, run, and sing the national anthem. They threw us into the psychiatric ward. I lost consciousness twice in the courtyard." He goes on to describe a horrific wave of beatings in which many prisoners were severely injured. Reports of Makmudov's hospitalizations in 2000 and 2002, coupled with this testimony, have led to serious concerns for his health and safety. International human-rights groups have urged his immediate and unconditional release from prison. He is an Amnesty International Prisoner of Conscience and an Honorary Member of the American, USA West, English, Canadian, and Dutch PEN centers.

Please join the international campaign calling for the release of Mamadali Makmudov by writing polite letters to:

His Excellency President Islam Abduganievch Karimov
Rezidentsiya prezidenta pl. Mustqkillik,
2, Oliy Majils
Republic of Uzbekistan

Siobhan Dowd, an author and journalist living in London, writes this column regularly, alerting readers to the plight of writers around the world who deserve our awareness and our writing action.

Only three photos survived my childhood, all of which have appeared alongside stories previously published in Glimmer Train. *Here's a picture of my daughter, Rorrie, blowing a kiss.*

George Makana Clark lives in Milwaukee where he teaches fiction writing at the University of Wisconsin. His collection of short stories, *The Small Bees' Honey*, was published by White Pine Press, and his work has appeared in the *Southern Review*, *Transition, Zoetrope: All Story*, and elsewhere. Clark was awarded a 2002 National Endowment for the Arts Fellowship in Fiction Writing.

THE STORY-GHOST

George Makana Clark

We traveled in our customary silence, listening to the pistons' rapid fire, the *dik, dik, dik* of bugs hitting the windscreen, the rushing wind. I breathed shallowly as the British Ford climbed into the mountains of Manicaland. After living in the lowlands, I could no longer fill my lungs.

The granite mountains seemed diminished now, sunken into the earth. We shot forth into a starless sky, the heat falling away with the horizon. A powder snow began to fall against the windscreen, unheard of in the eastern highlands of Rhodesia. Even the seasons had changed in the year since I ran away from home.

My father and I drove past the trust-land crossroads. The river of my baptism. The thorn tree where my umbilical cord was buried. I stared out the passenger window at the landmarks of my childhood, my reflection superimposed on the darkness without.

As we neared the bungalow, my father narrowly avoided a blind pedestrian who tapped his way along the highway with the tip of a closed umbrella. No one else was afoot. We overtook a lorry filled with soldiers, the lighted ends of their cigarettes floating in the darkness like rats' eyes. My father pushed the car to desperate speeds, drawn by an unseen force. Phantom shapes galloped alongside the car just beyond the tree line, flashing between the acacia and scrub mahogany, matching our pace.

Glimmer Train Stories, Issue 56, Fall 2005
©2005 George Makana Clark

• • •

The sensation of motion did not cease when my father turned into our drive and switched off the motor. We remained in the car a moment and listened to the ticking of the cooling engine block. Through some trick of shadow and perspective, the lightless bungalow appeared warped and swollen, the clapboards bowed outward with old secrets.

A familiar tightness spread across my chest and I nearly took my father's hand. Wordlessly, he roused himself from the driver's seat. I hesitated a few moments before following him across the threshold into the house where I would resume passing for white.

Inside, the story-ghost had become bloated, formless, ubiquitous. A seething, roseate mist that smelled of pipe tobacco. It followed me down the hall and into the bedroom where my mother sat immobile in her Queen Anne chair, bundled tightly in a shawl, regarding me in silence. An Italianate lamp hung by a chain from the ceiling, its spelter cracked during the voyage from Scotland. The gold-painted bulb reflected dimly in her eyes, making them iridescent. My mother refused to see what she could not understand, and so she was blind to the story-ghost that pinioned her to that chair.

Peter Pan was face down on the bureau, still open to the page where I'd stopped reading the night I quit this house. My mother looked at me expectantly and I realized that she was waiting for me to continue reading where I'd left off. I wondered if my year-long absence even registered on the woman, if time passed at all in that dark room. I switched off the air conditioner and read aloud from Chapter Nine, "The Never Bird," picking up the thread of the narrative: *In fanciful stories people can talk to the birds freely.* My mother interrupted the reading. "Come closer," she said, arms outstretched. I took this to mean that she couldn't hear me, so I read louder, *and I wish for the moment I could pretend this was such a story, and say that Peter replied intelligently to the Never bird.* I suppose one could look back on this scene in another light, one in which my mother had been aware of my absence and was reaching out to embrace her wayward son. *But truth is best, and I want to tell only what really happened.*

I collected the bedpan and left my mother with the story-ghost. The house had deteriorated alarmingly while I'd been away. The floorboards were sprung, the crown molding separating at the joints, clocks hung frozen against the walls. Dustwebs had collected in the corners of the kitchen ceiling and the pilot light no longer burned in the stove. I went outside to empty and rinse the bedpan.

An icy mist shrouded the garden, muting the rollers' nightsong, the bushbabies' cries, the light from the moon. A voice called out from the wilderness: "Divinations! Prophecies!"

I shut off the garden hose.

A figure moved toward me, tapping its way through the tangle of underbrush with the tip of an umbrella. It was the blind man that my father had almost run down on the highway. He wore a wool muffler and sunglasses, and he clutched a heart-shaped box in his free hand. "Pasts uncovered. Secrets unveiled. One dollar." He held out the candy box. "These casting bones belonged to my mother. She also was a powerful diviner, blessed by God. The future is here," he said, rattling the box, "your true nature waiting to be revealed."

He paused a moment, sniffing at the threshold. "This house is out of balance," he declared. "Perhaps one of your ancestors is aggrieved. For a dollar I can put it right."

I led him to the kitchen table and sat him down. The blind man shrugged off his coat and held the candy box before him. His divining bones continued to rattle in the box. There were words scrawled on the lid in a large, uncertain hand: *Omen reading. One dollar—One hour. No refunds after five minutes.*

The doorstep diviner half-rose, scratched his bottom, then settled back into the chair. "Let's kick on, then," he said. I watched him open the box, gather the bones into his hands, then cast them into the lid. He fingered the ossicles, rolling his eyes behind the dark lenses, making a show of it. "Bring me the dollar and I'll tell you what the bones say."

He reached out to take the dollar I held above his head, forgetting he was blind. I closed my fist around the bill and laughed. "I thought you couldn't see." He looked hard at me a moment from behind the dark lenses, then returned the bones to the box and closed the lid.

Long ago in Cape Town, when my great-grandmother grew too old
to be a bargirl, she too had become a diviner. In his library, buried in
the pages of *Readings for the Railways*, my father kept hidden a picture
of the woman, a pipe-smoking Xhosa woman, ritually scarred, seated
at a table as she read the future of a European—my great-grandfa-
ther?—whose back was turned to the camera.

"Go on," I said to the doorstep diviner, "give them a throw."

He looked down at the bones and shook his head. "We don't need
to pretend. Just give me the dollar." He shifted in his chair, reaching
deep into the back of his trousers to scratch vigorously. "Tapeworms,"
he apologized. The diviner looked at my fist, still closed around the
bill, then brightened. "Maybe I can help you after all. I know what
you want to know. All the boys ask me this question: What sort of
man will I become?"

"I'm already a man," I said.

"Oho! A man. I should have seen it straight away. A boy's soul is a
shifting, inconstant thing. In men, it becomes fixed." He pocketed the
dollar I put on the table, then resumed scratching his anus. "As a new
man, have you had time to learn what you are?" The diviner leaned
forward. "There's a way to find out."

My mouth became dry.

He put on his sunglasses and rose from the table. "Time for me to
leave. I want be home before the half-beasts begin their prowl. I sleep
in the baobab tree that grows near the highway. Come visit me there,
young friend. Bring another dollar and I'll tell you about a place where
you can go to see into your soul."

The doorstep diviner tapped his way along the animal track that
vanished into the bush, and I went back into the bungalow. In Cape
Town, in the days of my great-grandmother, it had been a house for
bargirls. My grandfather had the house cut in two and moved away
from the sea, overland to the mountains of Manicaland, leaving behind the brick foundation, a pile of sprung mattresses, and his African
ancestry.

I retired to my old room and stretched out on a proper bed for the first
time in a year, wondering if I might wake back in my childhood.

•   •   •

The sun rose on the first day of my return, a white dawn, shimmering and restless. I went out on the verandah which overlooked the glen. Nothing remained of my childhood. Loggers from the Forestry Commission had clearcut the old mahogany trees that once grew into the canopy of clouds, leaving the mountains naked. The tree trunks were stripped and sold to a nearby sawmill which produced industrial grade lumber for pallets and coffins. Shards of weak sunlight glinted on the rime-covered slopes.

A rough path had been forced through the dense foliage, as if by a herd of rushing animals. I followed it deep into the bush. Dead snakes were strewn by the pathside, their carcasses flayed. A wake of whiteback vultures fought over the pallid remains.

There was a disturbance in the earth, a soft tremor that made the bare soles of my feet itch. The grass rippled and whispered, a mystery on this windless day. An uneasiness settled over me as the whitebacks rose clumsily into the air, abandoning their carrion.

Then came the snakes. Pythons, spitting cobras, shield noses, puff adders, gaboons, mambas, garters. They surged from the tall grass in a panic, swarmed around my ankles, over my bare feet, their skin dry and glistening. The snakes vanished as quickly as they appeared, tails flashing, into the waist-high grass. I put my ear to the ground, and it was filled with a faint rumbling, a percussion of hooves that swelled until the earth shook beneath me. I dropped flat and still in the tall grass.

Perhaps thirty boys on horseback thundered past. Each carried a long pole with a thin metal hook on its end which they used to scour the bush, overturning rocks, poking into burrows, and whipping at the tall grass. Strings of snake skins hung from their saddles. These were the galloping shadows I had seen from the car window the previous night. The dense bush swallowed the riders, their mounts, and the thunder of hooves, leaving me to wonder if I'd seen anything at all.

I was still in my pyjamas when Mrs. Tippett approached the house. She was pallid almost to the point of albinism, translucent skin over a network of fine veins. It was my heritage, I suppose, this longing for achromatic women. Apart from a woven necklace of wind flowers, she was bereft of jewelry.

My father had been forced to ask the woman to care for my mother while he went to fetch me back home. Mrs. Tippett's husband, the Very Reverend, was founder and pastor of The Outreach Mission for Troubled Boys. Its chapel, rectory, dormitory, and stables neighbored our bungalow, perhaps a mile walk. The Very Reverend took in delinquent European boys and reclaimed them through scripture and horseback riding.

"You've come back, then," Mrs. Tippett said to me. She carried a frilly bible, a dish of ash, a tray of scrambled eggs gone cold. Her voice was atonal, disapproving. I wondered if this was because I'd left home, or because I lacked the strength of character to stay away.

"Yes, ma'am," I said. I moved nearer, close enough to inhale her breath.

"If I'd known you'd be here, I'd have made more eggs," she said. Mrs. Tippett's breath smelled of tinned peaches and beef broth. "Eggs is the Lord's food," she continued. "We're all of us eggs. In the spiritual sense, that is." The unmusical voice trailed away. "What the Very Reverend says, at any rate."

"Come in," I told her.

Mrs. Tippett paused at the threshold as she came up against the story-ghost. She crossed herself and quoted Job: *As the cloud is consumed and vanisheth away: so he that goeth to his grave shall come up no more.* Having thus reassured herself of its non-existence, Mrs. Tippett pushed through the story-ghost. I padded after her into my mother's room on feet numbed with cold.

Mrs. Tippett set the tray and the bible on the night table. She had sewn a purfled cover for the bible, quilted batting to soften the Word. The cover also served as a pin cushion for her sewing needles. While Mrs. Tippett tried to spoon the egg into my mother, the story-ghost turned one of the needles around, embedding it, point out, in the cover of the bible.

My mother had no appetite and Mrs. Tippett soon gave up on the feeding. I watched the woman spit in the dish of ash, mix in the saliva with her finger, then paint a cross on my mother's forehead. The air conditioner blew directly on Mrs. Tippett, freezing her breath and hardening her nipples. She opened the bible to read scripture. *But if thine eye be evil...* I moved closer, until the distance between us was less than the span of one of her pale, hairless arms... *thy whole body shall be full of darkness.* The words of Christ had been printed in red letters to set them off from the rest of the text. Mrs. Tippett's white fingers pressed into the quilted bible cover as she quoted from memory, her voice raised above the roar of the air conditioner, eyes locked unto mine. *If therefore the light that is in thee be darkness, how great is that darkness.* The backward needle stuck deep into the pad of her index finger, and the story-ghost drew nearer as Mrs. Tippett dropped the bible onto her lap, a fine spray of blood spattering across the page.

"Oh, life," she said.

I stared into the tiny droplets that punctuated the red text of the sermon, my own blood rushing. Mrs. Tippett looked up from her bible, stared below my waist, then turned away. "God forgive you," she said.

I spun round to face the wall, standing in my pyjamas beneath the disapproving gazes of my sepia ancestors, hands cupped over my groin, while I waited for the engorgement to subside. I noticed a palm leaf twisted into a cross that Mrs. Tippet must have affixed to the wall on a previous visit.

Oblivious, my mother picked at the cold eggs. "I can feed her," I said over my shoulder.

In the picture glass, I could see Mrs. Tippett tuck the Word of God between her arm and breast, her obligation discharged. "You won't be needing me anymore, then," she said. "I'll pray for you."

I listened to her quick steps against the floorboards in the hallway, the dishes rattling on the tray, the bang of the front door. My mother, un-saved, wiped the ash from her forehead with the back of her hand.

I stood naked inside my bedroom door and made muscles for the mirror, imagining myself standing naked before Mrs. Tippett. My pubic hair had begun growing, itching tufts that I scratched without relief.

Books crowded the shelf above the youth desk: *Goodnight Moon, Runaway Bunny, The Velveteen Rabbit*, stacks of thin Golden Books. Books for children. I carried them out to the trash heap, poured mineral spirits on them, lighted them. The books burned at the edges, smoldered, and went out. I poured more mineral spirits and the fire caught. The updraft lifted some of the curled illustrations into the air where they soared and flared, each page a hot breath on my forehead and cheeks.

When the fire was spent, I scattered the charred remnants of my childhood books, then went to my father's study. This room was the heart of the bungalow, a place where bargirls had once lounged at wooden tables or moved against one another on a small patch of dance floor as they waited to be chosen by any of the silent, drinking men who sat against the wall. The chair rails still smelled faintly of lavender. Peeling paper revealed glimpses of flesh-colored wall. This was also the room where my great-grandmother smoked her pipe and divined the blighted futures of those who entered that place. Often after hearing a small bit of his unhappy destiny, a man would place more money on the table and insist that my great-grandmother tell him more, and she would read on until his future was exhausted and he no longer had money left to spend on the bargirls. The study was a favorite place of the story-ghost.

Vast bookcases stretched from floor to ceiling, the topmost accessible only by stepladders that rolled along a track the length of each aisle. The carpenter had underestimated the weight of Western knowledge, and the shelves bowed and creaked plaintively each time a book was removed or replaced.

My father lay on the iron bed. My great-grandmother's story-ghost had settled on his chest. I stood in the doorway and watched him sink deeper into the mattress as the story-ghost forced him to heave and struggle for each shallow breath.

I browsed the shelves, taking down books at random: *Wealth of Nations, The Lost Horizon, Modern English Usage, Of Human Bondage, Technics and Civilization, Great Expectations.* Stories of lands and peoples, facts and myths, human and inhuman truths. Stories to instruct and stories to pass time. Stories for staying awake and stories for falling asleep. Stories for holding, for turning in one's hands. Stories like picture windows. Stories that wash over the reader. Stories to trouble the mind. Stories for men.

Awake now from his troubled sleep, my father stared at me without lifting his head.

"Go sleep somewhere else," I told him.

The story-ghost released him. Iron legs scarred the painted floorboards as my father dragged his bed into one of the empty rooms of the bungalow, thus abandoning the study, its books, and all authority over me.

For three days I read, letting the words wash over me. I fell asleep mid-sentence, picked up the narrative thread upon waking, chain-reading one volume after the next. Each book was a story-ghost, bound, covered, and shelved, and they all demanded an audience. Time thickened. Lifetimes passed before me. New words crowded out the old ones from my childhood. I tracked the days by the morning song of the rollers, the sound of the British Ford coughing to life as my father began his commute to Umtali, the midday stifle, my father's return, the night screams of the swifts. I left the study only to use the toilet and to drink water from the kitchen faucet.

Immersed in the books, I hardly noticed that the story-ghost had taken up residence in the study. The air smelled of sea salt and kelp and lavender. I heard the flutter of canaries' wings. Parrots cursing in tongues. A Victrola played from somewhere in the room, *This is my lovely day*. I listened as my great-grandmother's pipe-worn voice rasped along. *This is the day I shall remember when I am dying.* Somehow I knew the words. A heaviness stole over me, as if I were lying beneath a stack of woolen blankets. I let the book fall to my lap. *They can't take this away, it will always be mine, the sun and the wine, the seabirds crying.* The story-ghost had sent my father to bring me back to this place. I exhaled pipe smoke.

Perhaps I would still be lost in that room, the world a better place for it, had the lights not gone out. I left the study and went out onto the verandah to investigate. There were whispers and stifled giggles in the darkness. Small faces peered from the tall grass—Shona children, scaring themselves with their proximity to the story-ghost. I chased them as far as the highway. There I found a python hanging, blackened and eyeless, coiled around a blown-out power terminal where it had sought safety. In the distance I heard galloping hooves and boys hollering as they drove the snakes before them.

The moon had begun its descent: time for the half-beasts to rouse themselves. Unable to continue my reading, I allowed my feet to take me where they would.

In story there is direction behind even the most aimless wandering. My thoughts turned to Mrs. Tippett, her pallid flesh, and my feet turned toward the Outreach Mission for Troubled Boys. A light went on as I passed the rectory. I found myself hiding in a stand of fever trees.

And so I was waiting when Mrs. Tippett came to the window to stare out into the dark sky, her lips parted, heavy eyed, hair alive with the static electricity that filled the cool air. She cupped her pale breasts in her hands, giving them youth and lift, and for a moment she appeared a girl no older than myself. Her hand dropped to her belly, then below, out of view. She moved away from the window, leaving me no choice but to abandon the cover of the fever trees and take my place among the climbing onions that grew beneath the sill.

Mrs. Tippett drew the nightdress over her head and kneeled on the mattress, naked save for the necklace of wind flowers. Her lips worked in silent prayer, head bowed. I lowered my gaze to her shallow navel, the wispy pubic hair, my eyes following the direction of her prayer. It was my great-grandmother who had set us on this path, seeking ever lighter skin behind which to hide our race. My breath crystallized in the chill mountain air.

All my life, danger will come upon me when I'm looking hard in another direction. There was movement on the edge of my vision. A rustle and sigh of leaves. Shapes moving low and swift. Night adders writhed at my feet and the climbing onion came alive. Too late I heard the stampede of hooves, the whooping boys. I was still standing outside Mrs. Tippett's bedroom window when they burst from the fever trees at a gallop and lay into me with their long snake-catching sticks. One knocked me down. Another held my neck against the ground with its curved metal end. The rest beat and jabbed at me while I writhed on the hook.

Mrs. Tippett appeared at the window in a dressing gown and the boys backed their horses away as someone shone a torch into my face. A flash of recognition, followed by a shudder of revulsion. She pulled the dressing gown tight at her neck. The boys draped me face down over the shoulders of one of the horses, and in this manner, lying across a bed of snake skins, I was brought to the police station.

My father was of a generation that judged one another by their school colors, the shine of their shoes, the condition of their heels. He stood behind me on the morning I was to be brought before the magistrate, threading his school tie through my collar. A week had passed since my capture and disgrace, and a harmattan wind had chased the unnatural cold southward. My shirt was already damp with sweat.

My father looked over my shoulder and into the mirror. "You've grown in the year you were away," he said.

I felt suddenly small. "Not so much," I said.

My father guided my hands as together we tied a double-Windsor, passing one end under the other, round and over, above and through. In the mirror I saw him open his mouth several times, as if to speak. My father had been unable to look at me when the police brought me home after my arrest, but now he searched my eyes for something to explain what had happened.

"You can't change what you are," he said finally.

We shaped the knot, working it tighter around my throat. "There," he said, satisfied.

My father took me out onto the verandah and showed me how to polish my wingtips for the magistrate, melting the paste wax over a can of Sterno, dipping a shammy into the liquid and rubbing it onto the toe, into the crevice where the upper was stitched to the sole, working the wax in ever-smaller spirals until the shoes shined like satin. He had taught me to read. Spit like an African. Keep secrets.

I set down the shoes and together we stared up at the new sun, the dew glinting on the mountainscape. My father startled me by speaking without necessity: "There is sweet music here that softer falls than petals from blown roses on the grass." The words stuck in my mind coming from someone so unpoetical. Stories told in retrospective invite future memories, and time jumps the track. Long after his death, I would read these lines again in a volume of Victorian poetry. My father was only parroting Tennyson, but at that moment, on the verandah awaiting my trial, the words were his own.

Neither I nor my father spoke at the trial. A makeshift court was established in a windowless furnace room behind the headquarters of the district police. The electricity went out briefly, more snakes in the power terminals I imagined. There was a brief delay while a road flare was ignited. The usher bade us all rise, and I waited for an imposing magistrate in a powder wig and black robe to make an entrance. Instead, a slight figure dressed in khakis stomped into the room without acknowledging anyone. Sweat ringed her collar and armpits. She paid no attention to my tie and shoes.

I did not hear the magistrate's words as they were delivered unto me in the flickering light of the road flare. Rather, her assessment registered in my memory to be played back on future nights as I lay awake in my bed. The magistrate told the court that I was spiritually flawed and wanted character. A wide boy. Rhodesia would stand or fall on the strength of its young men and God help us all if my sort was indicative of the entire generation. She pronounced me a neurotic little thug who deserved a sound birching if it were left up to her, and so on. But fortune smiles on the wicked, second chance and all that. The Very Reverend had considered my circumstances. Absent father, afflicted mother, et cetera. No way to raise a white child. Monday next week I would report to the stables of the Outreach Mission for Troubled Boys for a period of no less than one year. Next case.

The magistrate's words kept me from sleeping that night. I quit the house, where secrets loomed larger than the thing that was hidden, and went to where the doorstep diviner lay in his sacred tree, his spine curved into the bough, legs elevated against the massive trunk. The baobab was riddled with beetles and ready to collapse. The diviner shimmied his bottom against the rough bark, seeking relief from the tapeworms.

I cleared my throat. "You told me there's a place I can go to look into my soul."

His foot slipped against the trunk and he nearly fell from the barren tree. "Maybe that's not such a good idea, now I think on it." He looked down on me for a moment. "God keeps us from such knowledge for a reason." He settled back into the bough. "When I was first born, my mother divined my true nature. It was a disappointment to her."

I held up one of my father's dollars. The diviner wrestled a moment with the temptation, then shook his head. "Better to find out at the end of your life what sort of man you are. It makes no matter then."

I climbed onto a massive root, reached up, and brushed his hand with the dollar. The diviner snatched and pocketed the money in one motion. "Oh, oh, oh. Are you certain you want to do this?"

The mouth of the trust land is lined with vendors' stalls and the graves of children killed by lorry drivers. Morning traffic flows away from such poor places and, unable to hitch a ride, it took me an hour to make the tagrag market on foot.

Shona street sellers squatted before legless tables, over kerosene stoves and cooking pots, beneath umbrellas, atop slabs of granite, in derelict cars, amid the expanse of transistor radios, paper sacks of fried takeaway, rows of sunglasses, plastic jewelry, soapstone animal carvings, bolts of garish broadcloth, crates of Castle beer, spools of ringspun yarn, gallon tins of Frytoll, woven placemats, and rolls of baler twine. Two soldiers played cards atop the turret of an armored car, the barrel of its cannon pointed into the crowd of market goers.

Long ago, the story goes, a little boy came here to beg. But trust-land Shona give nothing away, so the boy began to sketch the souls of passersby on bits of refuse paper that littered the road. Once captured on paper, he bartered the souls back to their owners in exchange for food. He grew fat on his earnings.

That is what the doorstep diviner had told me for one dollar.

George Makana Clark

A haze of gnats and dust hung over the market. I bought a beer from a vendor and took my place in the long queue of Shona waiting to discover their true nature. As I waited, I ate the purge nut the diviner had given me the night before. "It will help rid you of evil," he had explained, "so that your soul will perhaps appear less dark."

The Illustrator of Souls perched on a small hump of earth where the trust-land road meets the highway. His child-belly rested on his knees. Though competition was fierce among vendors for these choice spots, the boy had held this place uncontested for as long as anyone could remember. Beside him was a stack of flattened paper trash, a few pieces of charcoal, a transistor radio tuned to the African Service. Toothless, he chewed on a piece of biltong with gums as hard as bone. When my turn came, I placed the beer before him.

"Draw my soul," I said. The purge nut had left a bitter taste.

The boy picked up a piece of charcoal and, without looking at me, scribbled furiously on a paper sack. He tossed the drawing at my feet.

I picked up the paper sack and stared at the image. It was nothing more than a series of tiny, jagged lines blurred into a black smudge. There was a grease spot behind the image and some of the charcoal came off on my thumb. I breathed in the dust. The illustration stirred my guts and something surged into my mouth. I vomited onto the ground before the Illustrator of Souls, black bile that smelled of burnt milk and mildew and carbon and vegetable rot. Even the gnats would not light on it.

I kicked the bottle over, spilling beer on the boy's feet, and I ground his charcoal beneath my heel, leaving a smudge on the road identical to that on the paper bag I held in my hand. The Illustrator of Souls shrugged, his drawing validated.

An overland truck sped past on the highway, narrowly missing several children who shrieked with laughter as they ran out from between the stalls that crowded the shoulder. The vendors looked up, relieved that more valuable space would not have to be given over to graves for children killed in traffic.

•　•　•

Another sleepless night brooding in the study, the books closed and scattered at my feet, as I waited to be sent to the Outreach Mission for Troubled Boys, where I would join the pack of snake hunters.

My father brought me a tray of biscuits and quickly retreated. My mind clouded and I struggled to remember why I had run away from this place. I could no longer recall the details of my own story.

I sat in the study and listened to the footfalls of barefoot bargirls. Outside, seagulls screeched. The crashing of waves. My great-grandmother's voice: *A story, let it come.* The words came from my own mouth.

I was roused by a rapping on the study window, the doorstep diviner wanting to find out what I'd learned from the Illustrator of Souls. He looked past me into the thick miasm of story-ghost, then jumped back.

"God blind me!" He moved forward again, angling for a better look into the study. "How can you people live under a roof with this thing?" He scrambled in through the window. "Look how it pushes out the walls so." He passed his hand through the story-ghost.

"It's the spirit of my great-grandmother."

The diviner studied the apparition intently. "It's no such a thing, old friend. Your great-grandmother's long dead, her spirit gone some other place altogether. It's her story that throws this house off-balance. Was your great-grandmother a diviner?"

I nodded.

"Ehe! It's a terrible thing when a diviner gets separated from her own story. You live with this story-ghost?"

"Yes."

"Now there's real trouble. You need to do something. Quick-quick. Soon this thing will make you forget your own weak child's story." He sat down at the desk. "This is what I've heard anyway."

"My story's not weak. It's a man's story."

The diviner thought this was killingly funny and it took a moment for him to regain his composure. "This evil thing is eating your past and you're talking nonsense. It won't be satisfied until it has swallowed you completely."

Outside, a muster of penguins brayed in the surf. He was right. I

George Makana Clark

was living in my great-grandmother's story. "You're a diviner. Can't you chase it away?"

"Think! If I possessed such power would I suffer from tapeworms?" He stood and paced the study. The diviner slumped back into the chair. "My mother used to drive such things away." He seemed to reach a decision. "We should consult these." He removed the lid from the heart-shaped box.

"I thought you couldn't read your mother's casting bones."

"Truthfully, I never tried." He emptied the candy box on the table. "These are just old pork bones I boiled. I sold the others. Even so, I cannot leave a friend to be eaten by a story-ghost. Come bring me a dollar. Let's rattle the bones to get its attention." The diviner produced some pepper bark, a box of matches, and an ox-tail whisk. He pocketed the dollar and pushed me out of the study. "Everything, it's all right now. Goodbye, my friend. Remember that it was God who gave you your faults. And a life also, to spend correcting them."

I stood in the hallway. Wisps of smoke came from under the closed door as the diviner burned the pepper bark. I could hear the pork bones roll in the lid of the candy box. There was hand clapping, the swishing of the ox-tail whisk. He was working hard to give me my dollar's worth. Later there were voices, too low for me to hear, that sounded as if they were conducting secret negotiations. I fell asleep with my ear to the door.

The study was empty when I entered the following morning, both story-ghost and diviner gone. I searched the bungalow but the house was dead now, its lifeforce departed.

Days passed, sluggish and blurry, while I waited for my sentence to commence. I took to carrying my soul folded inside my breast pocket and it became my habit to brood over the drawing whenever I was alone. I sometimes looked for the doorstep diviner, pestering neighbors' servants, vendors at the trust-land market, tavern owners. No one would remember him, his existence erased.

Who can say why he offered himself up to the story-ghost of my great-grandmother? Perhaps he wanted a new past, even if it had once belonged to someone else. Or he was tired of sleeping in a tree with only his tapeworms for company. Or he did it for the dollar. Or a friend.

Some exorcisms are more successful than others. My mother remained secluded in her bower, unable to rise from her chair. My father took up pipe smoking on the verandah, and at these times, when he thought no one was near, he'd whistle a popular tune from another time. But such things were only the residue of the story-ghost. For as long as it stood, the bungalow would continue to whisper and creak, as old houses will, and I would lie awake at night, listening.

To this day, I'm more willing to show my ass than my face.

Oliver Broudy was born in New York, where he now lives and works. His stories have appeared in the *Missouri Review, American Short Fiction, ZYZZYVA*, and other journals.

THE BRIEF

Oliver Broudy

It was here in the wine shop that Christopher, a natty, some-what portly twenty-nine year old, met Saska Janjic, in the third aisle, squatting on the floor behind a display stand trying to cram a cheap bottle of wine into an already bulging shoulder bag. Behind the counter, a large black woman was watching the whole thing in a convex mirror, chewing a tiny piece of gum. She watched indifferently, with the half-lidded eyes of a cat, as though at any moment it would become too much for her and she would have to look away out of sheer boredom. Instead she reached for a phone beneath the counter and paged the manager. Christopher did not hesitate.

"How about I buy that for you," he said to the girl.

The girl turned and lashed him with her defiant eyes.

"Buy what?" she said, standing up. "What are you talking about?" She had an Eastern European accent.

Christopher pointed pleasantly to the bottle she was holding.

"I was not going to steal it," the girl said proudly. "*I* am going to buy it."

A stocky Asian man in a blue apron appeared at the end of the aisle, eyeing them alertly and holding a cardboard box. Christopher feigned interest in the wine and gestured to look at it more closely. It was a blush.

"Hmm," he said, and, turning back to the shelves, selected another blush a few shelves higher. "That's a nice springy wine, but why don't we get something a little nicer."

The man in the apron put down the box and started walking purposely toward them, but before he could say anything Christopher asked him whether the second bottle was really five dollars better than the first one.

The man stared up at him angrily, ignoring the question.

"Buy what you want and get out," he said, "and don't come back."

"Alrighty-roo," Christopher said, and began walking with the girl toward the counter.

"I don't want you in my store!" the man called after them.

"We're leaving, we're leaving," Christopher said, "right after we give you our money."

He put both bottles of wine on the counter and looked placidly at the black woman standing behind it.

"Why are you doing this?" the girl said softly, at his side.

Christopher honestly wasn't sure. Perhaps it was the jingling spring air. Or an unpredictable perverseness that sometimes afflicted him after sitting through another unhappy week of law classes. He was not a valiant person. Definitely not the sort to come regularly to the rescue of maidens. Let the dragons have them. He was deceptive, achy, mistrustful of himself, and as full of whispers as a cave.

"It's my good deed for the day," he said.

"Liar," the girl whispered.

Christopher agreed. "I am absolutely a liar," he said, loud enough for the cashier to hear. She looked at him severely.

"Y'all gonna get caught one day for real. He don't usually let people go."

"Eeee," the girl said, in subdued alarm.

The cashier rang up the purchases and put the bottles in separate paper bags, and then put these bags inside another bag, pink and plastic, while Christopher and the girl remained standing uncomfortably side by side like children assigned to one another. She was skinny and wolfish with dyed black hair pulled back in a lank pony tail knotted low at her neck. She had a slippery look to her, the look of a runaway. The zipper of her sweatshirt was misted with a rainbow patina.

"Do you have any cigarettes?" she said innocently.

Most Friday evenings were not spent this way. Most passed at home, drinking, reading through legal briefs. This was the ideal compromise between studying and carousing. The studying by itself was impossible because by the end of the week he had studied enough, and some part of him revolted. Carousing was unacceptable because he was almost thirty and no longer had the time to waste his evenings in bars exchanging words with people he wouldn't remember anyway. Both at once, however, proved the perfect solution—only on Fridays, however, when the week gave way like a door he had been furiously pushing against, and he felt himself reaching around for something to grasp onto. The alcohol made him feel grounded again and restored some sense of control. When he was drunk he felt heavy, he felt gravity sucking at him, as though with each pull from the bottle he was exponentially increasing his mass.

One of the pleasures of the legal briefs was the contrast between the formality of the language and the raunchiness of what it described—the way the language rolled over everything, regardless, pulverizing it into arbitrable bits. In the face of this grinding force the defendants and their crimes took on a forlorn air, like the jerking of puppets entangled in each other's strings. Christopher usually ended up pitying them, increasingly so as he reached the more supple regions of drunk. Here was the embezzler who risked everything for a pittance, here was the father who lingered too long tucking in his daughter, or the train engineer, drunk as he was on bad wine, who had failed to toot for the repair crew.

At a certain point the legalese became invisible, and the briefs began to read like a supermarket tabloid. What a circus it was! All these people out there walloping each other, scheming, grabbing, lusting, stealing each other's wallets. Defendant threw two women overboard five miles from shore; defendant struck victim hard with heavy stone, fracturing skull; defendant, in the guise of a practicing doctor, prescribed zinc oxide for cancer of the nose. Case after case, reports from all over the map, until it seemed that humanity was nothing but an unending parade of miscellaneous kidnapping, arson, bombing, drowning, bludgeoning, and fraud. Some part of him rejoiced in the mayhem. It made his head swim to think about it, the extent of the raucousness at large in the world, and how eternally engaged these forces of raucousness were with the forces of law. But even after the judgment was made and the criminal was sentenced, the judge would still be sitting there quietly shaking his head in amazement at the plain craziness of it all, about which, ultimately, the law could say nothing. What was this, then, that remained, that the final judgment left unsaid? What was this unadded element, this feeling of ruin? Why was it there, and what did one do with it? These were questions that were perhaps better answered by criminals than scholars. In each brief that he read there were hints of a solution.

On this Friday evening the feeling seemed to be everywhere in evidence: in the intensely rich, unpitted orange of the horizon behind the black buildings of Washington Square, in the lonely aspect of a linden clutching in its still bare branches a green balloon, in the plump reek of the hot-dog cart. All things seemed burdened with this oppressive significance, to which the only possible answer was alcohol. The great arch shone like alabaster at the bottom of Fifth Avenue. A cop sat creaking on a black horse, watching for dealers as women came up to touch the horse's warm jowls and look for a moment into its enormous brown eyes. Christopher and the girl snuck past him with their bottles of wine, which a waiter at a patio cafe had been kind enough to lean over and uncork.

Saska was not a runaway, as it turned out, although she was a refugee of sorts, from Yugoslavia. She still called it that, having abandoned all interest in her home country upon leaving it. She lived with her parents in Queens. Her English was pretty good, but he had to explain the term *kleptomaniac* to her. "Yes," she said. "That is me. I am that." And suddenly broke hunching over into a girlish giggle. The vertebrae of her back stood out against the blue cotton of her sweatshirt and Christopher felt the first stab of something terrible. They walked east through the park, and he discovered she had a habit of spitting, which he didn't find particularly attractive—a cultural thing, perhaps.

They walked toward St. Mark's, dosey-do-ing parking meters and dodging hipsters talking on cell phones. As they walked, Saska recovered the broken stem of an umbrella from a trash can and carried it with her, puncturing trash bags with it with one hand and swilling wine with the other. She was skinny as an otter with her boy hips, skulking along and rocking from side to side like someone treading on ice. He wanted to reach out a hand to steady her. He happily raised his wine and drank, remembering warm, spacious Princeton evenings, crossing the quad with a bottle raised like a horn. At the end of the block the sky was sinking into a plush indigo, and the air was possessed of that jungle sponginess that softens the sounds and makes everything blur and seem to move slower. The stoplights on Second Avenue shone a blissed-out blue-green.

"What do you mean, what do I do?" Saska said.

"Do," said Christopher. "You know. Work."

"I don't work. I live!"

They had come to rest on the steps of a walk-up on Sixth Street. It was more than enough on this liquid spring evening to just sit there pouring wine down their throats and watch the people walk by.

"Well, sure," Christopher said, "but what are your aspirations? Don't you want to be something when you grow up? Like an astronaut or something?"

"Why is that important?" Saska said, becoming exasperated. "I don't understand why everyone is all the time asking me this. Why can't I just be who I am? Why can't everything just be open and free instead of having to answer all these questions all the time. All you need in life is food and a place to sleep. Man. If I had food all the time I would be happy. That is the only thing."

"You sound like a hippie."

"I am a hippie," she said, straightening proudly. "That's exactly what I am."

"I didn't know there were hippies anymore."

"There will always be hippies," she declared, her dark eyes flashing. "There were hippies thousands of years ago. Hippies were the first human beings on the planet. All of the great religious leaders were hippies." She began listing them. "Jesus Christ, Gautama Buddha, Gandhi… All of these people."

Christopher leaned back against the stairs on his elbows, gratified. It was marvelous to hear these absurdities from her. His feeling of ruin had blossomed into a feeling of vast geniality. There seemed to be no end of room for absurdities, and each one was so correct in its own way. He was prepared to agree with them all. He stared upward dreamily, wishing there were stars to see.

"The one place where you need stars to be, they aren't," he said.

She did not reply. There was no telling, with her imperfect English, how much of what he said she understood. She seemed to understand all the words, but the various shades of irony and innuendo were lost on her, and almost everything, Christopher realized, was innuendo.

With an effort, he pulled his head back to level and began studying the opposite apartment building, a brownstone crawling with ivy—an ideal ladder for thieves.

"Can I ask you a question?" she said.

"Sure."

"Have you read the bible?"

"Sort of."

"Have you read the Bhagivad Gita?"

He shook his head.

"That is all about hippies." She said this in a tone of quiet conclusion. She appeared to be done with the conversation. He thought about getting up to leave. He could pick up another bottle of wine and go home to read. Thankfully he was sitting next to the girl and so could not see her face. It would be easier to leave her this way, not seeing the severe beauty of her face. Only her shoes were in his field of vision—worn brown boots—and her knees, the jeans crudely patched with vinyl ovals.

She pulled her bag onto her lap and began rummaging through it, then dropped it back down between her feet. It was an olive-green army bag on the front of which had been printed the word *Revolution*.

"What's that about?" he said.

"What?"

He pointed to the word.

"Revolution!" she said.

"What revolution?" He turned to look at her.

"The revolution, *man*! Overthrow the system! Free the people!" Her drummer-girl eyes flashed, but then, in a transformation that jarred something within him, she grinned sheepishly and produced a lighter to light one of the cigarettes she had convinced him to buy.

The People v. Reed. Guy A walks to work every morning at the Michelin tire shop where he has worked for two years. In order to get there he walks past Guy B's house. A walkway leads down the side of Guy B's house, beneath Guy B's bathroom window. The bottom of the window is six feet from the ground. Guy A is six foot, five inches, with his eyes at six foot, one inch. When he walks past the window, Guy B sees him, comes out of the house, and accuses him of peeping through his window. Guy A denies doing so, explains that he is simply walking to work as he always has. Guy B does not accept this explanation, and proceeds to verbally abuse Guy A. By this time, other residents of the house, including Guy B's wife and daughter, have come out of the house and are watching. Guy A again tells Guy B that he is just walking to work, and furthermore warns him that he has a gun. "You can't scare me with your goddamn gun," Guy B says, and positions himself to strike Guy A. Guy A shoots him.

The defense claimed that the killing was a crime of passion, and so merited leniency. The question was, were the facts and circumstances sufficient to arouse the passions of the ordinarily reasonable person? Christopher, who liked to think himself an ordinarily reasonable person, couldn't help wondering what the real story was. "You can't scare me with your goddamn gun." It was rare for a brief to contain the actual words used by the principals of the case. Usually everything was reduced to so-called facts and procedure. This, Christopher was given to understand, was the strength of the law; this was its power. In order to understand and manage the fates of criminals, it was necessary to become as least like them as possible: predictable, procedural, and dull. Still, one wished to know more. In almost every case the most important element seemed to be that which language could never describe. Each brief seemed to be an exercise in how elaborately the mention of this element, whatever it was, could be avoided. He would have liked to write his own textbook, with chapters on "The Desire to Kill," "The Desire to Rob Banks and Knock Over Old Ladies," or just "The Rebellious Impulse."

He put the book aside. He couldn't concentrate. He lay in his bed and studied the picture of Abraham Lincoln hanging on the wall, his studio apartment's one decoration. He had found the picture at a thrift store and discovered that he rather liked it in a strange way. The grim, reproving image stared down at him, but was no more able than the legal briefs to discourage him from thoughts of Saska Janjic. Various phrases of hers, in her exact, softly strident tone of voice, like someone waxing a bow string, kept echoing in his head and commanding his attention. He couldn't get free of her. It was as though some part of himself had got snagged on her, like a knit sweater on a splinter of wood. Christopher disliked not being in control of his thinking. He could foresee the weave of that ordered sweater getting pulled horribly out of shape. But there was nothing he could do, so long as the initial snag—no matter how small, a matter of mere threads—was beyond his power to lift free. He remained lying there, beneath the copious gaze of the sixteenth president, thinking about her, Saska Janjic, the rambunctious revolutionary with the dewy neck.

•   •   •

The pangs he endured after first meeting her were gone the next morning. They were, he decided, as he neatly threw back the covers and found his slippers with his toes, no more than the work of a small, toad-like gland tucked away somewhere in his chest cavity, which every now and then squirted some sort of astringent juice across the internal organs, thus precipitating the condition known as "heartache."

This flimsy thought, however, did little to protect him when she called to apologize for stealing his wallet.

She said, "I never steal from friends, but I wasn't sure if you were my friend. I think you are, though. Are you?"

"I'm not a liquor store," he said, irritably.

But he had been thrilled to hear her voice, that Slavic accent, that particular mewling way she had. At once he felt the hideous little gland contract, ejecting the vile juice.

In the days following, they went out boozing a few times, guzzling wine from paper bags and sitting on the steps of East Village walk-ups, scooping cheap Indian food from fast-food containers. He placed paper plates beneath his rear on the steps, and always brought along a wad of napkins, which amused her, and once she let him dab some curry from her chin. This bohemian living was not his style, particularly, but he participated with a tourist's enthusiasm. Usually he dined on frozen dinners.

The evenings usually ended, however, with him feeling more confused and uncertain than when they began. He didn't know if they were romantic or just friendly, and if friendly whether it was a friendship deriving from the somewhat avuncular tone he couldn't help taking toward her, or a friendship of equals, a friendship that, while it might not be romantic, might one day become romantic. He had the sense that, as a hippie, it was all the same to her, and this compounded his impatience.

"Who told you all that?" he asked her once, in an East Village bar, when she started raving about the "evils of the system."

"What system, exactly?" he demanded. "The government? The legal system?"

"Yes!" she said, looking back at him. "The government!"

"Or the traffic system? What about that?"

"That! Yes!" she cried, grinning jubilantly and pounding the table with her glass like a Cossack. "Everything!"

"What about the moon?" he said confidently, pointing out the window at the moon's reflection in one of the windows opposite. "Is that part of the system? The moon? Should we go and protest the moon?"

"Yes!" she cried, jumping up. "Absolutely! Let us protest it! Let us march against it! I don't like it!" She marched out of the bar singing a song in Yugoslav in a deep voice, and after a second he followed.

Outside the bar she stopped singing abruptly. "It is cold out here," she said quietly.

He held out his arms, and to his surprise she came to him and curled herself into his chest. He wanted to kiss the part in her hair but resisted the impulse.

"Wow," she said, her pickpocket hands stealing over him, quietly exploring his chest and girth. "You have some extra stomach here."

"I've been known to eat well," Christopher said, looking dreamily over her head and feeling her spare warmth. "I don't starve myself on celery like you."

"You should try fasting with me sometime. It is good for the spirit. It empties you out completely. Everything. Where did you get this coat? I like it." She inhaled deeply through her nose. "You smell like an old man."

"I am an old man," he said.

"I know that you are. That is why you do not understand the revolution."

The next day, halfway through a legal brief emphasizing the perils of *pro se* representation, Christopher jumped up and began furiously cleaning the kitchen. He doused the cabinet doors with a lemony cleaning agent and washed them down, and then got on his knees and scrubbed the gummy gray patches off the kitchen floor. He took the recycling down to the recycling bin and emptied the trash, and while he was out he stomped to the store to buy new light bulbs (until then having made do by ferrying the single working bulb from socket to socket). When he was done with all this he stood in the immaculate, brightly lit kitchen reconnoitering his soul, but the fact was still there, this mindless boiling-out of himself toward her, and all he could think was that now that he had cleaned his place it might be nice to invite her over for a romantic dinner. He wanted to smash something. She was just a twenty-year-old hippie living with her parents in Queens, a soup-slurping "revolutionary" who had never even heard of Che Guevara. A scrawny, unemployed kleptomaniac who dressed like an urchin, an ex-Hari Krishna, for heaven's sake, whose only interest seemed to be finding a way to get to India, where she could sit at the feet of some bald guru.

Yes, yes! some part of him cried in response. Exactly that!

All her weaknesses somehow resolved into strengths. Her spare, narrow, sparrow body—which he had so far only held, virtuously, like a father—seemed all the more precious, and lust and pity combined in him to form something more potent than either. He was compelled by the mystery of how a body as twiggy as hers could possibly contain the endlessness of sex that he longed for. The mystery seemed larger than it was because it seemed to promise an answer to other questions as well, questions he hadn't even formulated yet, such as whether his vision of himself as a lawyer was realistic, whether the "revolution" was in any way legitimate, and where she had acquired her revolting passion for mayonnaise, which he had seen her apply even to Chinese food. Whenever she met him she would come up to him pretending to be a panhandler, saying, "Hey, mister, can I have two dollars?" and then smile guiltily and kiss him, smelling of wintergreen gum. She lacked his years of higher education, but how wonderful it was once he had found a way to talk to her without reference to these things! To speak literally and without irony! What a relief it was, to be unburdened of the endless hodgepodge of history and laws and legal proceedings, and he wondered how love under any other circumstances but these was possible.

At the same time he had watched, appalled, as he had grown more enchanted with her, watched with a kind of detached amazement, like a semi-anaesthetized patient gawking at a surgeon's busy scalpel. He chastened himself doubly for putting his heart in the hands of one so young and fickle, an avowed Buddhist, among other things, whose main project appeared to be to depersonalize love and dispense it as indiscriminately as possible, like a stack of flyers for a shoe sale. It was this very Buddhist unattainability, a kind of coquetry of the eight-fold path, he reasoned, that had been his undoing. Until he could either secure her or master his own feelings, he vowed to make himself equally unattainable, and adopt a posture of being coolly aloof.

But then there he was, on the way to a Krishna temple, mooning on about her dark eyes.

"You have such beautiful dark eyes," he said flatly, without sentiment. "As black as coal." He had taken to accosting her with these hyperbolic compliments, even though she did, in fact, have beautiful dark eyes, the darkness of her pupils indiscernible from that of her irises, so that all the intensity of her girlish face came to gather there, in her raccoon gaze. There was something thin and wild about her, and something untrustworthy that perversely made him want to trust her. Her smile was like that of a toothy twelve year old, sneaky and bashful.

He stood before her now, and gazed at her as one gazes at a coin. He did this often, because of the response it brought. She didn't like it, and would shy away coltishly. She would refute it. It had become his sole advantage.

"What do you mean, dark eyes?" she said angrily. "Your eyes are dark, as well."

He smiled thinly and pulled their hips together so their belt buckles clinked. She was wearing a blue corduroy blazer with the back pocket of a pair of jeans sewn on the front. The blazer emphasized her long torso and skinny legs. They were standing on the corner of Atlantic and Flatbush, in Brooklyn, waiting for the light to change. To their right stood the clocktower building, displaying the wrong time in four directions.

170

"I am too advanced for this boolsheet," she said wistfully, looking over his shoulder.

He wound his arms around and under her blazer and drew her close. She puffed out her cheeks and made trumpeting noises, as if she were blowing up a balloon.

"That is a nice kiss," she said, surprised.

He kissed her again the same way, a kiss of great precision and intent that he hoped would do something to dispel the sheer amazement he felt at being this proximate to someone, basically a stranger, looking into her face and knowing he could never predict what she was going to do or say. He had never felt more in the present, or realized on what a tiny diamond the present balanced. The world carouseled around them and they stood on a point of perfect stillness. He wanted to find the source of this stillness, and to suspend himself there forever. He touched her neck, as though to somehow capture the thrum of her rushing blood, and she briefly closed her eyes, even as a car alarm sounded nearby. She let her face relax entirely, as if she was asleep. She hung on him, her cheek wedged against his shoulder, pushing open her pretty mouth in an idiot pucker. It was possible to quiet her, it was possible to hold her wildness. He wanted to place his ear against her and listen as though for some oncoming train.

Eventually he kissed her forehead, and she awoke, and began peppering him with kisses in return. He closed his eyes and turned his face to stone and let the kisses land.

"You are like a hummingbird," he murmured.

She drew suddenly back, distrustful again. "What is a hummingbird?"

"The way you kiss me," he said, opening his eyes, trying to sound casual, "like a hummingbird feeding."

"You are like a cow," she said decisively, as the light clunked yellow in the green traffic box.

"A cow?" he said uncertainly.

"Yes." She was serious. The light changed, and she took his hand and began crossing the street. He felt the impulse to just let go, the simplest impulse, to just open his hand and *detach*. But sneaking a backward glance at him she suddenly smirked and snickered, covering her mouth with her hand. There were times when she didn't look older than fourteen.

"A cow," he repeated, in a mock-offended tone.

"Yes!" she crowed, radiant. "You are exactly like a cow!"

She was practical, pragmatic, direct. She had to be. Since fleeing Yugoslavia, she had enjoyed precious little stability in her life.

But what could she possibly mean, that he was like a cow?

Before settling into Buddhism she had been a Krishna for a year or two. She had moved on, but she still liked to go back now and then for the food. The temple was located in one of the seedier parts of downtown Brooklyn. She loped along in front of him with her hands in her pockets. His first surprise was to find that the temple resided within a rather plain building, which might equally have housed the Department of Education. In fact, it seemed that some sort of city office was located in a building directly across the street, next to a park called the Seven Sycamores Park, presumably after the seven sycamores growing up through the asphalt. An abandoned shopping cart with someone's pocketbook in the top rack stood by the park gate. As they neared their destination, Saska began leading Christopher by the hand with a kind of canine excitement. Christopher followed after with an amused smile.

The inside of the temple, such as it was, was contrary to expectation as well, its decor of cinderblock and paneling suggestive more of a community center than cult spiritualism. From down the hall could be heard the raucous sounds of cymbals and chanting. To the right rubber-lined stairs led upward, with a thin chain across the landing and a sign saying, "No entrance without temple permission."

They were met at the door by the Krishna who had buzzed them in. He immediately recognized Saska and bowed to her, smiling. He was about Christopher's age, wore saffron robes and was, of course, bald. Christopher had always rather liked Krishnas. They existed beyond derision, in an absurd realm all their own, and nothing expressed this absurdity so much as their own baldness, or the combination of this baldness with their usual glassy-eyed good will. The Krishna who answered the door, however, did not appear to be the usual sort of Krishna, not least because his skull bore multiple dents thick with lichen-like patches of black hair. Nor was his look particularly glassy. Christopher disliked him instantly, especially the way he locked eyes with Saska and took both of her hands.

"This is my friend," Saska said to the Krishna. "He is happy to meet you. And this is my other friend, Akhandananda. I would like you two to be friends with each other. I think you will like each other. You are both such weird guys."

Akhandananda laughed. His teeth were all crowded together, as if fleeing some disaster transpiring within.

"She has a thing for weird guys," he said.

"It's true. I do. I like people who are different from other people."

"Well," Christopher said stiffly, taking in the Krishna's robes, "you're different all right."

"It all depends where you're standing," the Krishna returned, with his crowded smile.

Christopher bit his lip and said nothing. He felt that he had somehow been cast into the role of the conservative and unhip father figure, and was disturbed to find that something about the role agreed with him. He wanted to grab the Krishna—obviously just a punk in disguise—grab him by the collar and throw him across the hood of a car.

"So," Saska said, nodding her head awkwardly and smiling. There was something about the way she said this, something about her awkwardness, that instantly turned Christopher against her. He moved a step away from her. He suddenly wanted to get much farther away.

"I haven't seen you for a while," the Krishna said.

"Yes. Actually, I have been super busy. I am trying to find a job as a counselor."

"A counselor? A real job? Does that mean I won't be seeing you any more?"

Saska turned to Christopher, who had backed away even further.

"Actually," she said kindly, "maybe you should go ahead and check out the temple. I want to talk to Akhandananda about something."

Christopher nodded.

"Is that okay?"

"Perfect, actually," Christopher said with restraint.

"I will be there in just a second," Saska called after him.

It seemed at this moment that they were both equal strangers to him, Saska and the dent-headed Krishna. Obviously the girl didn't think twice about sleeping with as many people as it occurred to her to sleep with, and regardless of their teeth. Indiscriminate love: it was the Buddhist way, and—who knew—perhaps the Krishna way as well. Anyway, it didn't matter. She was a stranger. He didn't know her. And he was relieved to feel that he might not care. Perhaps this was because he had never known her, just as he had never known about her aspiration to be a counselor. Who could she possibly counsel? It was baffling, but not particularly distressing. On the contrary, it felt as if he had been somehow spat out of himself and set free.

As he walked toward the hallway he couldn't help looking back, out of curiosity, and indeed it seemed like he was seeing her for the first time.

"Christopher," she called after him. He knew she had nothing to say to him, that she was just calling out to him so he would keep looking at her. It was just another lie, the way she called to him. She was always calling him a liar, and this was why—because she was a liar herself. She was made up of lies. All of her gestures, her expressions, her half-smiles and thievery—even the way she walked was a lie. How could he have seen anything beautiful in this?

In the hallway, rows of shoes lay jumbled on the floor. With some misgiving, he added his own gleaming Nikes to the pile, and went inside. The room itself resembled nothing so much as a middle-school gymnasium, although somewhat more dim, with shellacked wood floors and a high ceiling from which dangling exercise ropes would not have appeared out of place. Folding chairs lined the circumference of the room, and above the chairs velvety paintings representing vignettes from Hindu mythology had been suspended against the lime green concrete. At one end of the room where a basketball net might have hung there was a puppet-stage-sized shrine. Between carved pillars wound with flower garlands two figures, a man and a woman somewhat less than life-size stood side by side amidst a craze of pointillistic ornamentation. The man had large, puppy-dog eyes, big pants, and a bluish, drowned-looking complexion. He was playing some sort of flute. The woman's face was all but invisible behind the tassels and silks of her complex headgear.

Roughly where the other basketball net might have hung, a high priest of some sort sat cross-legged atop a palanquin mounded with pillows. His eyes were closed, and he sat calmly with his hands raised in a prayer position in front of his heart. The chanting was being led by a small Indian man with horn-rimmed glasses sitting cross-legged on the floor before a microphone angled down. About a hundred people were gathered loosely around him. As the chanting cycled interminably through its variations, a queue of devotees shuffled in front of the palanquin, scooping handfuls of flower petals from a wooden basket and dispersing them around the base before moving on. Christopher joined the end of the line and began following the others forward. Every now and then someone would come in the door and kneel and put their rump in the air, the women's pocketbooks climbing to the floor, the men dropping to their stomachs and touching the wood with their foreheads, the soles of their bare feet curling upward with thick, horizontal wrinkles.

"What are you doing?" Saska said, sidling up to him. It was so loud with the chanting and the cymbals that she had to speak into his ear.

"Converting," Christopher said, not looking at her.

"Are you? You are going to become a Krishna? You are such a strange guy!"

Christopher ignored her.

"Are you mad about something?"

Christopher began humming along with the chant.

"Okay, whatever," he heard her say.

He stood in line behind a woman wearing a turquoise sari with a fork in her hair. When another woman approached him with a bucket full of flame he imitated everyone else and held his fingers over it and then touched his forehead.

This was all correct. The ritual was taking shape around him, and it appeared to be proper in every respect. Christopher was himself the object of this ritual, the purpose of which was to emancipate him from the last traces of his romanticism, and everything that sprang from it, including the occasional ruinous moods that made him want to get drunk and commit crimes. He had always thought that if he could just commit one big crime, it would be enough to finally satisfy the restlessness in his soul, and permit him to carry on with the business of living. And it occurred to him now that the reckless love he had felt for this miserable girl almost ten years his junior was this very crime. In this light, everything he had felt for her suddenly made sense. And it seemed to him only appropriate that the Krishnas would be the ones to help him at last bring about this transformation in himself, to provide the setting for the final extinction of his romanticism. Whether he had loved her or not was immaterial; she had delivered him to this absurd place, and he could even now recognize that he would one day feel thankful to her. He smiled, scattering flower petals, relishing his newfound indifference. Perhaps this was how Krishnas felt all the time, as though perpetually just freed from an embarrassing infatuation.

The chanting around him stopped, and the man with the horn-rimmed glasses chanted on alone. *Hare Krishna, Hare Krishna, Krishna Krishna, Hare Hare.* Christopher wondered idly if he was somehow being brainwashed. The ache in his heart had dissolved into something softer and no longer limited to his chest cavity. Could he really be free of her so easily? This was the perpetual question: not am I a fool, but rather how much of a fool am I? He looked up at the priest on the palanquin, admiring his otherworldly stillness, and then realized with a shock that the wax figure was not alive.

He looked toward the doorway just in time to see his beloved Saska trailing the Krishna with the bad teeth out of the temple and back toward the lobby. He trotted after them in his socks, catching up just in time to see them stepping over the chain on the stairs. He

176

paused at the chain only a moment and then stepped over. The stairs turned a corner at the top of the first flight and opened onto a small lobby exactly like the one below. A door to the right bore a sign reading *Men's Ashram*. The chanting and the ringing of the cymbals had grown fainter. Christopher stopped and listened. He proceeded a few more steps, hesitantly, and then stopped again, pulled up short by an awareness of himself. Who was he? A stranger, unknown to himself, proceeding into the unknown, chasing a kleptomaniac into the unknown regions of an unknown temple. He felt the temple watching him, like the black woman watching in the convex mirror at the wine shop. How small he seemed in that diminished reflection, a trespassing law student, a man in his socks, hesitating on the stairs.

The Holistic Healing Center where Saska volunteered reminded him of a college food co-op. It was an old building in SoHo with an iron front, tall ceilings, and hallways that smelled of candles and bulghur wheat. Flyers for holistic massage, crystal therapy, yoga retreats, and every other variety of new-age activity were posted on the walls. Further down the hall there was a small reception area where flute music played softly from somewhere, and a young man sat knitting behind a counter on which sat a vase of Queen Anne's lace. Christopher stood there quietly, watching a tiny green spider tinker among the blooms. Eventually the receptionist condescended to recognize him. Saska was to be found upstairs in the meditation room.

At the top of the stairs, beside a thick wooden door like the door to a sauna, Christopher recognized Saska's boots. He kicked off his shoes and placed them neatly next to hers, and went through the door.

It was dark and completely silent. A short corridor extended ten paces or so, and then opened out into a room on the left. It was so dark that he couldn't see anything. He walked blindly down the corridor and stood in the doorway, waiting for his eyes to adjust, aware that he was exposed and visible to whomever might already be in the room. There were no lights except for a dim, Buddha-shaped nightlight low on the wall behind what appeared to be a simple shrine. He stepped forward into the darkness.

Suddenly there was a squeal, and he felt arms around his legs and a head pressing against his thigh. He let himself topple forward, landing softly on the heavy carpet, and then she was on top of him, kissing him all over his face and neck. He lay back, his hands over his head, a lancing joy in his heart.

"Hi," he said.

"Hello!" she said. "What are you doing here?"

Slowly his vision was adjusting to the darkness, and he could see her dimly above him, smiling like a minx.

"I don't know," he said honestly.

"This is one of my favorite places. No one ever comes here."

He did not know what to say.

"Are you all right?" she said.

"I don't know," he said again.

"What is wrong with you, boy?" she chided. "Did you have a rough day?"

He tried desperately to organize his thoughts, to fend off this assault. How had she learned to speak with such vulgar innuendo? From which TV program? He found it impossible to reply. He had no thoughts, just a faint babble of voices, crabby and remote, overlaid with a debilitating gladness. The darkness of the room extended for miles around.

"Talk to me," she said, grabbing his nipples and twisting. "Tell me all about it. Do you feel old? Is that it? Is life passing you by? Do you often wonder what you're going to do with your life? Do you think about having children and dying one day?"

"Yes. To all of that."

"Really!"

"Yes."

With this he was able to lift his hands from the floor and touch her the way he had dreamed of touching her. He touched the sides of her, her ribs beneath the thin fabric of her T-shirt. He traced his fingers up to her shoulders and down to her narrow hips.

"How come you did not call me?" she said.

"I didn't think I was going to see you again."

"What do you mean? Why not?"

"I don't know," he said. "I am stupid." She bent down crouching over him and put her face next to his.

"And is everything okay now?"

He could feel her tangerine breath on his neck. What could be as fine as this, to be near her and to feel this electricity jumping from her cheek, to smell the rich incense on her clothes, to lie as still as an insect beneath the bootshadow of her pretty youth?

"Okay," he said.

"Are you sure?" she asked softly.

He squinted to restrain some emotion that ballooned in answer to this question. He touched the vertebrae rising from her back and kissed her, all of this without breathing. He wanted to feel her bones.

"Wait, what are you doing?" she said.

He said nothing.

She gasped. "What if they find out! They will hear us!"

"They won't find out," he said.

"Someone will come in!"

"No one will come in."

He repositioned a pillow.

"What are you doing?" she said.

"Punishing you."

"Have I been bad or something?"

"Very bad," he said, and then added, "Now you will discover what we do to revolutionaries."

"Long live the revolution!" she cried.

Quickly he unloosed her belt and shucked off her jeans. She squealed and tipped over backwards onto the pillows, and he followed her down, melting his tongue against the hair-pricked cotton of her Spider-man Underoos.

"Christopher," she said. "Can I ask you something?"

He waited in the darkness. The thought of locating his clothes and going back outside had plunged him into despair. He was remembering an exam on tort law he had to study for. He was remembering the Krishna with the bad teeth.

"What do you want to ask me?" he said impatiently.

"Nothing," she said. "Forget it."

He would not ask her again. He was withholding his own question about the Krisha, and so it was only right that she should withhold her question—whatever it might be—as well.

But she fidgeted next to him and eventually spoke anyway.

"Do you have any extra space in your apartment?" she said in a small voice.

"Space?" he said. "For what?"

"For me, Christopher. I do not need much space. Just a little bit."

"Wait, what are you asking? You want to move in with me?"

"I swear I am a good housemate," she pleaded. "I wash my dishes all the time and I am not loud. I just need a place to live for a little while. Christopher. You are my friend, right?"

"I don't know," Christopher said.

"What do you mean you don't know!"

"I mean I don't know," he said, as a sense of personal offense gradually dawned on him. Her request was the request of a friend, and without thinking he had assumed they had finally gone past that. He was angry with himself.

"I honestly don't know what you are," he said.

"Why are you so mean to me?" she said, rolling away from him. "I don't like you anymore. You are not my kind of guy."

"Maybe not," he said bitterly, still resolved not to mention the Krishna.

"Whatever," she said, mimicking some TV teenager.

"Whatever," he said, mimicking her in turn.

"You don't understand anything," she said. "You are just a stupid boy. You don't know what it's like."

"Know what what's like?"

"Whatever," she said sullenly.

"Whatever what?"

"I don't want to talk about it."

"Talk about what?"

They lay next to each other in the dark, not touching. After a moment he reached out and took her hand, despite himself. But she pulled her hand away.

"Saska," he said irritably. "Talk about what?"

A long moment passed in which she said nothing. He waited, and when she spoke her voice was different. It was hard; there was no pretense of friendliness or supplication.

"I have to move out, okay?" she said. "I cannot live with my father anymore."

Christopher waited, staring into the darkness.

"He is not a nice guy," she added eventually.

Christopher remained silent, trying to figure out what this might mean, if it was the truth or just another lie. Regardless, it was blackmail. She was threatening him with complicity in some unnamed heinousness unless he let her move into his apartment, which wasn't big enough for her anyway.

"I am going to get away from all of you assholes," she said, rising suddenly from the floor. "I am going to go to India."

Two days later he received the call from her. She was being held in the Court Building in downtown Brooklyn.

"They won't let anyone come see me," she said. "I am stuck here with these terrible people."

"What happened? What did you do?"

"I didn't do anything! It was him! That asshole!"

"Which asshole?"

"Akhandananda!"

"The Krishna with the bad teeth?"

"What? Yes! He is such an asshole!"

Christopher was silent, wondering whether he could accuse her now, let rip the searing indictment that was bunched in his throat. But to do so would only reveal how much he loved her, and this was something he could not do. Her ignorance was all he had going for him—that and the fact that she was in jail.

"Christopher!"

"Yes. I'm here."

"I'm in jail!"

"Yes, yes," Christopher said abstractedly.

"What do you mean, *Yes, yes*? I need you to help me!"

"What about Akhandananda?"

"What do you mean what about him?"

"I mean…why don't you call him and get him to help you?"

"What are you talking about! Why are you being mean to me! I thought you were my friend!"

Christopher considered hanging up on her. He felt like he could do it. He could cut loose right now, be free of her, and let the justice system finish the job.

"Saska," Christopher said, suddenly furious, "you can't sleep with two guys and expect one of them to sympathize when the other treats you badly."

"What are you talking about! He was never my lover! You are disgusting! I can't believe you are saying these things to me!"

There was silence on the line. Christopher thought she might have hung up.

"Saska."

Silence.

"Saska."

Again there was silence.

"Saska, I'm sorry. I thought from the way you…Please. Saska. Tell me what happened so I can help you. Just let me help."

"I don't want your help," she said sullenly.

"Saska," Christopher said.

There was silence on the line. Christopher waited, wondering if there was a timer on the other end, if her coin might run out. He pictured her with a sudden brutal clarity, squirming wretchedly in some white cubicle beneath the glare of some bull dyke standing behind her with a tape gun ready to bind her up.

"I was stealing things for him," she said finally, in a soft voice. "That is all. I would steal things and give them to him and he would sell them and give me the money. I needed the money to save it up and go to India, okay?"

"Okay. So what happened?"

"I don't know. I think Akhandananda was arrested or something, and he gave my name to the cops. I am innocent. I didn't do anything."

"I thought you said you were stealing stuff."

"Yes, but that is nothing! And I never took anything from my friends. I would never do that! Christopher, everyone here is against me, and I need for you not to be against me as well, okay?

"Okay."

"I don't understand what is going on. I called my father, but he is not going to help me. He hates me most of all. It should be he—he is the one who should be sitting where I am now. I cannot stand this place. It is terrible here. Everyone is angry with me. I don't understand! Why is everyone so angry? They took my fingerprints and they said they are going to send them to Albany by email. Now everyone will know who I am. I hate this country. This would never happen in Yugoslavia."

She started crying. Christopher sighed, looking at the ceiling, trying to think of something to say.

"I don't even know when they are going to let me go. I was talking to a policeman about it. I could not believe this guy. We were talking about spirituality, and he kept talking like he knew what he was talking about. But he didn't know anything. He kept saying that all things happen for a reason because of predestination, and then he started singing this song. I am pretty sure that he was crazy. I asked him if he had read the Bhagivad Gita and he hadn't even read that."

"Saska, he was a cop. Cops don't read."

"Yes, but he couldn't even tell me what was going to happen to me. He said the judge might not let me go because the case was complicated because so many other people were involved, or something. They took my shoelaces away, and my belt, as well, and now my pants are falling down."

She sounded pitiful. Helpless. For a brief second Christopher was back with her, clutched in the darkness of the meditation room.

"Christopher. Hello?"

"Yes. I'm here. What about bail?"

"Why did they take my belt away? Do they think I am going to hang myself?"

"Saska, what about bail? Can you pay bail to get out?"

"I don't know. I called my neighbor and asked him to talk to my father for me, but I know he is not going to help me. I should never have called him. As soon as he finds that I am here he is going to go into my room and steal all my stuff. Christopher! You have to go get it for me! Will you? You have to, or my father will take it."

"Take what?"

"All of my money! Everything I have been saving to get out of this place!"

"Okay. Slowly, Saska. Tell me slowly."

He heard her sniffling on the other end of the line.

"It is beneath my bed," she said finally. "In a box. All of my money is there, all the money that I saved to go to India. Christopher, you have to get it for me. If my father thinks I am locked up, he will go into my room and take everything. You can sneak in and go get it, and while you're there, if you see my father, you can kill him for me. I can't believe this is happening. I am never going to get to India."

Christopher chewed his lip, pondering.

"Christopher. You will do this for me, won't you? You will help me?"

"Well, sure, I'm just wondering whether it might be illegal, is all."

"What are you talking about?"

"Well, sneaking into your father's house. Breaking and entering. I mean, probably not, but—"

"I thought you were my friend!"

"Saska! Of course I'm your friend! I'm more than your fucking friend!"

"Please, Christopher, do not be angry with me. Do this for me and I will do anything for you. I promise never to call you again. I will let you live your life in peace."

"What makes you think I want that? Don't you understand? I'm crazy about you."

"Liar."

"I am."

"Then I will marry you. We will get married together. We can buy a house and you can become a lawyer and I can be your trophy wife."

"Saska. You don't have to marry me. I don't want a trophy wife."

"Yes you do. I know that you do."

Fregit intravit. The unprivileged entry into or remaining in a building or other structure with intent to commit a crime.

(1) Unprivileged entry. She did give him permission. "My house is above a dentist's office. There is a sign hanging there outside my window. All you have to do is stand on the fence and climb onto the sign. From there you can go through my window. I always leave it open."

This permission was not documented, however. Furthermore, she was not the owner of the premises; nor could she be called a lessee since she did not pay rent, and so there was some question as to whether she had any legal right to dispense access privileges. It would be necessary to demonstrate that all of the items in the room were hers, and that she had lived there with some sense of propriety for a significant length of time. Even so, there was the question of whether permission to enter through a window was the same as permission to enter through a door. It could be argued that permission to enter through the window constituted a tacit acknowledgment that she did not have the right to dispense legal access privileges.

(2) With the intent to commit a crime. In this case larceny. Defined as: the (A) trespassory (B) taking and (C) carrying away of the (D) personal property of (E) another with (F) an intent to steal it.

It couldn't really be called stealing if she had asked him to take it for her. The complication was that the money itself was ill-gotten, and so there was the possibility that he could be considered an accessory after the fact. But only if: (1) the money could be considered evidence pertaining to the original crime, such that removing the money could be considered hindering the cause of justice; or (2) removing the money constituted helping the felon "personally." And anyhow, (3) if she wasn't convicted of a felony, and she might not be if they couldn't link her directly to any of the thefts, or if they did not aggregate them into grand theft, then he couldn't be considered an accessory.

At any rate, the judge would have to bear in mind the mitigating circumstances, in this case the abuse, physical or sexual, suffered by the principal at the hands of her father. If this abuse could be established, the judge would be bound to view the principal in a more sympathetic light. It would be easy to paint himself as a good samaritan, especially as (4) there was no pecuniary gain, here, to himself. On the other hand, recall the case of Delk v. the State, wherein the defendant, motivated by vengeance, took the owner's jackass from its stable, led it twenty feet away, and killed it, leaving it lying there. In this instance, the absence of pecuniary gain to the defendant did not prevent a guilty verdict.

Christopher shuddered north on the Queens-bound G line, mulling the legal implications and enjoying his last moments as a law-abiding citizen. Already he felt the stigma of illegality, the pall of malfeasance gathering around. He felt his eyes changing, and wondered if they were changing to look like hers, that hunted look that he so adored. How amazing that these specific miracles of biology, the eyes, could also somehow register as abstract a quality as guilt! He looked around the train at the other riders, absorbed in their predictable and lawful lives. Across from him a young Asian woman was reading a magazine. As the train decelerated she stood up, leaving her magazine in the seat; but then, noticing him watching her, she picked up the magazine and tore off the address label, rolling it into a ball which she put in her coat pocket.

At 6:54 p.m., the defendant exited the Queens Plaza subway station and walked north on 29th Street. He located the house at 29-42 34th Avenue without difficulty, as it was clearly marked by a dentist's sign in the shape of a tooth. Name of dentist: Rupert Malanga, DDS. The house, the last in a series of two-story row houses, was positioned on the corner at the intersection of 29th Street and 34th Avenue. A traffic light regulated the minimal traffic at this intersection. From 7:02 to 7:15 p.m. the defendant repeatedly walked back and forth across 29th Street, waiting for the light to change, presumably in an attempt to verify the presence or non-presence of occupants in the house in question. There were no lights visible either in the dentist's office or in the windows on the floor above. A chain-link fence (height: 7') enclosed a three-car parking area to the east of the dentist's office.

At 7:15 p.m. the defendant crossed 29th Street and climbed the chain-link fence. Standing on top of the fence, he was able to brace himself against the brick wall and pull himself up onto the dentist's sign, which was secured to the brick by two metal braces. Straddling the sign and facing away from the building, the defendant here noticed that he was being observed by an elderly woman sitting at the window across the street at 29-37 34th Avenue. For some moments the defendant and the woman looked at each other. Eventually the woman looked away from the defendant. The defendant noticed that an unknown person had given the woman a cup of tea, which she proceeded to drink without further reference to the defendant.

The window through which the defendant gained entry was one of two smaller windows flanking a larger picture window. The smaller windows swung outward on a track mechanism. Upon achieving entry, the defendant dropped into a squat just inside the window, remaining there for two to three minutes. Eventually the defendant rose and went to the door of the bedroom (closed) and flipped on the light switch. This had no effect, as the light switch controlled a wall socket into which nothing was plugged. The defendant then proceeded to the bed, where a lamp sat on a night table, along with a copy of *Siddhartha* by Herman Hesse. The defendant turned on the lamp and then bent to smell the pillow.

It was at this point that Mr. Janjik presented himself at the door to the room. Surprised by the sound of the opening door, the defendant turned to face Mr. Janjik. After a long moment in which the defendant and Mr. Janjik confronted each other in silence, Mr. Janjik dashed from the room in the direction of the hall closet. The defendant at once fell to his knees and began searching beneath the bed, in a moment securing a small wooden box of Persian design. With the box tucked under his left arm, the defendant proceeded with haste toward the port of entry. It is to be assumed that it was the defendant's haste which caused him to slip on the window, precipitating his fall to the sidewalk twelve feet below.

Arms wheeling and looking around wild eyed in this second-and-a-half of half-flight for any chance of saving himself, he tumbled backward toward the pavement. Even then the mind reached out, calculating possibilities and hatching plans, conducting one last mad perusal of all the facts. The thoughts flew upward out of him like vines trying to attach themselves, but there was nothing to grab onto. A loud black crack brought all this to a halt.

When he opened his eyes again, Saska's father was bending over him, shouting incoherently. Christopher was conscious of having fallen and broken something. His body was no longer his to move. He lay there, oddly calm, looking up at the bilious face floating above him. At a glance he could see where she had gotten those magnificent dark eyes, and he smiled dimly at Mr. Janjik through the storm of language. Ah, Mr. Janjik, he thought forgivingly. What an unusual daughter you have. It must be difficult not to beat her sometimes. Janjik kept screaming, boring down until his face was no more than an inch away. He had wanted to introduce himself, but found he could not talk, so he simply smiled, and closed his eyes as a kind of drunken languor stole over him. In the midst of all the racket—the siren of the ambulance and the clamor of the EMTs—he felt oddly tranquil. And as the ambulance voyaged through the streets, the thought crossed his mind that, conceivably, he and Saska might one day end up in the same cell. A wave of hilarity swept through him. Gradually his hilarity ebbed, and he collected himself, shifting slightly on the stretcher. With his arms straight at his sides, he aspired to a certain stateliness, a certain silent dignity. His mind grew calm, and he imagined a long line of pretty adolescents throwing flower petals at his feet.

Here I am in my splendid lion suit: soft flannel fabric, mitten paws, orange polyester mane. Like everything I dragged around as a kid, the lion suit had that good milky-drool scent, but the mask, when I had it on my head, smelled even better—of starch and glue, with fine undertones of mothball. Encased in the lion suit I was Lion, and only those who quaked and addressed me as such—Who's that big scary lion?—might get a glimpse of my human face.

As a child I loved dressing up in costume. It was a good way to simultaneously take on the voice of another, to tell myself a story, and to make adults pay attention to me. (What kind of idiot wouldn't listen to a talking lion?) As a writer I'm still wearing the lion suit, metaphorically speaking, though perhaps I'm a little less lion-hearted in my approach than I was when I was three years old.

Allyson Goldin's writing has appeared in the *Madison Review, Black Warrior Review,* and *Harper's Magazine,* among other periodicals. She has served as a Jay C. & Ruth Halls Fellow in Creative Writing at the University of Wisconsin, Madison, and has received an MFA in fiction writing from the University of Montana. Currently she's an assistant professor of English at the University of Wisconsin in Eau Claire, where she lives, writes, and shovels snow with her husband, poet Jon Loomis. She is at work on a novel.

THE NAMES OF OUR
MANY MISFORTUNES

Allyson Goldin

All day long, David and a small pack of neighborhood boys had galloped in and out of the house. ("Such energy!" his mother had said, looking weary.) This was February 22, 1942—Washington's Birthday, and so no school in Los Angeles. The boys stopped only for Cokes and peanut-butter sandwiches, and to argue theories about what exactly was going to happen at nine o'clock that night on the Beverly-wood Park baseball diamond. All they knew was that the Army would be holding an educational event—a demonstration of something or other—and that everyone in the neighborhood was supposed to go see it, or else.

"Prob'ly they're gonna blow up some bombs."

"Not a chance," David said, "too risky for the old folks." He clutched his hands to his heart in mock cardiac arrest. This made the other boys laugh. Gathered in front of the kitchen corkboard where David's father had pinned up the Army's invitation, they stood breathing hard from their games outside, small chests rising and falling inside slouchy cotton shirts. They studied the flier's block letters: *You and all members of your household are urged to attend, in patriotic service to our nation.* David reached up and put his finger on the big words to read them aloud: "'*An educational demonstration designed to enhance community defense.*' See?"

he said, because to him it seemed obvious. "They're going to teach us to shoot machine guns from the roof."

"They aren't either," his mother said, standing at the sink, drying cups.

She'd shaken her head at him—she did that a lot—but the other boys looked at him with their mouths open, ready to believe.

It had been a great day, thought David, and it wasn't over yet.

Now, at eight thirty-five at night, his supper eaten and the holiday from school long since finished, it was finally almost time to head to the park for the Army's demonstration, almost time to see who was wrong and who had been right all along. David wanted to think about that, about who was going to win (*rat-a-tat-tat!*), but his mother, the killjoy, was calling him, needing to know—of all things—whether he was dressed warmly enough.

David's mother, Hannah, stood in her son's bedroom holding his folded pajamas. "Why don't you wear your PJs with a jacket over top?" she said to him when he appeared in the doorway. "Then you can pop into bed as soon as we get home." She thought this was an excellent idea, a streamlining of the hours before she could sleep. Hannah was tired. The week had been hard, and she wasn't looking forward to this demonstration—wasn't up for any endgame Army theatrics. She feared the worst: gas masks; meat rationing; the issuing of first-aid kits full of gauze, antiseptic, and tape; instructions on how to stanch the bleeding; advice on how to tell a fatal wound from the kind a person might survive.

Pajamas? David looked at her horrified. He said she was—what a mouth on an eight-year-old boy!—*cracked* if she thought he was going out to the baseball diamond in his PJs. Not on her life, no way José. "You are always trying to *humiliate* me," he said, and his mother clucked her tongue to hear such a ten-dollar word from her own skinny kid. David was small for his age, with olive skin and kettle-black hair that seemed to grow faster on the very top of his head, where his curls boiled over. He had a very good head on his shoulders—everyone said so—the smartest boy in school. "What we have here," his teacher proclaimed to Hannah one afternoon, setting her two chalky hands on David's shoulders, "is an enthusiastic, lifelong reader."

This was no surprise to Hannah. She had been a reader once herself. During the summer of 1930, after the stock market had crashed and just before she had married her husband Henry, she'd read the Webster's dictionary from cover to cover while working the counter in her father's paint store. It was such a dry summer, that year. Even the sky seemed strapped, too poor to offer an evening rain. Sometimes dusty men would cup their hands to the front window and peer inside, looking to see if anyone was there. Hannah kept her eyes on the columns of words: *almoner, clonus, febrifuge.* Sometimes she practiced her new vocabulary on her father. He had bad diabetes and sat in the back room soaking his purple foot, mixing pain medicine and gin in a blue milk glass. "*Tincture.* Noun, singular," she said, watching him stir his concoction.

"Young lady," he said, "you give me a pain in my ear talking Chinese like that."

Twelve years later, listening to her son David pronounce a four-syllable jewel—*hu-mil-i-ate*—Hannah could hardly remember any of the old fancy words she had loved. She spoke the plain talk of carrots for lunch and starch in the wash. "Okay, fine," she said to David, "wear what you want." She laid his pajamas out on the bureau so they would be ready for him when he got home.

David's grandmother went to see that the stove was turned off, the refrigerator shut tight. From the hallway, she heard David say something smart alecky to his mother, her daughter. He'd used a word she didn't understand. She stopped and watched him stalk out of his bedroom in a huff. "David!" she shouted. The name was the same in Yiddish and in American. She motioned for him to come over—a crook of the upturned finger—and when he did she pinched his ear and examined his face up close. This was how she communicated—prodding an arm, wagging a finger, slapping a knee. Her grandson, she thought, was developing a good, strong jaw. She patted his cheek and pointed to the bathroom, her gesture translating: *Go. Wash.*

"Criminy," said David.

"Let's go!" shouted Henry, her son-in-law, from the foyer.

The grandmother knew Henry hated to be late. He expected them all to come running like dogs looking for leashes.

He could forget it. She passed right by him as she moved through the house, and she didn't hurry or acknowledge him. Neatly dressed in a white blouse and a gray skirt, she was wearing neither her hat nor her sweater, by which she meant to clearly demonstrate to anyone who cared to notice that she wasn't going to any Army demonstration. At her age, she'd said to Hannah, what could possibly need demonstrating? She had known corsets and washboards, borne three children, nursed them through fevers, survived an attack of the kidneys, and, from her hospital bed, watched the maimed men come back from Europe, her own brother, not so lucky. She had kept the Sabbath holy every week, except for once—God forgave her if her children didn't—many years ago when, on a hot Saturday afternoon, she kicked her husband out of the house for all of his boozing and philandering. Him she had not taken back, not ever, not when he lost his vision, not when he lost his leg, not even after he died. Now her youngest, her only son, Hy, had enlisted for this new war, and—she should pluck out her eyes—wasn't that enough to see?

In the kitchen, she checked the icebox twice. She didn't like anything to go to waste. The insulated door made a sharp, cold exhalation when she shut it firmly, as though she had made it pay sudden attention.

"Let's shake a leg!" boomed Henry, though he knew he should not be yelling, should not be rattling Hannah's nerves. Still, why the hell was it they always had to wait until the last possible minute? His wife, his son, his mother-in-law—did none of them know the pleasure of being a little bit early, of having time to park the car and walk without hurry, of getting a good seat for once in their lives?

He waited, tapping an impatient toe on the foyer floor. Henry had laid the linoleum in the foyer himself. He had also framed and hung the heavy front door. This was his new house in his new neighborhood where tonight the Army would be demonstrating something important, and he planned to arrive with his family in time to be settled and ready at exactly twenty-one hundred hours Pacific Standard Time.

"Let's get a move on!"

Earlier in the evening, he had put on a tie, then taken it off thinking perhaps it was too much, and then put it back on again, deciding, on second thought, that the demonstration at the baseball diamond might be a solemn occasion. Preparation for bombings was no laughing matter. And anyway, it was better his new neighbors see him looking overdressed than looking shabby. There was a war on, after all, which made everything one did seem more noteworthy. Also, the summons to the demonstration had been sober enough. It came as a cardboard flier, printed and undersigned by the municipality and the Army Local Office No. 71: *You and all of your family are urged to attend…*

Henry, exempt from enlistment, believed in the war. Wasn't everything, wasn't life as they knew it at stake? And if you believed the rumors from Europe (Henry worked with a fellow named Lemkin whose letters to his sister in France were returned to him, the addresses struck through by bolts of black ink), wasn't the war for them, as Jews, an even more personal affair?

When the notice of the demonstration had come, Henry had pinned it to the kitchen corkboard himself and told his wife at dinner, "We are going to this thing. *All* of us." He'd gestured toward the private side of the house where his mother-in-law ate her meals alone, off her kosher plates and forks, under the paltry light of a single burning candle. She would not sit at table with them in a kitchen where spoons which stirred cream into the morning coffee appeared later the same day in bowls of lamb stew.

The old woman's stubbornness hurt Henry's wife, and obliged all of them, out of Hannah's strange, injured guilt, to attend monthly Shabbat dinners at Hannah's sister Marla's house, where the kitchen was kept hot, hot, hot, and strictly kosher. Marla ignored Henry on purpose, and her obese husband Sol sniffed loudly while he ate.

"Does he plan to digest his food inside his sinuses?" Henry asked once, complaining to Hannah after one of these meals.

"We have to eat as a family once in a while," Hannah said, as she always

Allyson Goldin

did when Henry objected to the journey to Marla's, or to the company, or to the stultifying meal. He'd argue: "*We're* not the ones preventing meal-time togetherness, you know. Your mother could come out of her hole once in a while. Your mother could show some flexibility." But there was no reasoning through this problem. Reason—mighty solver of conflict and builder of nations—did not apply in this case. It only led to the battlement of Hannah's aghast expression. She looked at him, on these occasions, as though he had just slaughtered a bunny rabbit in front of her and handed her the bloody knife. "Oh, for god sakes," he'd say.

But Henry loved his wife, and decided, when he got right down to it, that a dozen dinners a year with Marla and Sol wasn't such a burden to bear. On the other hand, he felt that as the head of his household—as the one who had in fact built, with a few of his friends, every wall, floor, joist, and ceiling of his home—he was entitled once in a while to get his own way. He made his message plain and clear: "We are *all* going to this demonstration. No exceptions."

David washed his hands and face and dropped the towel in the sink. Here, in his parents' pink porcelain bathroom at the back of the house, was some privacy and quiet. He could do what he wanted while he was alone, so he pressed his thumb into the soft metal belly of the Colgate tube. For three weeks he had been looking forward to the demonstration, maybe even more than he looked forward to fireworks and fishing trips and presents from his Uncle Hy, who would soon be leaving to fight in the war. Today, all day, he'd felt the tingle of excitement, like radio static under the skin, and no matter how fast he ran and played it didn't go away. Surely, even if the Army wasn't going to issue him his very own machine gun, he would be allowed tonight—at last—to fire a real gun loaded with a real bullet.

With the demonstration so close, his anticipation had become pleasurable. He wanted to stay in the bathroom for a little while more, wanted to feel his own heart beating, and think about things without having to talk. He'd heard his father shout, "Let's go!" and, "Shake a leg!" but David knew from long experience that his father would yell

196

and yell, would rattle his keys, and then, finally, would stalk out the front door as though he were leaving everyone behind and go start the car. This last, the roar of the Chevrolet, always sent him and his mother running. There was time.

He glanced around. Someone—okay, maybe it was him—had left his mother's Webster's dictionary on the back of the toilet. He liked the book, leather-bound, red, smelling lightly of sawdust and glue. Plus, there were things tucked inside: pressed pansies, faded coupons for stuff like light bulbs and nail polish, and once he had found a note written in his mother's hand. It said, "Meet you back here at three o'clock. Sorry!" He grabbed up the heavy book and sat down on the edge of the bathtub to have a flip through, but he stopped at *C* thinking of a word, what it meant and how it was spelled.

Cancer. David knew cancer, knew what it was. Of course, dummy, everyone knew what it was—a disease! A disease where your whole body turns black and you blow away like ashes from a fireplace. Still, David didn't know *exactly* what it was—did it start with a *C* or a *K* anyway?—and he wasn't going to ask his mother, who had shaken her head sadly when Aunt Marla, dropping off his cousins for the day on Wednesday, had followed her down to the rumpus room. He could tell they had secrets by the way they shoved him out the door, and so he ran around to the window to spy. Marla reached her hand out toward his mother and put it right *there*—right under his mother's armpit. "My god," she said, feeling around like a doctor does. She pulled her hand away and clasped it up against her own big boobs. Then she whispered something loud enough to hear. "Do you think it's…" This is what Aunt Marla had said.

He found what he was looking for on page 200, between *campground* and *candid*—but he didn't know *tumor, propensity,* or *malignant.* This was the trouble with dictionaries. They led you around by the nose.

David stuck his finger in the book to keep his place and flipped to *M.* Then he heard his mother come into her bedroom. It had to be his mother; his father was ready, and would not leave his post in the foyer. Her bracelets clinked.

Please, thought David, please leave me alone.

• • •

Hannah had seen that her husband was wearing a tie and his dress shoes, and so she had hurried back to her bedroom to find a scarf and some earrings, and to change her blouse, which was spattered with spinach at the sleeve. She should change her shoes, too, she thought, but she worried about mud. All those people walking over the baseball field—surely the grass and the dirt would emulsify. It had been so damp lately. Mornings, the lawn was slick with dew.

She would bring a coat. A sweater. No, a coat, and the green scarf, and she would not change her shoes.

It was hard to know how to dress when one didn't know what the demonstration would entail. What was the point of all the mystery? Mrs. Rassmen next door said that whatever the Army did, she was sure the noise of it would scare her poodle, who was bound in that case to pee all over his bed. Mrs. Levy at the bakery joked that the Army had a golem, god forbid. "A golem with a Social Security number," she said. Mr. Levy said he pictured marching drills, Army officers lining all the neighbors up into single-file lines and helping them to march in formation—left, right, left—never mind the mud. But of course this was ridiculous! Even he said so. What advantage could there be in teaching the neighborhood to march? Probably, Hannah thought—and she felt a chill—it would only be another informational session about how to survive an enemy attack. For this they had to gather in the dark of night? Ever since Hawaii was bombed, she and her neighbors had been receiving pamphlets and had been practicing the blackout drills. She already knew what to do: get David down to the rumpus room and press her body over his. In her opinion, these Army men could better spend their time playing pinochle than explaining to mothers what to do if bombs were to fall around their children. Mothers knew.

Hannah took a fresh blouse from the closet, cranberry colored, and began to unbutton the old.

Evil in nature, influence, or effect, read David in the bathroom. *Passionately and relentlessly malevolent: aggressively malicious. Tending to produce death.* This definition was at the bottom of page 721, and he had to run his finger under the lines to read them. The book teetered on the knobs of his knees, and the words sounded loud to him, like the voice of the baseball coach, who, when he wanted the boys to do push-ups, shouted, "Hit the deck! Hit the deck!" David lifted his eyes from the page. He blinked, trying to keep the loud words from colliding with the sounds of his mother in her bedroom. Suddenly, the dictionary toppled backward and fell, deadweight—first on its side and then on its front. It made two loud thumps and slid out to the center of the bathroom, with its pages splayed from the bottom like an Oriental fan.

"David!" shouted his mother from outside the door. "Is that you in there?"

David scrambled to pick up the book. A couple of the pages had ripped. Also, his mother's flowers, pressed and folded into wax paper, had scattered over the floor.

"Stay there. Don't come out until I say so. I'm changing."

"Okay," said David. He couldn't believe his luck. He gathered up the pansies, put them back between the leaves, and smoothed out the dictionary. The ripped pages were hardly noticeable, unless you turned right to them, which didn't seem likely since they were buried deep, deep down into the center of the book.

Hannah stood beside her dressing table in her brassiere, which hurt her, or maybe she only imagined it did. Dr. Burns had said, "Don't touch," but she couldn't help it. She slid her left hand under the thick elastic strap, and pressed her fingers over the lump that lay under the skin at the top of her breast just at the edge of her armpit. It had been there for maybe a week before she had mentioned it to Henry. It felt like nothing. A nothing like the end of a potato lopped off, a small dome of vegetable matter. She was to have her biopsy tomorrow.

Dr. Burns had come over to examine her after poor Henry, rubbing his forehead, had called him and had said in a controlled voice, "I'm sorry to bother you at home, Doctor, and on a Sunday, but…"

Dr. Burns was a kind man. "It's probably nothing, honey," he'd said. Hannah had looked up from where she'd lain on her bed and studied Dr. Burns's face to see what she could see. Her husband, her hale and proud man-of-reason, had echoed Dr. Burns like a clerk receiving instructions—"Probably nothing." Hannah had watched Henry's worry fade from around his tight mouth. He'd nodded his head and believed.

"Twenty to nine!" shouted Henry, and he knew he shouldn't be shouting, but great God almighty. What was taking his family so long? He jangled his keys, cleared his throat. "Let's move it now! Let's get going!"

Everyone in the family heard him.

Hannah put on her blouse and buttoned it quickly.

David sat down on the lid of the toilet with the Webster's dictionary on his lap.

The grandmother shrugged. She walked through the pantry and back to her room, avoiding the foyer where she knew her son-in-law's blood pressure was rising. Let it rise, she thought, he's young and strong. She hung her cardigan up in the closet and sat down at the card table to read her Yiddish newspaper, an expensive paper full of bad news. The pages were yellow and brittle, and the ink, if you set your hand on it, smeared. The grandmother read it, as much as possible, with her hands folded in her lap.

Henry felt a film of sweat emerging in the small of his back. The house had fallen suddenly silent and this drove him crazy. It spoke of a lack of progress, maybe even of *backsliding*. It meant, he was sure, that nobody in the house was listening to him. Henry took a deep breath and held it. He paced a few steps back and forth, making much of his footfalls. He looked at his watch. He would call for them one or two more times and then he would go to the car, he thought, except that he could not leave without them, could not even pretend to leave without them because, first of all, the whole family was expected at the demonstration, and second—Henry wasn't an ass—he was *not* going to walk out in a temper the night before his wife's biopsy operation, come hell or high water, even though she said she felt fine; probably she was fine. *I feel fine*, she said, whenever he asked, and the simple sentence made him want to kiss her with the urgent passion of a man who has been on a terrible, long, and dangerous journey. *There's my girl, there's my girl!*

This was a good sign—wasn't it?—that Hannah felt all right, or said she did? Henry couldn't tell. There was no way to predict one way or another, but it couldn't be a *bad* sign, could it? Nobody knew. The difficult thing was that nobody knew anything.

When Henry had walked Dr. Burns to his car Sunday evening after Hannah's examination, the man had said it, plain and simple: "We won't know anything until we have the biopsy results."

"Sure, sure."

"Henry," he'd said, turning and stopping, "these things are sometimes nothing, sometimes cysts that go away by themselves, but then they can be something, too—I know I don't have to tell you. And then I just want you to be prepared. As one friend to another. It could be a very hard year."

Henry had known Dr. Burns for a long time, for half his life at least. Dr. Burns had been the most popular family doctor in Boyle Heights, Henry's old neighborhood. He had attended Henry's wedding, had brought David into the world. When Henry and his family had moved to Beverlywood, Dr. Burns welcomed them in high style. He and his wife Rose threw them a dinner party—candles and linens, a whipped chocolate mousse—and made a champagne toast. Now they all went to the same synagogue. Dr. Burns would be at the demonstration, too.

"I understand," Henry said. They were standing in the driveway, their white shirts stark against the black night sky.

"Right now, keep her calm, keep her positive. Life should go on as usual, but keep things settled down. Don't let her get too excited. I'm going to try to get her in for the biopsy on Friday morning. I want you to come along. Friday will be all right?"

"Fine," said Henry. "Yes. I'll be there. We'll both be there."

Dr. Burns clasped him on the arm and ducked into his sedan. Henry patted the car as the Doctor drove away.

But Henry didn't go back inside immediately. He stood for some time in the darkness looking at his house, at the way the lights poured gold through the windows and splashed onto the front steps. Since moving in, Henry had stood on those steps, feeling his large feet resting on the brick that rested on the cement that rested on his land, his property, the piece of Los Angeles that was *his*. One could stroll the perimeter of his property for a good two minutes. One could dig down and down into it, clear to the center of the Earth, given strength and time. It seemed to him a crying shame, nowadays, that a man looking at the handsome glow of his home had to wonder, right away, what the same glow might mean to an airplane pregnant with bombs.

Hannah came out looking for him, squinting toward the driveway. She stood in the wash of electric light pouring through the front door. It soaked her—the light—turning her green pantsuit vivid as moss, illuminating the tips of her ears and her fingers, and lighting up the thin silver chain that swam over her collarbone—a moon snake. Henry's bricks and concrete and dirt, the whole measured tonnage, all of it would melt away in time, he knew. He went to his wife—one, two, three steps toward her—and then she could see him, and she was smiling her half-smile, one hand on her hip, as though nothing in the world were wrong with her.

"I thought you got lost," she said, and Henry put his arms around her, and smelled the lemony scent of her hair, and kissed the hot skin at the back of her neck. When she eventually said, "Okay, Mister, I've got dishes to do," Henry still wouldn't let her go.

And so what was he thinking, bellowing at her like a ship's captain the night before her biopsy? He would go get his wife and walk her to the car. He'd loop her hand into the warm crease of his elbow and together they would shepherd the boy and the old woman to the car—ten, fifteen steps—and the four of them would ride calmly, sweetly, to the demonstration at the neighborhood baseball diamond. It started in seventeen minutes.

How hard could that possibly be?

Hannah looked away from her vanity mirror where she was doing a rush job on her lipstick and heard her husband's heavy footsteps coming down the hall. A moment later Henry appeared in the doorway.

"How're we doing?" he said.

This wasn't like him, to be barging in on her this way.

"Ready," said Hannah, but the word sounded brittle even to her. Henry's new vigilance was driving her crazy. It was scaring her, and was that really necessary? She turned, drew a tissue out of the box, and blotted her lipstick. "I just need a purse."

"Okay, sooooo, get a purse." He smiled a smile like David might smile when forced to stand for a photograph, and Hannah didn't like it, Henry's masking his impatience so obviously—coddling her. She went to the bureau and found her black clutch.

"Henry," she said, annoyed. "Go find your son."

"I'm *here*!" shouted David from the bathroom. Hannah had forgotten him. He burst through the door holding the dictionary, which he hot-potatoed to his father. "Let's go, for crying out loud!" He looked at his mother accusingly. She did not know why he seemed so angry with her tonight.

"Okay, head on out," said Henry, tossing the dictionary onto the bed. It bounced once and settled. David ran out into the hallway, feet pounding.

"Why don't you go start the car," Hannah said to Henry. She scrambled to transfer her wallet, comb, and lipstick from the big purse to the small. Henry stood stiffly with his hands spread wide at his sides. "For god's sake," she said, "don't just stand there. Go!"

David's grandmother heard her grandson whipping through the house and knew it was time for the family to leave. She turned the front page of her newspaper and continued to read with willful serenity, even as she heard David circle back and then saw him, out of the corner of her eye, standing in the doorway on his two skinny legs. He said to her, "Ready?"

She looked at him with mild interest and then turned back to her paper. *Pogrom*, it said, first paragraph, page two—an article about the War. *Pogrom*: a Russian word, darker than Russian bread, a word too dark to see by. She stared at it and, for no reason at all, thought about the diabetes that had taken her husband's leg. She had not visited her husband during the end of his life, but her daughter Hannah had. The day after the amputation, Hannah had come back from the hospital and said, "Pop wants his leg back, to bury it or something, but the hospital told him it's already gone." Hannah had spoken this sentence in a tone of amused derision—*Crazy Papa! What can you do?*—but the grandmother had been filled with deep sorrow and regret, worse than knowing her husband was having affairs, worse than the grief of a brother's youthful death. This was a sorrow that felt meant for her alone, as though she had been designated to mourn for all of her own lost mercy. *Has my heart really grown so bitter?* She concluded that it had. On that day, she took to her bed, and she stayed there for such a long time that her daughter had to ask the doctor to bring over some pills.

David stood waiting and rocked on his heels until his father came up behind him. "Bubbi's not coming with," said David.

"What's this?" said Henry, taking over his son's place in the doorway.

"*Ich gai nicht*," said the grandmother.

"You have to go," said Henry, glancing at his watch. Eight forty-seven. There was no more time. Unless they left within two minutes, they would officially be late. "Everyone has to go." *Late, late.*

"She won't come with," said David.

"All *right*, son. Keep quiet." His voice came out graveled and loud. He had roared, though he hadn't meant to do it, hadn't meant to talk above a whisper, but here was Hannah, rushing to the scene. "Don't run!" he told her, yelling again.

"What're you barking about?"

"Bubbi wants to stay home," said David. He was shaking his hands at the wrist, his fingers flailing in an anxious blur.

"Oh, Ma," said Hannah, "come on. It's time to go."

Henry walked into his mother-in-law's room, went to her closet, took out her sweater, and handed it to her. His mother-in-law raised her hand, dismissing him as she might dismiss a plate of cookies at the end of a long lunch. "*Ich gai nicht*," she repeated.

"Why are you going to make this trouble?" said Hannah.

"No," said the grandmother. She would speak their language if they needed to understand her better. She looked to where her daughter stood. "No, no, no, no, no." She was not going out to consort with people from the Army. The Army was no friend of hers. And besides, what did it profit an old woman to go into the dark of night among strangers? She could catch pneumonia. Treading over unfamiliar ground, she could trip and fall and break a hip. She might see someone from the old days and have to explain. Worst of all, she could encounter, for the first time, things she couldn't explain, shadowy things, and then what? To die confused and disoriented? These pogroms, these "modern wars"—she intended to keep out of them. She intended to eat a piece of the only slightly stale cake she kept in *her* room for *herself*, off *her* plate, with *her* fork, alone and in peace. "For-*get* it," she said in her throaty, thick-tongued accent.

"Mother!" said Hannah.

In Henry's hand the grandmother's sweater shook slightly. He was looking down onto the top of his mother-in-law's head where, in certain patches, he could see her scalp coming through, threadbare. Since they had moved into the new house, Henry had thought of his mother-in-law, at certain uncharitable moments, as a shoddy old chair that ought to be cast out onto the front lawn for scavengers. He pressed his lips together, and turned to Hannah, who shrugged. "Well," he said—but he wanted to bellow his anger, he wanted to hiss a string of vile words. He hung the sweater on the back of her chair, and, sweating with the effort of containment, walked back to his wife and son. "If she's not going, she's not going," he said. "There's no sense in all of us being late."

To everyone's surprise David punched the air with his fists and screamed and howled. "She *has* to go! We *all* have to go! We have to go *together*! How can you let her stay? How can you leave her here? We have to go *together*!"

The grandmother got up from her chair. What had gotten into the boy?

"David, honey. It's all right," said Hannah. "Are you afraid we're

going to get into trouble? We're not going to get into any trouble."
She leaned down to rub David's back, and she looked up at Henry. "I
think he thinks we're going to get in trouble," she said.

"Hey, buddy," said Henry. "There's nothing to cry about here. There's
nothing to cry about. Everything's fine. Stop crying now." Henry felt
disoriented. It was as though David had taken the rage from his own
throat. "Come on, little man. Let's go get some air." He picked up his
boy and headed for the front door.

David twisted against his father's arms and then, all at once, collapsed over his big shoulder, and let go with his sobs. He cried so
hard, he couldn't mark his father's footfalls through the foyer, out of
the house, down the steps, across the walk. He rubbed his face into
the rough gabardine of his dad's sport coat and smelled camphor. His
father clasped him close. David felt the big warm hand on his back,
the same hand that sometimes held a fine nail in place, risking the
smash of the steel-headed hammer. David cried.

"Oh, you're a heavy one," said Henry.

His mother followed, unfolding a handkerchief.

His grandmother, stubborn old woman, closed the front door behind them.

They were not late. People drifted into the demonstration until nearly
twenty after nine, so Henry and Hannah even had time to wait in the
car until David's breathing had quieted to a subtle sniffle. Folding chairs
had been set all over the baseball diamond, and volunteers from the
Army recruitment office helped with seating. Floodlights, hung from
poles or from the chain-link backstop, provided plenty of illumination.
Not too far away, a generator hummed. The volunteers handed out
small pamphlets which read: *Black out the windows! Block out the enemy!*
On the backs of these pamphlets were cartoon pictures of wide eyes
open in the dark. "Don't worry," the volunteers said. "There are no bad
seats." Henry and Hannah and David perched themselves on a small
stand of bleachers from where they could see everything.

Henry looked at his watch as people he recognized from the synagogue jogged in from the side streets. Mrs. Rassman and her husband

strolled. Dr. Burns and his wife were two of the last to arrive, but they didn't hurry. They walked together calmly, expressions placid, maybe even a trace bored. Henry felt his own face flush. Shouldn't there be more concern for schedules? The Jews of Beverlywood assembled slowly.

Hannah put her hand in Henry's.

David hung his head a little. He didn't want to meet his friends with his face still red from crying.

At last a man in a splendid blue uniform—black belt, white gloves, and a hat set so precisely on his head he must have used a level—strode out onto the green lawn. He stopped a yard or two behind third base and stood stiffly, facing the crowd, feet together. David examined him. He didn't seem to have a gun. He didn't, on David's closer scrutiny, seem to be carrying any weapon at all. How could a soldier not have a gun? Didn't a soldier, whose days were dangerous, at least get to carry a pistol for protection, like any corner cop? David had a fearful feeling then, a feeling that the soldier standing before them was about to be killed, that someone hidden, perhaps crouched at that very moment behind the bleachers or between two rows of seats, was going to step out and shoot the soldier in the head—a quick spray of blood over the outfield, the body dropping like a rag in a butcher shop. This demonstration would be a demonstration of how easy it was to die. Don't be stupid, David told himself, but he was afraid. He turned to his mother.

A voice sounded then—not from the soldier—a voice low and reassuring, emanating from everywhere through a circle of small speakers: "Thank you for coming tonight, ladies and gentlemen. The following is a demonstration designed to help you understand the importance of the blackout drills your neighborhood will participate in more and more frequently. To enhance this demonstration, streetlights in this sector of the city will be turned off in approximately thirty seconds. At that time, the lights illuminating this field will also be turned off, and hopefully it will be good and dark. For your safety, we ask you to keep your seats and remain quiet, please."

The lights died with an audible pop and hiss. Everyone waited. Hannah drew a breath, put her arm around David. He trembled, poor thing. She held him closer, pressed him into the side of her body, the palm of her hand covering his ear. *My baby.* How she wanted to go home, tuck him in like she did every night, say the things she always said: *Finish your homework? Brush your teeth? Sweet dreams, my little boy.* But they were at the baseball diamond in the middle of the night—Why? What for?—and the crowd was silent. She felt Henry tighten his grip around her fingers. No one said a thing. Hannah feared any second there would be a sudden, earsplitting noise…

Many years from that night, when David was himself a father and a doctor of internal medicine, living in a big house full of books that overlooked the ocean, he would say to scientist friends, "I don't know why, but a woman always knows beforehand when she has breast cancer." In the silence that followed his statement, while his scientist friends looked at him, faintly amused, he would remember the night of the demonstration, when a single soldier—a boy, really—had stood alone on the dark baseball field, had lit a small candle, and had held it at chest level. An amplified voice warned them of danger: "Do you see how much light a single flame makes?" That was the gist of it—but what David recalled most vividly was how the moon was only a shred of fingernail in the sky and how, as they had driven the slow three miles through Beverlywood on their way to the baseball diamond, all the people on the sidewalks had looked like elegant shadows against the silvery fronts of newly built homes. In particular, David remembered how kind his father and his mother had been that night in the car, each with a hand upon him, calming him, reminding him about how much he had been looking forward to the demonstration, and of how much fun they were all going to have. His father parked and didn't make them hurry. His mother dug mints out of her purse and unwrapped three sweet, hot pinwheels—one at a time. She wiped David's face with her handkerchief, looked into his eyes, and smiled. *Pumpkin.* His father tousled his hair and called him *my man.* David saw the two of them looking at each other over his head.

"Let's go," said his father, finally, opening the car door.

It was the last night—the night before they all knew the names of the many misfortunes that, even at that very moment, were flying down upon them like a net cast out of heaven.

My world seems beautifully in order, which must be why I look so happy: lots to read, arranged in a nice fan, and the only doll I ever owned, Tiny Tears, at rest. My brother had an enormous collection of comics, including the Classics Illustrated *ones. He must have been in a very generous mood to trust me with these; and so all was well throughout the house.*

Katherine Vaz, a Briggs-Copeland lecturer in creative writing at Harvard University, is the author of two novels: *Saudade* (St. Martin's Press, 1994), a Discover Great New Writers selection by Barnes & Noble; and *Mariana*, in six languages, selected by the Library of Congress as one of the Top 30 International Books of 1998. Her collection *Fado & Other Stories* won the 1997 Drue Heinz Literature Prize. This is her second story in *Glimmer Train*.

THE LOVE LIFE OF
AN ASSISTANT ANIMATOR

Katherine Vaz

A naked woman got hidden inside every film. Nathan Porter knew that; everyone knew that. The animators would slip one drawing into every episode, and the speed of the film made her disappear. She was there but not there. Spreading her legs or holding her bare breasts—the animators got bored and it was their fun. Maybe children watching their Saturday-morning cartoons were getting dirty pictures imprinted on their brains. But soon enough everyone gets to carry around desires so deep that often he doesn't know he's having them.

Did anyone ever die in your arms? That was a question often put to Nathan after Vietnam. People needed to look at someone who had looked at that. They wanted to paint a few scenes and run them together, to enjoy the shudder at a distance, coloring in the details at their leisure—the jungle one hundred shades of green. *Did you kill any babies. Did you have to duck.* He was tall, six-five. Six feet by the time he was thirteen in Michigan, lying under the piano while his mother played sonatas, like George Sand listening to Chopin. Nathan was growing so fast his bones hurt if he stood too long. He'd eat a quart of strawberry ice cream at a time, but the pink film barely soothed him, and once he'd screamed because he hadn't asked to be skin and bones and hunger. It was sexual in a way he couldn't define when people said, *Tell me what it was like*, and their eyes widened. He was one of the lucky ones, he said. Built like a jackknife, his eye level higher than most, on one of the first helicopters out of Saigon. No one had died in his arms. He never connected the bullets he fired to the sound of a man falling. He would never tell anyone about the girl in the sand. He would not let people bury her in the starring role, the best part of the movie they were begging Nathan to insert into their heads. That had always distinguished him: a far-reaching code on the subject of betrayal.

He also possessed a disturbing aptitude for patience. Nathan suspected that it came from an inability to accept certain truths, a belief that if he only waited long enough the world would see the wisdom of what he wanted, and some dovetailing of fate would bring it to him. At the University of Michigan, he had perched in a tree for five hours to win a keg of beer for his dormitory. He once did sketches of a nude woman for twenty consecutive hours, after the rest of the class had left, because he had to capture her perfectly, and the model wanted to be caught perfectly, and he fell a bit in love to discover that her ability to fix herself and not move matched his own.

That was how he ended up, after the war, at age twenty-three, as an assistant animator at the Delmar Studios in West Los Angeles. The work required drawing skills and maniacal patience. Nathan's Uncle Sid, in story development at Disney, called East Lansing with news about the job; everyone wanted to pry Nathan out of his dark, childhood bedroom with its Wolverine pennants. *Union wages. Benefits. California's fried white sunshine.* Nathan couldn't admit that he wanted to be a famous artist, and assistant animation seemed a suitable bluff. One more night of his mother making him Ovaltine and he would sob worse than the time that his Jack Russell terrier, Dorothy, had run under the wheels of a car before he could save her.

Delmar Studios, a low-lying, yellow building, was on Pico Boulevard and bore the spray paint of the Sawtelle 13 gang pushing west and the Santa Monica 13 gang going east. Before the janitor painted yellow again over the letters, Nathan could size up who was winning the night wars. Yellow over black over red—the toxic skins were piling up. The studio was one of the lesser ones, with one minor cartoon series and one hit, called *The Hive*, about bees who solved animal crimes.

Nathan perched at his light board in a small room with Jen and Barbara, the other assistant animators. The lights stabbed brightness through their eyes and burned into their skulls. Nathan would do his time, and, instead of coveting a promotion to animator, he'd try for character development, the highest-paying job. Then he would quit and paint for the rest of his life. His patience wasn't dutiful so much as calculating. He had ambition. There was no point in having spellbinding patience unless it was attached to a leap ahead.

He hardly spoke to the women flanking him. Barbara was a collector of slights, real and imagined, and her flesh expanded to contain them. Jen had dots for eyes, a round head, thin lips, and short brown hair with bangs, like a child's drawing of a woman. They both enjoyed disliking their husbands, and then did all they could to impart to Nathan that he could not claim to be a true adult until he drank deeply from the cup of marital bliss. Every afternoon at four, Jen's daughter called to report that she was home from school, and Jen chanted, "I love you, Mathilda. Did you hear me? I said, 'I love you, Mathilda.' What do *you* say? Remember our talk? *I love you.* What? Louder, dear."

When Nathan closed his eyes, his parents were still waving farewell to him through their double-paned windows. The Remington bronco rested on the cherrywood table. At the vanishing point while driving away, he turned, and a jolt of realism almost undid him, to see them reduced to small figures under glass, contained in a paperweight. In his mind the house shook and covered them with a flurry of gold glitter.

An animator would draw: *Jen looking at phone. Then: Jen talking into phone.*

The assistants were the in-betweeners. They drew each incremental stage between the main poses, tilting the tracing paper to go a fraction farther into the action, ten steps of a phone closing in on an ear. A mouth redrawn ten times in the spaces between "I L-o-v-e Y-o-u." Replicating life at its slowest speed. Honoring every nuance of motion. Spending days on the wings of flying bees. The cell painters recreated each step in color. When speeded up, the cells blurred into continuous action. *Answer the phone, I love you.*

Nathan defrosting enchiladas at his apartment on Kiowa off Bundy. Na-

than alone in bed. Thousands of steps in between, drinking a beer with *I love you* ringing in his ears, jogging on San Vicente Boulevard, *I love you, love, love,* Nathan at his Uncle Sid's in Pasadena, a shipshape Arts and Crafts bungalow, enduring stories from World War II, the last true war with a real enemy, Nathan hurrying away, not trading stories of his own. He must protect the girl in the sand. Nathan at home, painting irises in oils and throwing them away; after Van Gogh, who can dare a purple flower? Vincent was loved by his brother, but it did not save him. *No one loves you enough, Mathilda, and I like you for knowing it.*

Nathan meeting a woman. Nathan at their parting. An average of three thousand animated steps per day and still the film misses half the beats.

The glaring, unmoving sky made him sneeze. *You're allergic to the sun,* said Becky, a girl with a black mini-dress and green sunglasses. He met her in line at the Westward Ho Market. A scratcher in bed. A three-week affair. Affair? Collision. *Fucking A, the sun hates you, how can you stand your bad luck?*

One morning at work, a high voice entered him, right through his skin. It was coming from someone unseen, in the hallway. He had the odd but not disagreeable sensation of something familiar that he could not name. It was a shock that he first took for pain and then realized was pleasure; it hurts when the clay cracks off a man who's been dead. Right away he felt he was wrong; the sound was high but it was low, too. The voice had everything at once—but not in a jumble. Articulated. He surrendered. Who could describe it?

The music of it was so generous that it also lit up Jen and Barbara. Jen said, "Oh, good. I guess Mrs. Delmar has come back."

Violet Delmar owned a prize voice. She'd narrated an opera series for television and got called in to do wildlife programs, Disney heroines. Her voice-over for a Tide commercial was said to earn her fifty thousand a year from residuals. She had already been streaming into Nathan's head for years. Journalists tried to capture her tone with overused words—*silk,* say—but silk was silk and Violet was Violet. It was reasonable to think that Norman Delmar had taken money out of his wife's voice to open his animation studio.

214

Nathan first saw her inside the sound booth, recording tracks for some female roles in the cartoons. She was in her late thirties, and although she wasn't heavy, she had hips that no amount of exercise would reduce. Though this was utterly foreign to him, he found himself not unmoved by such a predicament. Her red hair seemed prematurely thin. She had on a white blouse and a denim skirt that hit mid-calf, but that a woman could unbutton up the middle as high as she liked, and Mrs. Delmar undid hers to slightly above the knee. Her stockings had vivid designs.

Nathan was among the employees who arranged their coffee breaks to listen to Mrs. Delmar. She usually came in at ten in the morning to do her recordings. There were Sam Edelson, an animator, a cell painter named Lisa, and Liz from Accounting. Nathan had a mild crush on Liz, who was forty-eight but was still wearing white lipstick and dying her hair jet black. He was fixated upon the beauty mark near her left eye. He commented about the high and low of Violet's voice, and Liz grabbed his arm and said, "That's it! Every word's got top notes and bottom notes. Like a perfume does."

Notes, perfume—their connection was a mystery to him.

One time Violet finished early and emerged from the booth, and Sam broke into applause. Violet blushed rather horribly. Nathan accepted this as the condition of people who are not quite beautiful. They are particularly shy when reminded that they are stuck forever in their own skins. Her earrings were orange fish, like garibaldis. She caught Nathan's eye, as if the woman who was a famous voice needed help in knowing what to say. He blurted, "Where does it come from?"

What did he mean? Star power? Her voice? Getting paid for being purely who you were, because of some innate quality?

She appeared grateful, and touched the front of her neck. He wasn't sure how she understood what he had asked, since he didn't know himself. "My mother sang me very nice lullabies," she said. "They got stuck in my throat instead of my head."

She was awkward at even this type of minor parting, and said, "Goodbye, my lovelies," the sign-off from *The Hive*. She put on a sun hat with cherries, the kind on sale at seaside resorts.

When he climbed back into his chair to resume work, Barbara said, "Isn't Liz married, Nathan?"

He stared at her. "To a nice man. As you already know."

"I was just wondering if you did."

"I didn't know it was against the law to speak to married women, Barb."

"She probably just needed help ratting her black helmet," said Jen.

"Liz is terrific," he said, loudly. "I like her."

They looked pale and boiled as they stared down at the lights, and traced such precise stages of larks in descent that they seemed to be gunning them down in slow motion. He would never comprehend why it made him such an unusual breed, to resist attacking a friend. To refuse joining the mob in feasting. *Why are the fish hurting that one, Dad? It's sick, Nathan. We'll remove it so it can die in peace.* He loathed anyone who could savage you behind your back and then look you in the eye. Part of this was virtuous, but most of it wasn't. He hated trying to guess what was going on inside someone, what someone really thought of him. Jen could be cruel about Liz's hair and then go have tea with her and nothing would seem like betrayal. Jen and Barbara would age right here and dissolve into X-rays while the Sotel 13 and SM 13 armies battled through the night.

His chance to escape arrived with the news from Liz that the studio was about to close contracts for two new shows, *A Rare Bird* and some space-age thing. Barry Wills was the inventor of characters, but would need to hire one new person, maybe two. Nathan had drawn a portrait of Liz that she had tacked up in Accounting, and she would never speak to him again if he did not apply for the job. "Hurry up and get famous, Nathan," she said. "I want to sell your picture of me and retire from this dump."

He handed his portfolio to Barry Wills on the same day that Violet Delmar stopped coming in to record voice-overs. She was out auditioning for movies, and it was not unpleasing to think of her taking the next step upward in a sort of parallel ascension to his own. The question remained whether she would, with her shyness, cross over from being a hidden star—in lesser avenues—to a visible presence.

"Good luck, Mrs. Delmar, and good luck to me," he announced while standing at his sink, eating a fried-egg sandwich.

Barry Wills kept him waiting—days of pretending not to see Nathan strolling by his office. Wills had a room to himself, where he read scripts and dreamed up creatures that got stuck into the memories of children.

Nathan went to the planetarium ("Why Mars Looks Like Fire") and met a medical student, Jasmine, who laughed about her parking tickets and moving violations. Was this a good thing, he asked, for a future doctor to collect moving violations? Didn't that imply harm? *It implies speed, that's all.* She asked about the medics in Vietnam. He said tape, glue, hacksaws, screaming, what did he know. *What do you know, Nathan? Do you like drawing bees and fish?* She called him "tall and handsome" so that it sounded like a species. They were eating trout and drinking cabernet in a place with a tin ceiling to collect and crush the din and pack it into ears. He excused himself and stood at a urinal in the men's room, trying to figure out his dismay. He was having dinner with a pretty girl who would go back to his place with him. Glancing at the other men pissing, he had it: he could send any of them to sit in his place and Jasmine would not notice. He could be anyone sufficiently good looking and sexually alert and "interesting" in his work. The right thing to do would be to climb out the window, but he saw Jasmine for a while before they moved on.

It was three weeks before Barry Wills left a note for Nathan to come talk to him. Wills worked at a draftsman's table with his back to the door. After a lengthy minute of waiting to be noticed, Nathan said, "Mr. Wills?" The room was a startling red with white trim, and gave the appearance of welcoming you inside lean meat. Awards and sketches of Barry's famous characters were in gold frames.

Nathan's brief career as an assistant animator had already alerted him to the infinitesimal steps within a single motion, and his pulse adjusted itself to the exact cadence with which Barry Wills put down a pencil, straightened, and turned from his drawing board. He looked unsure as to why Nathan was in the building, much less filling his doorframe.

"You asked me to come and see you, Mr. Wills."

"I thought you were Jewish. What kind of a Jewish name is Porter?"

"It started out as Tannenbaum, sir." He cringed. Sir? "My grandfather thought it would be more American to name himself after his job."

"Hotels?"

"No. He was a porter on Amtrak."

"A white man?"

"Well, yes. I suppose so." On an animation board, this entire minute would be discarded as action spun in the wrong direction, a miscue of calibration. "With the new contracts coming in you'll need—"

"Right, Porter, you can help me carry my burden." He located Nathan's portfolio in a stack of papers and opened it. Cartoon birds, safari animals. Nathan had included a sketch, done in red crayon, from his marathon session in college, which Wills held up. "This isn't bad, Nathan. As a sketch. As a woman, she's fat and red. What exactly am I supposed to do with it?"

"I wanted to show you what I can do, I guess, Mr. Wills."

"To show that you're better than what gets done here."

"That's not what I meant."

"Sure it is. You probably are better than what gets done here, Nathan."

Wills took a marking pen and redid a sketch. "A vulture with a garland?" He changed the garland into spikes. "Cute is Disney. Cute is out, Nathan."

"Okay." He didn't think the vulture was cute in the way that Barry meant. The script named the vulture Daisy and Nathan had thrown a garland over her head. A touch literal. He had things to learn. Barry deflated the round bodies of the remaining animals and then stuffed them along with the red nude back into the portfolio so that it looked like a badly made sandwich and slung everything onto a cabinet.

Absurdity dropped Nathan into something close to wonder. He had seen the fall of Saigon and Barry had survived Normandy, and they were discussing birds with garlands. A man could rise up from where he stood, but that hardly meant he had planted himself in the right place. But at the moment Nathan had no idea what to do except move forward from where he now was. "Will I have a chance, Mr. Wills? To work with you?"

Barry trained his watery blue eyes on Nathan. "I'd say you have a good chance, Mr. Porter."

He returned to his light board, blinking with surprise. He fell into the rhythm of presenting Barry Wills with sketches, waiting for a week, making an inquiry, receiving revisions. Barry would not give him a definite no or yes about moving up; he insisted that Nathan tend to the artwork and not worry. Liz once looked at his revisions and said, "Gosh, Nathan, what do I know? Mr. Wills must be right. But I liked your first version better."

Sometimes Barry Wills treated Nathan to his revision lessons in the animators' room, so that Christian Harvey, Jim Thornley, and Rob Klein could witness Nathan's schooling. The place had the feel of an elephants' graveyard, though Nathan liked Sam Edelson, a quiet man caving into slow-moving alcoholism, four, five shots a day so that he didn't feel hardcore, but got to kill himself by inches. He was preferable to Jason Ridley, a twenty-eight year old who wore engineer's hats and was already aware that his brilliance would never convert to anything outside of cartoons. One afternoon, while Nathan watched Barry redo one of his drawings, Jason said, "Have you heard? No one wants the boss's wife."

Violet's auditions were not going well. She had read for ten film roles and drawn blank after blank. What blasted open was like a strange, howling sound chamber—filling with jibes from Christian, Jim, Bob, Barry, and Jason. Imagine the Famous Voice presuming it could speak as a Famous Actress. At least in the sound booth her legs stayed invisible. That huge ass, in a romantic lead? That face?

The outpouring transpired with a breathtaking speed, faster than Sam or Nathan could form words, and it was right then that Norman Delmar stepped into the room. The silence that passed over them was still saturated with taunts. Nathan had never experienced so sharply how words could stay drifting in the air, attaching everywhere like dust.

"Norm," said Jason. "Esteemed boss man. We were just wondering when Violet's going to be a star."

Norman glanced around at their faces. His eyes were light gray when you glanced at him, but a deep gray when you looked right into him. He was average height, but had the bearing of a coiled spring. Nathan could see the calculations clicking inside Norman's head. He had missed the cracks about his wife, but suspected that things had been said that should not go unanswered; he also had to make light of things they hadn't intended for him to hear, or there would have to be a tiring, low-level war. What he said, mildly, was, "Hey, she'll strike it rich if she knows what's good for her."

Nathan said, "What a thing to say about your wife."

Norman's face tightened, but they were all distracted by a person striding by the doorway, no more than a flash of her.

Nathan went into the hallway and saw Mrs. Delmar in her hat with the cherries, hurrying away. He wasn't sure if she'd heard only him, or nothing, or the entire exchange. She couldn't have heard the stupid insults; her husband came in afterward, and would have seen her standing there.

"Mrs. Delmar?"

She stood but not did turn around, like a child told to wait. Nathan had to walk around to the front of her. Her skin was a liability. She couldn't hide inside it. Her whole body was scarlet. She took off her hat as if she had a sudden inkling that people saw her as ridiculous, and she said, "Yes?"

"I just want to ask if you're okay, Mrs. Delmar." He took the hat from her grip and put it on her head. "It looks nice on you," he said.

"Vi?" It was Norm coming up the hallway, but not very fast.

"What does 'okay' mean, Nathan? Men and their 'okays.'" Everyone in America knew that voice as detached, but he knew it as attached to someone.

"Men aren't okay. You are. I hope," he said.

She smiled. There was a gap between her top front teeth, and her eyes were shining. She put the fingertips of one hand on his chest and said, "You are too, I hope." It was like an echo with three sides to it, a dimension to sound that he'd never heard before. A voice had come from inside him, and he had given it to her, and she was giving it back to him, but not before she'd restrung the tones with a low joy and high sadness.

Norman arrived. "Dear?" he said. She was silent, but took his arm, and Nathan drove home and drank enough Guinness to blacken his bones.

When he was called to Norman Delmar's office, he wondered briefly if Barry Wills had finally, after a month of torture, decided to elevate him to an inventor of characters for *A Rare Bird*. It was one shard of a thought, no more or less real than what actually occurred, which was for Norman Delmar to open his mahogany entertainment center and run the film for a new episode of *The Hive*. He hit the stop-action button and pointed. Imbedded in the film, invisible at full speed, was Nathan's red nude.

"That your work, Nathan?"

"It's my drawing," he said, "but I didn't put it there."

"You think this is funny? Smart guy?"

"You know the guys...do this. Worse, usually."

"Worse? So making fun of my wife is fucking okay?"

Nathan had a falling sensation, like those animated moments when an animal goes off the cliff and stops with false hope in midair. "I don't know why you think that's your wife, Mr. Delmar. I did that in college."

A heavy redhead. Large hips. A round face. *That's my wife.* Good enough. Norman needed a reason not to look at Nathan anymore after Nathan had shamed him, and here it was. Norman Delmar and not some Jew boy would be the one defending Violet from now on. Nathan took his severance check and walked past Barry Wills's office. Barry had his back to him. Nathan paused—what could he say? Why did you do that to my sketch? He had no idea who had brought it to Mr. Delmar's attention, but that didn't matter. Mr. Delmar was going to be looking for something, and it had been handed to him sooner rather than later.

Liz burst into tears when he kissed her goodbye, and even Barbara and Jen seemed stricken. Sam Edelson said, "You're better than here anyway, Nathan," and Nathan said, "Take care of yourself, Sam," and that was all. He stole a stapler and some pencils. He contemplated phoning Jasmine, but he was haloed with the scent of failure and she would wrinkle her nose.

Lying on his bed, drinking beer, losing track of the hours, he listened to the phone machine broadcast his Uncle Sid's voice: Whadja do? Something about a naked woman? They're even laughing about it at Disney. For Christ's sake, I get you a job and you screw up. Look, get over here so Beth can feed you. Hey, kid? You okay?"

Men and their okays.

He sat at his easel, painting women in their daily lives—naked. Naked women buying oranges in the market. Naked women kissing cartoon figures. Naked women weeping while the clothed family ate a turkey. His brush stopped mid-air when pealing over the phone machine and filling his small rooms was the voice of Violet Delmar. "Nathan? I would like you to have lunch with me." His first thought was that Norman Delmar got to wake up every morning and hear those sounds. His second thought broke down into a grief that was muscular: If Uncle Sid had heard the story, probably Violet had as well. She might think that Nathan had been making fun of her.

When he met Mrs. Delmar at Michael's, an outdoor cafe in Pacific Palisades, the ocean was motionless and the wind had died. The décor was blue and white. It had been so long since Nathan had entered such a composed scene that it felt wrong. Mrs. Delmar, already pink from the sun, was in a white blouse and navy skirt, with stockings decorated with palm trees.

She stood when she saw him and grinned. She didn't seem angry with him. He did not want to eat a hamburger in front of Mrs. Delmar, but he could not think of what he wanted. "I'll have what you're having," he said.

"You may not want that, Nathan," she said. "I get the consommé." She patted her midsection. "I'm reading for parts. I have to compete with girls who look half my age. Some of them *are* half my age."

"You look fine, Mrs. Delmar." He had no idea what consommé was. His mother had used cans of Campbell's beef consommé to make gravy.

"How old are you, Nathan? Do you mind my asking?"

"I'm almost twenty-four."

"I'm thirty-eight. Guess what happens. My agent gets me a reading, and I confirm it by phone, and they say, 'Oh, wait—you're—wait, don't tell me. You're very familiar.' But when they walk into the reception area, they keep looking around, and I say, 'I'm Violet,' and their faces fall. Like this." She did four or five faces for Nathan. "They say, 'Your voice doesn't match you.'"

"How can your voice not match you? I mean—it's your voice."

They laughed. "Well, yes, it seems that way to me, too, Nathan."

Mrs. Delmar asked a waitress in a polo shirt and shorts for two orders of the Consommé Aurore and two glasses of chardonnay. The waitress stared and then thought better of asking Mrs. Delmar who she was.

So this was what it was like, going places when you were famous but not quite. People heard her as they might stumble across a memory only a little beyond their grasp. She must hear it constantly: *Oh, haven't we met*—? He knew she'd say, *Why, yes.* Because, in a sense, she'd entered their ears at some point to stay for good. Days might go by before the answer came: *Yes, it was the famous American voice, I should've asked how she herself would describe it. But why describe a song instead of singing it? Why describe a person who is right outside a door instead of opening the door?*

She said it was all a bit unreal, because she had wanted to be an opera singer. "I had the size, the projection—you have to be born with that," she said.

He said that wanting to be an opera singer was a good dream.

"The problem is that you can't be good. Or excellent. You have to be world-class outstanding. I have a pretty voice, I know that, but I have no idea what I can match it to that means something."

He voiced his sympathy for the man with the thirtieth-best record in the hundred-yard dash in the Olympics. He took off his jacket and muttered that he wanted to be an artist, and then he went into shock. His buried secret, never uttered to anyone, had been given to a woman whose husband had fired him. It was a relief that the wine and soup arrived. Two filaments of white meat floated in a brown soup tinged red. How did she live on this stuff?

"What I mean is that I know what it's like to be good at something but not good enough," he said.

"You're more than good, Nathan. I saw the—I heard about

the—oh, dear." She put down her spoon and he put down his. She stretched her arm toward him, belly-side up. He saw the blue veins, the strings that attached to other strings to make up her vocal cords. "Nathan? That…picture. You shouldn't have put it in one of the children's—"

"Mrs. Delmar, I don't know what you heard, but—"

"Nathan, was that woman really supposed to be me?"

"Mrs. Delmar," he said, "God, no. God!"

She tasted her consommé. "This is very nice, Nathan. Try it."

"Why did you think it was you? That I would do that. To you." What infernal heat in California. Sweat spilled from under his arms to stain his shirt a wet dark blue. The top of her bent head showed patches of scalp, and he had an impulse to knock over this bowl of fancy beige water and kiss the bareness and ask if he could put his tongue in the space between her front teeth.

"Because I'm a silly woman," she said. "I thought it was…you know, hidden. For me."

He drank half his wine, and it instantly flowed into his head. He set his glass down and looked at her. She seemed ready to cry.

"Then it was," he said. "Sure, Mrs. Delmar." A Valentine not available to the naked eye. "Why not," he said. He got her to look up.

The consommé surprised him. It had one taste, but also several others. He'd thought of tastes as single items. Mrs. Delmar explained that this was the beauty of something simple, that it contained the work of immense clarification, the richest part cooked out of the marrow, the glistening that came from knowing how to whip in egg whites that collected the sediments and got strained out. The word didn't come from "consumer" for consuming, the way many people thought—Nathan had never thought of it at all, he assured her—but from "consommer," to consummate, since it was the summing up of the essence out of bones, this pure, complicated, simple thing.

She asked him about Vietnam, and he almost told her about the girl in the sand, but he didn't, and her gaze read clear through to his troubles. She was the smartest woman he had ever met, much smarter than barrel-ahead Norman. Nathan could not bear that she might have overheard anything in the animators' room. "Mrs. Delmar? Did you hear? What we said. You know. Me. Your husband." He regretted his stupidity; Mrs. Delmar's face trembled.

"It's Violet. You can call me by name."

"I don't know what got into me. Violet. Forget what I said."

"But that's just it, Nathan. I can't ever forget things. I actually don't know what Norm said. I heard you saying what you did. So Norm had to have said something sort of bad. About me. Right? You've seen through me. I thought, I'll have lunch with Nathan, and somehow without putting him on the spot, it'll come out. There. I've said it. Now you won't think much of me."

"Listen, Violet, I don't blame you for wanting to know, but it's better to ignore things like that. Norman's a nice guy."

"Is he? It's funny. Someone who's supposed to be close to me said something awful, and I should ask him, but I can't."

He watched her fighting the divide from her husband: She'd have to decide whether to forgive him, or if this discovery would undo everything.

"The least I can do is not let them take your job away," she said. "That's another reason I wanted to talk to you."

"Never mind about that. I learned a lot from Mr. Wills."

"You sure did. I heard he was redoing your sketches. If you were that terrible, wouldn't he have told you to get lost?"

Nathan sat back in his chair. His ideas about Wills had been vague—something to do with letting Nathan know that getting into the club meant going through a wringer. But it had not been clear until right now, words matched up correctly to nuances, that Wills had not tormented him because he had no talent, but because he did. Barry wasn't going to let some boy saunter in and outdraw him. And he seized his chance to do Nathan in. He'd be almost grateful to Wills for this primal lesson if he were not also stuck with no idea of what to do next.

"I appreciate everything you've been saying, Mrs. Delmar. I really do," he said. "I should have seen it coming. The ambush, I mean."

She insisted on paying the check. "You'll call me," she said, "if you want my help? With finding work?"

He said that being fired was for the best. He shuddered. He was turning into the typical American, convinced that when doors slammed shut, magical ones opened that guaranteed an ever brighter future.

He walked her to the parking garage, but when they reached her car, she turned to him and thrust her head against his chest and began to cry. Her voice twisted into an animal sob that started from some far place inside her, and she kept her face buried against him.

"Mrs. Delmar?" he said. He put his arms around her.

"I'm embarrassing myself. I'm acting like a fat, weepy old fool."

"You're nowhere near being a fool, Violet," he said. "You're nothing but wonderful."

She stood back from him and smiled, and his hands were huge enough for him to put them on either side of her face and use the thumbs to clear the tears away. She had green eyes.

"Goodbye, Nathan," she said. "I'll go home now."

Home. Time to go home. "Me, too," he said. "Goodbye, Violet."

Nathan got a job as a mail carrier, since it allowed him to wander the streets with a clarified purpose. He guessed at the lives of people on his route without reading postcards or looking too closely at letters, since that seemed a violation of a trust. He received a letter of his own, from Mrs. Delmar.

> Dear Nathan,
>
> You bring me good luck. Not long after our lunch, I got a part in a movie. I'm to be a raging alcoholic, the kind of role that starlets take when they're forty, and everyone thinks they're brave for being raw. So—raw I shall be. Norman seems pleased on my behalf. I hope you'll forgive me some day for troubling you with my woes. I know that awaiting you is much success and happiness.
>
> Fondly,
> Violet

Nathan asleep alone in bed. Nathan discovering the difficulty of painting something complex that is at the same time clear and simple. Maybe he was an animator as early as his boyhood, every time he sprinted, commanding the pines of Michigan to become a blur. The edges of them bleeding, concealing the owls and reducing a fox to a dot of fire. Maybe he was learning even then that he was the one running and running, but it was the place that was flowing fast away from him. Maybe that red sketch really was Mrs. Delmar. Before he met her, he was dreaming her up, sitting there hour after hour trying to get her just right. Already he was dashing through bursts that said, *Love, love, lily-of-the-valley*, whenever his mother sprayed her blue atomizer and he'd dash through the cloud of the air changed, and he thought, *She pressed a button and out came perfume that stays in a cloud.* Only later could he animate the connection, that a past action can linger and become more itself in the present, actual particles of sweeter air, followed by a million in-between steps, until he learned that perfume has properties called top notes and bottom notes, that these were waiting in the blue atomizer all along, though he knew nothing about it at the time. His grandpa took Nathan on train rides and pointed through the window as the wheels rocked them almost to sleep. *There they are, the Great Plains, the forests, Nathan, the white clouds like hats for the mountains, the lakes, the invisible borders. I want to guard it all. I love trains because they carry me over the land*, and Nathan was the guardian of the terrain of his grandpa's face; in the dining car, he brushed crumbs from his grandpa's white mustache. His eyes are my lakes, his skin my country. *Don't look down, Nathan, if the motion makes you sick; eyes up, straight ahead, at the horizon.*

Except that keeping a head up can get it blown off. Nathan lifts his eyes from books about Vietnam when the grunts are too streetwise; maybe it was just his luck to be in a company of boys who probably also came from the edges of pine forests, carrying pictures from their senior prom as they stared down, looking for tripwires. No army buddy died in his arms. He was looking at the horizon and was not the first to see the girl in the sand. Sergeant Whitcomb had pulled her from a tree, a Viet Cong girl with a rifle, maybe sixteen, and he had her black hair in his fist. Nathan hadn't heard her rifle. She'd missed someone's head, Lopez's, maybe, because he kept running his hand over his skull and saying, *Christ.* He'd felt the heat of a bullet, as close a layer as it gets without furrowing open your scalp. Lopez wanted nothing to do with her, and he and Nathan were the ones, when the Sergeant ripped off her black trousers and started going at her, who were saying, *No, don't.* Then it was someone else's turn to rape her, but it was on a bed of sand, and her head was going under. *It's better when they're dying,* said someone, *the cunt goes into spasms.* Just the girl's pussy in the air, and her head below the sand, making the sand move. Lopez and Nathan were the ones pulling someone off her, and Nathan pulled her head out of the sand. She said some words he didn't understand, but that didn't matter. The voice is true and clearest when it's the body speaking. Her face was free, and her crotch and nostrils were bleeding. *Speak. Speak. Speak.* She looked right at Nathan and said some word that he tried without luck to have translated back home. Her breath did some indecipherable refiguring of the air. It might have been saying thanks, or cussing at him for ninety seconds more of life, because right then Whitcomb said, *Porter, I don't want to shoot you, so I'm going to have to shoot her, you dumb cocksucker,* and he rammed his AK-47 up her vagina and blew off her head. She didn't die in Nathan's arms. She had her last minute of life in his arms, and then it was Lopez screeching and vomiting, and Nathan cleaning him up. Two weeks later, the length of an American vacation, he was home, away from something so far out of the narrative sync of his life that he did not understand why a scene so removed should now become the central bottom wailing note to everything he would be condemned to do.

He stopped wandering the streets with the mail during the invention of claymation. He did well with a short feature, *My Troubled Year,* which he co-wrote with someone who'd been fired from a different cartoon studio. No one could believe how claymation worked. You manipulated a clay figure, a hair's breath of an action forward—it was like assistant animation, except in a third dimension—and you shot film, and then you moved the clay again, maybe against a new clay landscape, shot film, and edited the million frames so that your hands and every trace of you were removed, and the time speeded up. It took forever. People thought it was magic because no one could believe that anyone would have such patience, close to insanity. Nathan adored it: he was invisible, but lifeless clay was suddenly walking and speaking, arms and legs going like mad. Their film was about a housepainter who falls in love with a Gloria Swanson-type actress, a sort of Little Tramp meets *Sunset Boulevard*. The colors he paints her dark manor revive her. In the final frame, he kisses her, and they both turn bright red, as if their kiss is spilling over to cover their bodies, their insides taking over their outsides.

He and his co-author won an Oscar for Best Animated Feature.

Nominated that year for Best Actress—though she did not win—was Violet Delmar, for her role as a hard-drinking, pill-popping loner, a portrait so at variance with his memory of her that he called ten *Delmar, N.*s in the phone book until he got her voice, which made him hang up.

She must have forgiven the old dunderhead. Norman seemed less knowable to Nathan than the clay figures that went warm from his continual grasping. Violet was a famous voice looking for proper vessels, and Norman was the one with plans for it, Norman the well-ruddered force, his cartoon studio a mere step toward owning a studio that made movies with real people, not animated ones. Nathan knew that his reduction of the Delmars couldn't be entirely true. Anyone that Violet could stay with had to have, imbedded in him, some persistence of affection. That scene in the animators' room could be slipped into a long-running marriage as a flicker that vanished, swallowed up by the far view, making it into a mature, un-Nathan kind of love.

Nathan married Doreen O'Malley six weeks after meeting her. She was hired to design a look for some claymation figures in his next film. At first he resisted, but then he had to admit that she had fleshed out inanimate clay better than he could on his own. He liked her. She was his age, slender, and her tennis shoes had those dangling balls at the heels that made him think of a dog's gonads. She exploded his adolescent image of Catholic girls with their knees together, mumbling prayers; she was a smoker, drinker, and fierce kisser. He had his worries: she could eat minestrone for a week and then curl her lip at it. After working on a screenplay fifteen hours a day for two weeks, she put it away, never to be spoken of again. He took this as a personal warning. She might be too much in the mold of a classic volleyball player to love with complete comfort, and as a costume designer she was not so much dressed as outfitted. But she was also staggeringly beautiful, a throaty singer. Doreen went to bed with him after their second date, and didn't seem to fall in love as much as prove she could swallow him whole, if she wanted. He decided that would suit him fine.

The speed of the years would have taken his breath away if he had stopped to notice, though at some point, in the general fast-forward of his married life, a diagnostic backward glance confirmed that he and Doreen were on schedule. The surmountable lull in affections arrived right when their twin boys did. The affairs that he and Doreen managed were few and slight, designed as secret scenes played out quickly, off the main track, though a day came when he figured that Doreen was in love with someone who had no plans to take her from him, because he found her crying, and when he put his hand on her shoulder she did not shrug it off. It seemed the position of someone very young, who had not yet spent sustained time with anyone, to imagine that closeness always arose from proximity, that what someone actually thought of you was one collapsible, portable revelation away.

Galleries in Los Angeles and San Francisco sold his drawings and paintings, including some of his old nudes. A solo show at the Corcoran in Washington led to some galleries in New York, and he acquired a minor following. "You're B-Team," Doreen said, "but impressively B-Team, Nathan." It was cruel, except that Doreen was more vicious about her own small victories in costume design, and one day she simply quit and announced that it was time for her to start *being* instead of *doing*. She would go in reverse. This meant that Nathan would need to *be* less and *do* more himself.

He took the leap to sculpture, chunky Rodin knockoffs that Doreen did not like until the *Los Angeles Times* wrote a good review. At the Kryker Gallery, filled with Nathan's statues of naked men and women, he saw a girl with acne, and the world froze. He was back to being a teenager—this girl was walking around with his body, the days of him wearing his anxiety on his face, his insides boiling, every hour an agony of waiting to outgrow it. Doreen looked at her, too, and whispered to Nathan, "I'd kill myself." A variegated chill pierced him. He had married his enemy.

He followed the gentle rise in the fortunes of Violet Delmar, the brief coverage in the movie magazines and calendar section of the *Times*. She had done well in two more movies, but remained on the fringes. And then one Sunday, he opened the paper and saw a photo of her at a premiere, on the arm of a young actor. The caption read: "Seen around town: Ed Kincaid with the woman who will always be The Voice." She looked worn but happy, not a bad way to forge ahead to appealing exhaustion. Away from old Norm.

He received a postcard with crowded writing:

> Nathan!
>
> I bought a painting of yours here in New York! Norman's rare-bird show did well. He's producing movies now. We're divorced-but-friends. I've given up guessing what's next; they keep wanting me to play blowsy lost women and I keep saying no. To try for other things, I've lost weight, which is a torment—*a torment*—but no "other things" appear. I know you're very very busy.
>
> You've done animation and you've done sculpture. Have you thought of kinetic sculpture? You'd be perfect.
>
> Love & the rest of it,
> Violet

He was haunted by her underlining of "a torment," and by the doubling of the word "very," and he kept backing over the image of her at a desk, writing those high-nerved things. What was "the rest of it"? He had no idea how to reply, and kept the postcard in his jeans until Doreen threw them in the wash and the card got pounded down to its fibers.

He thought of flying to New York, punching out the Kincaid guy, and making life-detonating love to this woman he scarcely knew, after a speech about living to the point of ruin, since everyone got ruined anyway. Instead, he buried his father; he applauded his boys, Kyle and Jeff, when they graduated from high school; he moved his mother to a care home when she sank into dementia. Instead of getting butter for her bread, she did this: Stood. Walked to refrigerator. Opened door. Forgot why she was there. Remembered. Picked up the butter, and so on, until he wondered why she didn't scream.

One evening, on his way to meet Doreen at Le Louvre, a restaurant in Westwood, he got caught in traffic so thick at the cross of Barrington and San Vicente that he had time to step from the driver's seat. A bicycle ahead on the sidewalk made him abandon his car and run to the scene, where the man who had hit the cyclist was saying, "The ambulance is on its way. I've called. Okay? I've called." Nathan looked at the man, and at the Latino fellow with blood streaming from his mouth, and said, "*Habla inglés?*" When the cyclist shook his head, Nathan said, "Then I'll keep talking. Save your breath, but don't shut your eyes. I'm not a doctor but whatever you do you shouldn't fall asleep." Around them rose what Nathan thought of as the L. A. symphony, a helix of the sounds of horns, furious leanings, and when the cyclist stopped breathing, Nathan sealed his mouth to the mouth of the dying man. He'd learned CPR in the army. The sun beat down and Nathan looked up and breathed into him again, and when the cyclist's lungs inflated, he smiled weakly at Nathan. Nathan would never figure out what possessed him to say, "*Soy un padre.*" He was grateful to Doreen. Otherwise he would not have learned about absolution, about wanting to be forgiven for your entire life when your final minute arrived. Nathan used his terrible Spanish to indicate that he'd left his clerical collar elsewhere. The cyclist grinned. He knew that Nathan was not a priest. The ambulance arrived and took the cyclist away. The driver talked to the police, and when Nathan was free to return to his car, nosed to the side of the road, he sat behind the wheel, weeping with horror and relief. The man's blood was on the front of his shirt. But no one had died in his arms.

Doreen was later than he was to the restaurant, and when she plunked down, she said, "There was an accident. Fucking mess. Then I saw glass and police and I thought, *finally*. Now everything can lighten up." She saw the blood on this shirt, but he said he'd had a nosebleed.

That's what Californians did: voice relief when they came across an accident, because it meant that now their own progress would be clear. He'd done it himself any number of times. The mystery of not-moving was met; the cars could flow on. You could wait for years, but eventually an essence of a place would show, the leakage out of its bones. This would become California for him. He refused to eat for days, even after calling the hospital and hearing that the victim had survived. When he confessed the truth to Doreen, she argued that this was an ordinary city story, and the man had lived, and Nathan should get over it. "But it's *my* ordinary story," he said. "A man was going to die. He bled on me. He didn't know the language. It's my fucking *ordinary* story, and it's *his*, and it's the story of this entire *non-fucking* place."

His first kinetic sculpture consisted of men tied up by their wheeled feet, their heads on a revolving platform as blood flowed out and got recycled back into them. A tape recorder played yells, shouts, screams. Doreen informed him that he was sick, but the sculpture ended up in the Museum of Modern Art in New York. *Life* magazine took a photo and mentioned that artist Nathan Porter insisted upon using the animal blood from slaughterhouses, and that *City Limits* was a fine entry into the school of noisy art with a real voice. When Doreen said she was proud, he felt worse than if she'd followed through and left him. Her marriage counseling consisted of the assent of others.

He saw pictures of Violet with a new boyfriend in Paris; he read mixed reviews of her in a new movie, which ended up precipitating a decline for her, right as his own fortunes as a kinetic sculptor rose.

He received a postcard:

Dear Nathan,

I saw your shockingly beautiful work in *Life*. I admired the screech in it. You gladden my aging days. I saw a picture of you and Doreen in some society page; I'm forgetting where. I hate forgetting so much! Now I've run out of time and money and so back to L.A. I take my worn-out hide.

Love,

Violet

He wrote a letter back, using the address of the hotel, the Esmeralda in the Latin Quarter:

Dear Violet,

That "shockingly beautiful" move came from you. Mostly I have no idea what to do next. I'm happy to hear you're coming home. I am sorry for not tracking your whereabouts to say that your movies have been nothing but wonderful, though they make me worry about you. This means you are good in what you have done.

Love,

Nathan

It was returned "Addressee Unknown." She had already vanished.

On Nathan's twentieth wedding anniversary, he surprised Doreen with a weekend in San Francisco. Her daily routine now consisted of drinking steadily from five in the afternoon until falling asleep at midnight, and when they were trying to have a quiet argument about her ordering a second champagne in the War Memorial Opera House before taking their seats for *La Traviata*, he heard, "Nathan? Is this really you?"

He had heard her voice at regular intervals on film; he had seen her in the newspaper and movies; but he had not seen her in the flesh for two decades. He took a moment before turning to her, playing it out a measure or two, the different sound of her actual voice. She would now be about fifty-nine. He moved arm, body, eyes. Violet Delmar was standing against the railing near the bar, holding a tumbler of sparkling water. Time had gone a desirable way with her. Her red hair was thicker, and she looked thin and healthy, but she still had those heavy hips, and she wore a sapphire ring instead of a wedding band. He walked closer, with Doreen following him. Violet had even closed the gap between her front teeth. He wished she hadn't. But he admired that instead of being in black eveningwear like everyone else within eyesight and earshot, she was in a beaded rose-colored gown that seemed to end in a fishtail behind her. He stammered, "Are you here by yourself?"

"Why, I believe I am. But you know that saying, don't you? 'Sometimes the best company is being alone.'"

"I do," said Nathan. "I know that saying."

Violet shook Doreen's hand and said, "This is a wonderful surprise."

"Yes," said Doreen. "Who are you? I recognize your voice."

"She's done movies, since the voice," said Nathan.

"What?" said Doreen.

Violet laughed. "I have the same old voice, it's just moved around a bit, that's all. Never mind. None of that matters."

"We're here for our twentieth anniversary," said Doreen.

"Then congratulations," she said. "You've outdone me. Norm and I still talk, but we only managed nineteen years. Shall I buy you a drink?"

"No," said Nathan.

"Yes," said Doreen. "He's no fun, but I'm lots of fun."

Doreen downed a whisky, and he and Violet had clear, plain water, and in the minutes before the bell to call them to their seats, Doreen's conversation with Violet washed over him as if he were underwater and the words roared on the liquid surface: Queries and answers, all about Norman doing car-crash movies while Violet did "dark, small pictures," and then Doreen's drunken exhortations about "*being* versus *doing*." Right as the bell sounded, Nathan said, "It's torment. You wrote that to me. About torment. You look great."

Violet stopped and touched his face. Her green eyes turned large and wet. The great American voice took a startling leap, because there was no sound, no sentence spoken aloud. Just the reverberating of her insides, going through her hand and into his skin.

She turned without a word and left them.

When the opera was over, Nathan could not find Violet to say goodbye. In the car, Doreen mimicked Violet's voice, though she was nowhere near hitting any of its tones. "You've outdone me, Nathan."

"What?" he said. "What was that for?"

"It's not as if I think you're pure as the driven snow, Nathan. You can't just say, Gee, it was good to see one of my old girlfriends. Or new ones, or whatever she is. But I guess in this case *old* would be the word, but now I'm being mean, but I can't stop myself. She seemed lonely. Fuck."

"Fuck what?" he said. "She isn't a girlfriend, and she wasn't one in the past." What was he doing, testifying before a Senate subcommittee? "I've never slept with that woman, Dorrie, but she's a good friend," he said, though this, too, struck a note that was perfectly true and curiously wrong.

"You don't sleep with me either, Nathan!"

She went crazy. He almost crashed the car. So little between them had anything approaching vehemence that her fury stunned him. The outpouring continued at the hotel through the night and into the morning—*Torment, what was that about?* Because Doreen knew herself what torment was, and he replied that her torment was that she needed more to *do*, that she did nothing all day anymore, and it had taken her voice away from her, and she screamed that that's what *he* had done, with his fucking embarrassing, grotesque statues dripping blood, and he said he thought she was proud of all the notice he'd received, and she said that he made assumptions because he was so *stupid* about women, as for one little example he imagined they wanted to be *saved*, and he said, "*I'd* like to be saved," and she yelled, "Then join Jews for Jesus," and on and on, until she was hoarse and couldn't speak, and they both lay on the bed, holding hands, having finally reached a simultaneous splicing of themselves, as every married man and woman managed sooner or later, at that juncture of wondering if it showed strength of character to soldier on with the choices made, to submit to the long promises littered with difficulties and unhappiness, or if strength of character meant admitting a rupture was beyond repair. A picture of a little sailboat was over the bed.

Nathan having a brief encounter in which he felt love. Nathan alone in bed. In between: The pretty stranger below him, naked, running her hands over his bare arms, crying, with him saying, Did I hurt you? I didn't mean to hurt you. With her touching his hand as he cleared the hair and tears from her face, while she murmured, *I picked you across the gallery. It's my fault, because I had the feeling you'd go somewhere with me. I wasn't wrong, was I?*

No, she wasn't wrong.

Everything is more for me right now. More sad. More happy. My husband got killed three years ago in a plane crash, and I picked you across the gallery to bring me back to life. I'm sorry to get teary. I hear men hate that. They say, "Oh, no, this one's a weeper."

No, he was sorry she was crying, but that was all right. It was the screamers he didn't like. No one likes the screamers, with their fake Oh, God, oh, God, I'm dying. Could he see her again? Had he helped her at all?

Yes, he had no idea how much, but she couldn't see him again, because she was awake now, and that meant she was in agony. *I'm just here with you for a moment. I'm very grateful to be in pain again. Now I get to quiver like an iron bell hit once hard. The day says, "Welcome back to dawn," the night says, "Welcome back to midnight."*

That's very nice, he said. Not the feeling, the way you put it. The words you used are sweet. Thank you.

Thank you, Mr. Porter.

While he helped her dress, she said, *Tell me how it works. Animation.*

He felt far too far from speech. So he took a sheet of paper from the motel's desk and wrote: *This. Is. The. Way. It. Works.*

And then:

ThisIsTheWayItWorks.

He explained that digital imaging now rendered the task of assistant animation virtually obsolete. What he'd done for a while in his history no longer existed as necessary. Not such a different fate from most people's. He told the pretty stranger about the habit of the animators of hiding naked women, but now with VCRs, freeze frames, the obscene drawings got caught. Her parting words were: *I heard last year that some artists threw in a beaver shot of the lead cartoon female in a half-real, half-animated movie. They thought it was invisible, but there was hell to pay.*

Nathan in his bathrobe alone. Doreen out without saying where.

Nathan watching an ancient rerun of *A Rare Bird*. Rory the Rare Bird had a splat of mustard-colored hair, and did oafish things out of gallantry, which made the chorus of raffish sidekicks twitter with an amusement that Nathan would be condemned to hear into dotage. He gave a bleat of anguish that was pointless, since he wasn't within shouting distance of another living being. The *rara avis* was batting his eyelids at a red-breasted, waddling cardinal. Nathan's hair wasn't the color of Rory's, and he didn't wear glasses, but he knew how to read through the thin veil of a story's camouflaging details: There he was, in love with Violet Delmar. It was that clear. Those soused animator bastards had seen his insides and smeared them onto film. Eating shredded wheat on a Saturday morning, while wondering how to ask his wife for a divorce now that their sons were in college, had been planned as a time waster. And yet suddenly he was thrust into the second half of life, when you are meant to carry a grief that you will be permitted to survive, but from which you will not recover. It coincides with the time when it occurs to you that waiting does not always segue into the triumph that everyone agrees should be accorded to patience. That was when Doreen returned home to find him watching cartoons and sobbing, and from then to the final dissolution of marriage, to being alone in his bed, seemed the work of hardly a minute.

Nathan Porter was to see Violet Delmar exactly one more time in his life. It was two years after his divorce. He was forty-nine, and Violet was sixty-three. It was during a phase of shame for him, when his kinetic sculptures had made him a name and did well, but not well enough to pay for everything. He told a friend who owned a catering business that he would help out now and then for extra money.

While working a party in Bel-Air, picking the toothpicks from the hors d'oeuvres off a lawn—the kind with cellophane frills in red, yellow, and blue—he heard a voice that made him wish the earth could open and swallow him. The voice was calling his name. He was in a monkey suit that he had hoped made him invisible.

She still had a lovely smile. He had not seen it in so many years that it put his breath high enough to block the greeting churning in his throat. Her face was radiant enough to soften the mild, normal lines—she did not seem old so much as deepened, but her hands looked troubled by a stiffening and, distressed, he simply took them in his own hands. She was wearing a wedding ring different from the one for Norman, so he managed to say, stupidly, "You've married someone." They both laughed.

"Well, Nathan," she said. "I've thrown myself at you and—"

"Right now? Or that time in the garage. I didn't want to take advantage of you when you seemed unhappy."

"Oh—men and their 'I only want to be happy.' What does that mean, Nathan?" she said, grinning. "Our timing has always been incredibly off. That's all okay, isn't it? Isn't that just our story, yours and mine?"

He touched the side of her face because he hadn't been thinking clearly enough to do it the night in the War Memorial Opera House. He loved how they spoke in echoes; he loved that she didn't even forget the time in the hallway with the business of men and their *okays*. He wanted to say that she had been so long the underside of his every waking moment that he did not understand why their scenes were so few, with so many years in between. But those scenes had expanded, every second and every gesture of them opened into its own reel, and it was those other times—those other years—that sped up and out of sight.

Speech seemed to exit him by force, but when uttered it barely reached her ear, so that she had to lean her head on his chest. "I really don't see, Mrs. Delmar, how I can go on," he heard himself saying. He saw a man approaching them, carrying a light coat. He knew that would be her new husband, an older man, coming to collect her and take her toward old age. "What's it like," he said, "to speak, and that's enough to be famous and adored, just for being who you are? What's it like, to be beyond words?"

"Not so famous, Nathan. Not so adored."

She was being called away. Her new husband was drawing closer.

Violet Delmar squeezed Nathan's hand. He leaned down and did not quite manage a kiss, just the placement of his face against her face. She put her hand on the back of his neck, where his hairs were standing straight up. "Oh, Nathan," she said. "Whatever will I do, if I think you haven't gone on. Only don't go anywhere just now. Dearest, who can say why—I just know you've always cheered me so immensely."

Sometimes you didn't have to be moving ahead to the next thing, the next scene and minute. Occasionally you could stop. You could stop where you were, stay where it mattered. He wanted to say her name, to hear the sound of it in his own voice, but sometimes it was best to give up speaking. Violet Delmar's husband was a stone's throw away, but Nathan quit looking at him. Nathan was too far imbedded in the scene he would imbed within everything for the rest of his days, here in this ill-timed moment, with the surprise of her, with the much-storied woman alive in his arms.

The Last Pages

Anna Hauschildt Behrmann (our father's mother's mother's mother) and her son, Henry August Behrmann, reunited in Germany after twenty-six years of separation. Circa 1912. When Henry had been just sixteen, he'd accompanied his father, Claus, captain of the Estanislada, *on a shipping journey to Australia. Seasick for the entire trip, he begged his father to leave him there rather than force him to endure the two-month return trip, to which his father reluctantly agreed. Claus drowned at sea before this reunion occurred.*

It was ironic, growing up in Iowa in the fifties, and not speaking Iowan.

Our family lived in a suburban neighborhood in Des Moines. We four kids went to public school. When I was invited to the houses of my junior-high-school friends for supper, it was embarrassing not to know how to converse with their families. At our table, my older brother Tom would share with us the things that interested him the most: the special language in the soliloquies of *Hamlet* by Shakespeare, the killer last stanza of "The Circus Animals' Desertion" by Yeats.

After supper, the songs my friends played on their living-room hi-fi sets were forty-fives working their way up to the Top Ten Hits on the Hit Parade. In our house, the songs were hidden in the music of John Coltrane. "My Favorite Things" was the easiest to pick out. With patience, I did, eventually, learn to hear the beautiful and familiar strains of "Greensleeves" aching away within Coltrane's sheets of sound.

Tom became a poet and co-founder of the Des Moines International Poetry Festival. By that time, I could identify this important

influential relationship as one of being mentored. By that time, it was also disorienting and difficult to concede that the world we lived in valued so little of the music and poetry on which we lavished our youthful intensity. All this time in the middle of Iowa, we'd been speaking in a rare dialect—and the dialect wasn't Iowan.

—*Lucia Nevai*

Me and Tom in 1948, ages two and four, at our kiddie table, several years before he taught me to love John Coltrane.

242

In the Vumba Mountains, in my childhood, a visit from a doorstep diviner was a common occurrence. I remember one who claimed that the dead have no respect for chronology, and for this reason even new houses have at least three ghosts. And if you live in the house in which you'll die, he explained to me, one of these spirits will be yours. Here's a picture of my Milwaukee bungalow, built in 1929. It's the first house I've ever owned, a place where people lead agreeable lives and all the ghosts stay quiet.

—*George Makana Clark*

When I told my daughter Christy that "Wormwood" was finally being published after all these years, she produced photos to prove it had taken most of her lifetime. Decades gone, the world changed in ways we couldn't imagine then, the people in the story still fighting the same endless battles. Four of those people survived to appear in my upcoming novel, *The Poison Makers*.

Storytelling is family tradition. Going back generations, much of our collective history comes from the repeated stories of our elders. The sensory triggers in "Wormwood"'s setting connected my generation and my daughter's, exposing latent emotions that must've grown similarly inside us both. Not uncommon in the same family. Such connections exist on various levels in all stories, of course, and bind strangers as closely as lovers or children or grandparents. It's one reason we tell them—a vital part of why they're so important. A world without stories is probably impossible, but written stories have sure taken a beating in the decades since I sat on a rooftop watching the sun sink into the Caribbean, trying in my own clumsy way to make words tell why people are so different and so much the same.

—*Jimmy Olsen*

Pictured here during story time is my daughter Christy Rice. Her eldest son Gabriel (six) looks down from above, but not necessarily at the book. Emma (four) sits with sister Natalie (three) on her lap. Sophia (two) is devouring both hands at once, and in his stroller a short distance away, but outside the frame, is Lucas (one). Christy's husband Jason took the picture after only eleven attempts. He's a patient man.

My narrative is unusual in its multiple perspectives. Whose story is it, after all? Hannah's? David's? Henry's? This question bugged me for months, and I tried lamely to change the point of view to that of a single character.

Well, I'm a little dense. It took ages for me to see that the story's soul resided in its multiple perspectives, in its assertion that a story does not *belong* to anybody but to everybody at once.

"The Names of Our Many Misfortunes" is dedicated to my father, Richard Goldin, shown here befriending a chameleon in Madagascar.

—*Allyson Goldin*

My stories lately have been about people who are relatives of one another, descendants of Jewish immigrants who came to the United States from Eastern Europe at the beginning of the twentieth century. Ruth Hillsberg is their granddaughter, and she appears in several stories. Ruth never forgets that she's in a family, but she's usually at odds with one or another member of it. She's interested, too, in words and writing: here, she works as an editor; elsewhere she reads "The Waste Land." When I began these stories. I wanted them to reflect my own childhood in a family of recent immigrants, and also the culture I discovered in books and in school. That is represented by a set of repeated tropes that make an elaborate pattern, like the pattern of repeated words in a sestina, a Renaissance Italian poetic form. You can't see the pattern in any individual story, but I can tell you that each story includes a glass of water, a map (which may be wrong), a sharp point, an exchange, a cord, and a mouth.

—*Alice Mattison*

Photo credit: Paul Beekman

246

This is the view from my bedroom window in a house in Harrisonburg, Virginia. I lived there for two years with some great friends while I was in graduate school about five years ago. The silos are part of the old Westsel Seed Plant, and the trainyard lay just beyond those buildings. It was an odd place to live, very smelly and noisy sometimes. But then again a family lived in that white house, the train tracks running through their front yard. I was glad to be where I was. This story was born there.

Everybody has met someone before who made them think, "Boy, this guy was born in the wrong place or time or both." This story is dedicated to my buddy Thom Kyger—drinking buddy, employer at one time, constant friend, and one of the true originals. I learned many things from him, and I'm lucky that he was stuck there in that cow town with me. He's moved away now, too, and doing well, but it doesn't matter. The wrong place will follow him wherever he goes.

—*Matt Bondurant*

Ballroom dancing is my avocation. Eight years ago, I started taking lessons, goaded on by a friend who said we should both take "the fun pledge." Oh, those first terrible moments in front of a full-length mirror, stumbling through the rhumba! Since then, I've advanced to the big ones: Foxtrot, Viennese Waltz, Quickstep. Competitions both here in Santa Fe and at other cities in the Southwest combine terror and delight, which is what my writing, at its best, offers its readers.

—*Sally Bingham*

My Grandpa, though gone now, still inspires storytelling and certainly the love of a good tall tale in our family. We still recount the story of the Disastrous Fourth of July Company Picnic where, using a secret recipe, Grandpa concocted a huge vat of root beer. What happened next was a scene fit for the movies: Grandpa ladling out his beloved root beer, his friends, coworkers, and neighbors one by one turning green, setting off a peristaltic chain reaction up and down the rows of picnic benches. Grandpa never did figure out what went wrong with that batch of root beer, and it was a long while before he was invited back to the company picnic.

After he retired, Grandpa applied for a residence at a center directed by a Benedictine nun and a board of Quakers. In the suggestion box at the bottom of the application form, Grandpa wondered if they could organize an all-female nude football team, which they could call The Fighting Quakers. His application was unanimously accepted, though nothing came of his suggestion. But that was all right with him, as he was far too busy anyway: he'd fallen hopelessly in love with the first-floor nurse. When he discovered she loved black licorice, Grandpa, the consummate hunter, lined the first-floor hallway with bite-sized pieces, setting a trail that led to his door, where he sat with a birch fishing rod strung with a long black rope of licorice.

—Gina Ochsner

My friend Norb, who is eighty years old, really did use to drive here and there with the dogs in the trunk of his Buick, along with the guns and the other hunting gear. When you ask him about this, he says, "I've been putting the dogs in the trunk for longer than you've been alive, and not a single one of them has ever had a bad thing to say about it."

The dog in the photo is named Ike. The dog that came before Ike was Nixon, and the one before Nixon was Tyler. Nixon and Tyler are buried in those woods beneath a wreath of red plastic flowers. Every so often we leave them treats, a practice that puzzles Ike enormously.

—*Abby Frucht*

I wrote my Nathan story because love is irreducibly strange. Even when its scenes are played out, its absence creates a persistent presence.

My ex-husband, Michael Trudeau (on the left; he hit a time-release on his camera, and I'm next to him), took these photos on the day that Books & Co. closed in New York, in June 1997. Steven Varni, next

to me, was the manager, and Varley O'Connor, then his wife, a novelist, is beside him. Neither couple is together anymore, though Varley and I are good friends and Michael and I still love each other.

Doesn't the bookstore look haunted by emptiness? But books and stories do go on, and love finds its strange way: I promised Michael that one day I'd see these into print, to show what a fine eye he has, and what he captured on that day of endings. Love sometimes goes off the shelf, closes the door…but it stays alive, wandering in the world.

—*Katherine Vaz*

Photo credit: Michael Trudeau

*Our father's favorite photo of his mother, Anna Catharina
Elisabeth Theodora Giffey Burmeister, who passed on in 1980.*

COMING SOON

Her mother died at age one hundred and one, after a four-course lunch at the Waldorf Astoria, where she went every day for lunch. The waiters loved her, though she insisted on wiping her mouth on the edge of the tablecloth.

from "Sabbath Queens" by Yosefa Raz

It used to be that music was always quiet like this. Nowadays, as we all know, music can be listened to over and over, at any volume. Not so back in Beethoven's day. Back then, music like this still seemed magic to whoever heard it, and the world was altogether quieter.

from "The Best Man" by Mark Cunningham

He saw his friend's face, too, bright as day: the man he would become, skinny legs giving way to muscle, face lengthening, turning angular and not unhandsome, forgiving his American friend for what happened, because life is long, and in it there is always dark as well as light, and a friend, no matter what has happened, is always like the sun.

from "Ombra" by Bruce McAllister

He was driving down the old Cotter Road, making a beeline for the incident, though he didn't know it just yet.

from "Disappearances" by Catherine Ryan Hyde

The most likely answer is that I was tired of third person at the time, and needed a change. Isn't that mundane? But sometimes we do make artistic choices for mundane reasons.

from an interview with Mary Yukari Waters by Sherry Ellis

252